CAT'S PAW

D0828972

ROGER SCARLETT was the pen name of Dorothy Blair and Evelyn Page, whose five novels are remembered today for their emphasis on detailed maps and puzzling plots. The two women were one of the first same sex couples to co-write mystery fiction.

CURTIS EVANS is the author of several studies of classic crime fiction, including *Masters of the "Humdrum" Mystery*, *The Spectrum of English Murder*, and *Clues and Corpses: The Detective Fiction and Mystery Criticism of Todd Downing*. He edited the Edgar-nominated *Murder in the Closet: Queer Clues in Crime Fiction Before Stonewall* and blogs at The Passing Tramp.

CAT'S PAW

ROGER SCARLETT

Introduction by
CURTIS EVANS

AMERICAN MYSTERY CLASSICS

Penzler Publishers
New York

Published in 2022 by Penzler Publishers
58 Warren Street, New York, NY 10007
penzlerpublishers.com

Distributed by W. W. Norton

Cover image: Andy Ross
Cover design: Mauricio Diaz

Paperback ISBN 978-1-61316-283-5
Hardcover ISBN 978-1-61316-282-8

Library of Congress Control Number: 2021923407

Printed in the United States of America

9 8 7 6 5 4 3 2 1

INTRODUCTION

IN 1929, youthful New York cousins Frederic Dannay and Manfred Bennington Lee, under the pseudonym Ellery Queen, published their first detective novel, *The Roman Hat Mystery*, and with startling celerity became leading lights of that dazzlingly ingenious literary epoch known as the Golden Age of detective fiction. Although the two men behind the celebrated pseudonymous author constituted the most prominent mystery writing "couple" of their day, there was another couple—one united not by family ties but by bonds of intimate companionship—that soon followed in Ellery Queen's distinguished wake: life partners Dorothy Blair (1903-1976) and Evelyn Page (1902-1977).

Between 1930 and 1933, these two women, both of whom were but a couple of years older than Dannay and Lee, published five superlative puzzlers under the pen name Roger Scarlett. Yet, although they were well-received in their day, the Roger Scarlett mysteries until recently had been forgotten—outside, interestingly enough, of Japan, where Roger Scarlett was championed by the great crime writers Seishi Yokomizo and Edogawa Ranpo, leaders in Japan's embrace of "authentic" (i.e., fair play) detective fiction after World War Two.

Like the influential English detective novelist Dorothy L. Sayers, who graduated from Somerville College, Oxford, Dorothy Blair and Evelyn Page were educated at elite all-female institutions, the former woman at Vassar and the latter at Bryn Mawr. Both schools formed part of the loose association of northeastern American women's colleges known as the "Seven Sisters," comprised of, in addition to Vassar and Bryn Mawr, Barnard, Mount Holyoke, Radcliffe, Smith, and Wellesley. Whether or not the detective story truly is the "normal recreation of noble minds," as the English barrister and author Philip Guedalla is reputed by Sayers to have memorably put it, during its Golden Age it was undeniably the addictive plaything of the highly educated.

The ancestral lines of both Dorothy Blair and Evelyn Page went back as well to the northeastern United States, the traditional intellectual citadel of the country. Dorothy's father, dashing, mustachioed James Franklin Blair, was a Pennsylvania native who after graduating from the University of Vermont College of Medicine initially practiced at the State Farm Institution at Bridgewater, Massachusetts (today the Bridgewater State Hospital for the Criminally Insane). After completing further studies at Harvard Medical School and the School of Medicine at Trinity College in Dublin, Ireland, Blair, back in Bridgewater, wed Elizabeth Pickering Healey and departed with her in 1902 to Bozeman, Montana, a town of some 3,500 people and home to the Agricultural College of the State of Montana (today Montana State University). There Dorothy was born the next year, followed four years later by a sister, Betty, who died tragically from a heart ailment at the age of fifteen.

Before settling permanently with his family in Bozeman, Blair purchased the Bozeman Sanitarium, an ornately gabled and turreted thirty-two room private hospital erected in 1894 at the cost of over $30,000, which he promptly renamed, in an unabashed show of self-assertion, the Blair Sanitarium. Dr. Blair achieved considerable prosperity in Bozeman, evidence of which can be seen in the construction as his family's domestic residence of a stylish brick colonial revival structure complete with a glassed-in sunporch and a second-story ballroom. He also sent his attractive blond daughter Dorothy back east for her education to Vassar, located in Poughkeepsie, New York, whence she graduated in 1924. At his death in Bozeman nine years later, Dr. Blair left his widow and daughter an estate worth, in modern value, over three quarters of a million dollars.

Although comfortably circumstanced on account of her parents' ample wealth, Dorothy upon her graduation obtained a position as a junior editor at the Boston publishing firm of Houghton Mifflin, where she met the similarly situated Evelyn Page, a graduate of Bryn Mawr College near Philadelphia, four months Dorothy's senior who came from a socially prominent family in the City of Brotherly Love. (Evelyn's late father, William Hansell Page, had been a tea broker, surely a fitting occupation for the pater of a writer of classic mystery.)

Oddly enough Evelyn's family home on Locust Street, where her mother Sarah Sherrerd Page resided until her death in 1932, was just a five minutes' walk from the residence of young pharmaceutical executive Richard Wilson Webb, who in 1931 published the first of his Q. Patrick detective novels with another young bluestocking from a prominent Philadelphia family, Martha Mott Kelley, a recent graduate from Radcliffe.

A couple of a years later, Richard Webb in England would

meet another newly degreed collegian, Hugh Callingham Wheeler, and together under the pseudonyms Q. Patrick, Patrick Quentin and Jonathan Stagge, the two men would become, along with Dorothy and Evelyn, the only same sex couples collaboratively writing Golden Age detective fiction of which I am aware.

At Bryn Mawr, Evelyn, an energetic five-foot-three brunette with a severe bob cut, had been active in student athletics and other school activities, playing water polo and field hockey. Also, during her senior year, she served as class vice-president and treasurer, as well as managing editor of both *The Lantern*, the college literary magazine, and *The Sportswoman*, which was among the first American sports periodicals devoted exclusively to women's athletics. After graduating magna cum laude from Bryn Mawr and earning a BA in 1923, she went on to obtain an MA at the same institution three years later and edit the alumnae magazine.

By 1928, Dorothy and Evelyn were living together in a flat in the Beacon Hill neighborhood of Boston where, like all those vaunted mystery-devouring statesmen, scientists, archbishops, professors, and captains of industry of the day, they perused detective fiction for relief from the tedium of copy editing at Houghton Mifflin.

Concluding, after reading an egregiously poor example of the crime craft, that they ought to be able to make a go of writing detective fiction themselves, the two women left the publisher's employ and retired to a charming remote early-nineteenth-century farmhouse two miles outside of the village of Abington in northeastern Connecticut. The next year, they completed their first essay in the genre titled, appropriately enough, *The Beacon Hill Murders*. It was accepted by Doubleday's Crime Club imprint and published in March 1930, about seven months after *The Roman Hat Mystery*.

At their Connecticut farmhouse during the early 1930s, the couple would write an additional four mysteries for the Crime Club—*The Back Bay Murders*, *Cat's Paw*, *Murder among the Angells* (this one long a particular favorite of Japanese connoisseurs), and *In the First Degree*—and they would reside there together until their deaths in the 1970s, long after they had ceased penning detective fiction. (In another odd coincidence concerning Richard Webb and Hugh Wheeler, Dorothy and Evelyn's farmhouse domicile was located only ninety miles east of the eighteenth-century farmhouse in the Berkshire Mountains of western Massachusetts, where the two men moved in together after World War Two.)

In 1934—ironically the year which, in retrospect, saw the cessation of their brief mystery writing career—Dorothy and Evelyn at their Abington farmhouse entertained Wesley Griswold, a twenty-five-year-old features writer for the *Hartford Courant*. His long article on his visit, published on December 2, gives fascinating details of what the two women's writing partnership was like, while also providing intimate glimpses of their personal relationship. (Griswold himself would later become an editor at *The New Yorker* and *Popular Science*, a successful antiquarian writer, and the life partner of UCLA librarian and art collector Brooke Whiting.)

According to Griswold, Dorothy and Evelyn typically spent from four to six months plotting and writing one of their mysteries, with Dorothy—"a fair-haired native daughter of Bozeman, Montana, who affects tweeds and sweaters….and is hospitable in a breezy Western way"—outlining the story and Evelyn—"a small, well-groomed brunette with a Vina Delmar coiffure and a quiet but keen sense of humor"—doing the preliminary writing at her typewriter. However, Dorothy kept her hand in this phase of the job as well, "smoothing out snarls in the action, adding drama to the discovery of clues and finesse to the solution of the crime. She often sketches a crude graph which indicates where the peaks of suspense are to be raised."

"At this point the meticulous process had still only just gotten underway: in story conferences which intrude upon meal time and overshadow evenings set aside for rest and recreation, it will have been mutually decided that the first draft will have to be revamped.

"Miss Blair then tackles this task while Evelyn Page taps her way to the end of the story. When it's complete the two authors attack it together until they are satisfied that it's plausible, exciting and that not too much has been given away before the conclusion."

Clearly Dorothy and Evelyn were not adherents of the haphazard "I just plot it as I go along" or "When I start the book I don't know who the murderer will be" style of mystery writing. In her conversation with Griswold, Dorothy made clear that she, like Frederic Dannay and Manfred B. Lee, belonged to the then influential traditionalist school of S. S. Van Dine, creator of the Philo Vance detective novels, which in the 1920s were national bestsellers in the United States. Like Van Dine and Ellery Queen, Dorothy regarded "the concoction of crime stories [as] a fascinating game, a sort of super jigsaw puzzle." Dorothy commented to Griswold:

"The hardest job in writing a detective story is to protect the murderer from discovery.... Of course we employ the normal number of red herrings, but only to test the reader's mettle. We prepare one character for the dumb reader to fasten his suspicions upon, another to mislead the slightly more intelligent murder mystery fan, and for the really smart reader, with whom we have the most fun, we lay a trail of clues which, if he's as adroit as he thinks he is, will lead him directly to the criminal. It is our plan to give this reader every opportunity to make his own discovery, so that, when he has finished the book, he can look back and see exactly why he should have thought the murderer guilty."

Evelyn insisted to Griswold that their detective novels, constructed as they were upon a series of virtuoso artifices, did not require an "exhaustive knowledge of police procedure," because as mystery writers she and Dorothy were concerned not with documentary realism but rather "the perpetration of the crime, the suspicion cast by its occurrence on friends or relatives of the deceased and the discovery of clues leading to the guilty person."

While allowing that the "police are necessary to us in our crime puzzle, of course," she added that "we should only confuse ourselves and the reader by explaining in great detail just what they were doing and why." Dorothy amusingly admitted that her strongest memory of their research excursion to Boston's Middlesex County Courthouse had nothing to do with cops and criminals but rather concerned "the difficulty we had in finding a parking space."

When laboring over one of their detective novels, Dorothy and Evelyn usually spent their mornings writing in their "well-lighted study in the southeast corner of the house. They had no set schedule but Evelyn noted wryly: "We seem to start later each day."

The name of Roger Scarlett, they divulged, had been derived by them randomly from a Boston telephone book, back when they were looking for a name for their pet bulldog. When they began writing their first detective novel, they simply appropriated the name for their *nom de plume*, rechristening their bulldog "Podge." Being confirmed animal lovers, Dorothy and Evelyn upon their move to Abington added to their burgeoning menagerie two black cats, dubbed Liberia and Congo, and an enormous Newfoundland named Puck, who provided security for the isolated abode, the two women having let their gardener go not long after their arrival.

"The best excuse for having a man about the place," they informed Griswold, "was the sense of security and protection he afforded, but Puck's formidable bulk serves this purpose very well." When the local postmaster brought the first Roger Scarlett fan mail to the farmhouse at Abington, asking Dorothy, who answered the door, if she and Evelyn "had a houseguest by the name of Roger Scarlett," Dorothy announced to the bemused gentleman that she was Roger Scarlett. "She's sure he still thinks she has lost her mind," wrote Griswold.

Dorothy and Evelyn proved quite self-sufficient with neither man nor maid puttering around the house and grounds, womanfully coping "unaided with forty acres and two ponds, and the painting, plastering, preserving, cooking, washing, wood chopping, and gardening pertaining thereto." Griswold noted approvingly that the couple's "literary hideout" was enlivened "with cheery chintzes, rich mahogany American antiques and bright Oriental cabinets and prints. Nearly every room in the house has a fireplace and a great pile of freshly cut logs is heaped on the front lawn."

Perhaps mystery writing proved too economically incidental to this idyllic pastoral existence for the couple to continue to yoke themselves to its rigors. With the death of Evelyn's mother in 1932 and Dorothy's father in 1933, they may simply have felt no financial need to continue writing detective fiction. For whatever reasons, however, the pair's last detective novel appeared in 1933. Dorothy and Evelyn produced no more books of any sort together after the publication of the last Roger Scarlett mystery in 1933, yet they kept active intellectually.

Both women, but particularly Dorothy as we shall see, were friends of bestselling regional novelist Mary Ellen Chase and her life partner, medieval historian Eleanor Duckett, both of whom were professors at Smith College in Northampton, Massachusetts. Dorothy and Mary Ellen Chase had originally met in 1916, when the twenty-nine-year-old Chase, a native of Maine, was teaching primary school in Bozeman, where doctors had sent her to cure her tuberculosis. A thirteen-year-old Dorothy—whom Chase later recalled as a "girl in a red coat in the snow of Montana, a radiant memory"—had been one of Chase's students.

Over three decades later, in 1949, Dorothy, now forty-five, reintroduced herself to the sixty-one-year-old Chase at Smith College, where her partner Evelyn had been hired as a professor and she was serving as a reader. The delighted Chase wrote of her encounter with Dorothy: "I like her hugely, and we had an exciting three hours. She is most attractive, tall, healthy, and looks thirty-five though she must be forty-five. I do not know when I had so thrilling a day."

Chase, who was then writing a commissioned biography of John D. Rockefeller, Jr.'s late wife, Abigail, engaged Dorothy as her research assistant on the project, with Rockefeller's full approval. She wrote much of the book at Dorothy and Evelyn's farmhouse near Abington, effusively declaring that the abode was her "shelter in this whirlwind, the one material means by which the book has been accomplished."

"During their collaboration on the book," notes Chase biographer Elienne Squire, Dorothy and Chase "became lovers" (with the knowledge of their own respective companions), and they traveled together to Europe for a seven week holiday that Chase termed the "New Experiment." Those weeks, wrote an enraptured Chase in her personal journal, "will always be borne within us. They have meant everything to me and I know they have meant the same to her."

Dorothy later would stay at Windswept, Chase's home in Maine, for several weeks in the summer of 1951, when Duckett was conveniently away in England researching a book, and the pair would spend a couple of months together in France in 1953. Over the rest of her life Dorothy, whose "astute mind and sunny disposition" utterly "captivated" Chase (in the words of Elienne Squire), served as a reader and, one might say, muse, not only for the books written by Chase and Duckett, but for those written by her companion Eleanor, who led a far more visible public life than Dorothy.

During 1938 and 1939 Evelyn contributed an interesting book review column to the *Washington Post*, taking notice mostly of mainstream fiction, although she allowed the occasional mystery to make an appearance. Mainly on account of its appealing central character, an elderly English gentlewoman and amateur sleuth, she favorably reviewed the short detective fiction collection *Mrs. Warrender's Profession*, written by the prominent English socialist intellectual couple Douglas and Margaret Cole. Perceptively she pegged as the "best baffler" in the collection "The Toys of Death," which nearly a half-century later was anthologized by Martin Greenberg and Bill Pronzini in their book *Women Sleuths*.

During the Second World War, Evelyn served consecutively as an aircraft inspector for the Navy Bureau of Aeronautics (1942-1945) and a sergeant in the Women's Army Corps, or WAC (1945-1946). In the postwar years she boldly stormed the groves of academe, obtaining a PhD at the University of Pennsylvania in 1952 and positions at Smith College (1949-1956) and Connecticut College (1956-1964), where she was an assistant professor of English and history. Additionally she served for four years (1956-1960) as principal of the Williams Memorial Institute (today the Williams School), a girls' prep school affiliated with Connecticut College that was founded by nineteenth-century New England feminist philanthropist Harriet Peck Williams.

In 2017, art critic Lucy Lippard affectionately recalled taking a course in creative writing at Smith College in the fifties with a "wonderful woman named Evelyn Page. She wrote detective stories under the pseudonym Roger Scarlett with her partner Dorothy Blair. She limited us to one violent death per semester—that was the easiest way to wrap up a story."

Three times during the 1960s, Evelyn secured appointments as a Fulbright lecturer at overseas educational institutions, initially at Mashad, Iran, and later at Seoul, South Korea, and Saigon, South Vietnam. Having developed a taste for Asian sojourns, the globetrotting Evelyn was visiting Morocco in 1977 when she died suddenly on the 13th of December en route from Casablanca, little more than a year after Dorothy had passed away on September 5, 1976, committing her ashes to her partner of four decades. (Mary Ellen Chase preceded her two younger friends in death by just a few years, expiring in 1973, while Eleanor Duckett died in 1976, at the venerable age of 96.)

During her later years Evelyn published two more books: *The Chestnut Tree* (1964), a gently satirical novel concerning life in genteel Philadelphia society during the early twentieth century, and, just a few years before her and Dorothy's deaths, a historical literary study, *American Genesis: Pre-colonial Writing in the North* (1973), which is still cited in scholarship today.

In her acknowledgments to *American Genesis*, Evelyn circumspectly thanked "Miss Dorothy Blair" for the "time and attention" she had "generously spent...in reading and criticizing my manuscript." Although they had published only five Roger Scarlett detective novels over a short span of four years during the midst of the Great Depression, the two clever women behind Roger Scarlett remained, to the end of their lives some four decades later, the closest of collaborators.

In their debut Roger Scarlett detective novel, *The Beacon Hill Murders*, Dorothy Blair and Evelyn Page introduced their brilliant series sleuth, Boston police inspector Norton Kane, along with his avidly admiring chronicler, a staid attorney named Underwood, who provides narration in the first three novels of the series and appears as well in the fourth. Also debuting in *The Beacon Hill Murders* are the dutiful if not overly perspicacious Sergeant Moran and his dim minion in blue, McBeath, cops of the conventional "flatfoot" school who witness Kane's dazzling feats of deduction in the first three novels in the series.

Physically Kane, a confirmed bachelor like all the best sleuths of his day, is described as possessing ugly features, although he is graced with "thick black hair" and a "fine forehead," along with the sensitive eyes of a visionary. Clearly Dorothy Blair and Evelyn Page modeled Norton Kane and Underwood after affected aesthete Philo Vance and his worshipful pal Van (not to mention Sherlock Holmes and Watson), to the extent that the authors soon came to worry that they had made Kane too arrogant and condescending to the lesser mortals around him. ("Philo Vance/Needs a kick in the pance," famously quipped poet Ogden Nash of Kane's famous model.) "We found we were making him too disagreeable," Dorothy confided to journalist Wesley Griswold. "When he began to annoy us we figured the irritation of the public was probably greater than our own. Lately we've been trying hard to sweeten him up."

Similarly recalling the detective fiction of S. S. Van Dine, Inspector Kane in the Roger Scarlett yarns invariably is tasked with elucidating a murder or series of murders taking place among denizens of an old mansion or brownstone townhouse. (All of Van Dine's mysteries are set in New York, while Scarlett's take place in Boston.) As in Van Dine's books, lavish floor and room plans are provided. In *Cat's Paw*—the middle child of Roger Scarlett's five distinguished criminal progeny, originally published ninety years ago in December 1931—Kane, along with his loyal chronicler Underwood and his assistants Moran and McBeath—is tasked yet again with solving a diabolically clever murder in a mansion filled to the rafters with genteel suspects.

The novel has the most unusual structure of the Inspector Kane series, being divided into four parts: the first part, "The Question," being a short prologue; the second part, "The Evidence," a depiction of the days of family discord leading up to the murder; the third part, "The Case," Moran and McBeath's ultimately stymied preliminary investigation; and the fourth part, "The Solution," Kane's dramatic exposure of the culprit. Only the prologue and the final section are narrated by Underwood, although the middle parts, told in the third person, ostensibly are written by him for the perusal of Kane, who has just returned to Boston from an overseas trip to take over the investigation.

In the section of his nationally syndicated "Book Survey" column devoted to detective fiction, future Pulitzer Prize winning historian Bruce Catton—having come down with a confirmed case of Scarlett fever, as it were—deemed *Cat's Paw* "another good one," based upon a classic murder mystery situation (found in such outstanding examples of the form as Agatha Christie's *Hercule Poirot's Christmas* and Georgette Heyer's *Envious Casca*): "The eccentric old uncle gives a house-party to his nephews and nieces, and gets done in just after announcing that he's going to change his will. The suspects are singularly hateful, and you keep hoping that all of them are guilty. The result may surprise you, though."

With *Cat's Paw*, Roger Scarlett continued his generous habit of lavishing floor and room plans upon readers of the Norton Kane series, in this case providing an endpaper map of the second story of the Martin Greenough mansion, an anachronistic survival along Boston's Fenway, a thoroughfare laid out by the great Victorian landscape architect Frederick Law Olmsted along the southern and eastern edges of the Back Bay Fens in the Fenmore-Kenway neighborhood of Boston (home, from 1912 onward, of Fenway Park). The forbidding mansion in this novel is a "huge Gothic house" surrounded by a "high stone wall," which in turn is surmounted with "threatening spikes of broken glass." Understanding the intricate physical mechanics behind Roger Scarlett's mansion murder is essential to any reader attempting to descry a solution to the puzzle; yet so is comprehending the novel's fairly complex (for the genre at this time) character psychology.

Cat's Paw is the most obtrusively subversive as well as the wittiest of the Roger Scarlett novels. Elderly cat fancier "Cousin Mart," as he is known to his relations, resides in improbable sin with a decorous middle-aged woman, the respectably widowed Mrs. Warden, to whom he is not married, scandalizing, much to the reader's amusement, the flummoxed Sergeant Moran when the policeman arrives upon the scene.

Cousin Mart himself, in the classic manner of the mystery murderee, enjoys sadistically baiting his outwardly docile but inwardly seething dependents, a fatal indulgence. On the occasion of his seventy-fifth birthday he gathers before him his paramour Mrs. Warden, nephew and niece George and Anne Pickering, nephews Francis, Blackstone and Hutchinson Greenough, Hutchinson's wife, Amelia, and Stella Irwin, formerly affianced to Francis and currently keeping company with Blackstone, to announce that, after a decade of cohabitation with Mrs. Warden, he is shortly going to marry her and change his will.

At this point, readers will know that Cousin Mart is not long for this world. Can they beat Norton Kane to solving the riddle of Mart's ingenious murder? As a puzzle, this superbly constructed detective novel, like those of Ellery Queen from these years, is a true tour de force, with Kane dramatically calling out Martin Greenough's killer literally in the last line.

—CURTIS EVANS

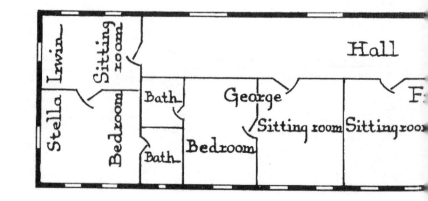

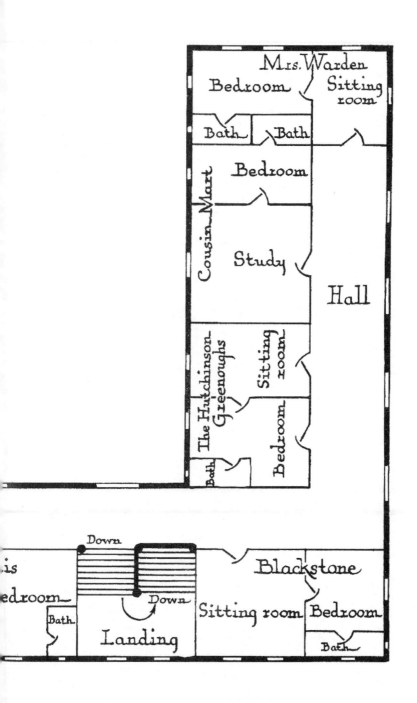

CHAPTER I. PROLOGUE

THE QUESTION

I HAD received Kane's wireless message and had sent him my reply. That had been thirty-six hours ago, when Kane, returning to Boston from a vacation abroad, was on the steamship *Scythia* off the banks of Newfoundland. Now, as I sat waiting for him in forced patience, the message that had come from him flashed again through my mind:

"Get in touch with police on Greenough case. Find out everything, everything. Kane."

Well, I had done that, I had found out everything I could find out. I glanced over toward my desk to assure myself for the hundredth time that my sheaf of notes was still there—those notes that formed the skeleton and even the flesh of the story I had to tell him. It was as strange and monstrous a crime as any Kane and I had followed together. But I felt that I was ready, that there was nothing he could ask me about the case that I could not answer, except for one question—who did it? That riddle, Kane, as inspector under the Bureau of Criminal Investigation, must solve for himself.

In the time that had passed since my receipt of his message I had entirely abandoned my clients and my law practice to devote my thoughts and imagination to the affairs of the Greenough family. That had not been difficult, for the curiosity of a whole city was centered on the crime which I was privileged to study at first hand. Not I alone had been swept off my feet by the combination of legend and truth, reticence and masquerade, which old Martin Greenough had so carefully and so mockingly built up about himself and which had brought him and his family to so shocking a climax. The press and the public were hourly clamoring for more news and fresher news, but little enough of the case had leaked out to satisfy their demands.

With Moran, the police sergeant in charge of the case pending Kane's arrival, I had been able to probe into the strange happenings on the Fenway estate. We alone knew the situation as the Greenough family knew it. Between us we had pressed the inquiry farther, perhaps, in our desire to serve Kane, than he himself would have pressed it. Both of us had worked with him before and were trained in his methods. If Moran, the good-natured, objective sergeant, lacked subtlety, and I, a lawyer, born and bred into caution and convention, lacked his magical daring and acuteness, we tried to make up for our defects by our willingness to learn and our eagerness to pick up every stray scrap of information. Kane was one of those who, without asking, command devotion.

It was growing late. The hot afternoon sun cast slanting shadows across the dusty streets. Kane's steamer must have docked by now, even allowing for the delays of quarantine and the customs.

I began to check the things I must tell him. Over and over again in my mind I turned the faces, the speeches, the actions of the people with whose lives I had suddenly become intimately concerned.

"Taking a short nap, Underwood?" I should not have heard the words if the warm, amused voice in which they were spoken had been less characteristic and less familiar.

"Kane!" There was nothing I could say to express the pleasure I felt at seeing him, the long, loose-jointed, angular New Englander with whom I had spent so many absorbing hours.

As soon as I had shaken hands with him, I seized the pile of notes from my desk. "Here is——" I began eagerly.

But Kane, when he had thrown his coat and hat on the sofa, waved me aside, smiling, and fetched out a crumpled package of cigarettes. "Have one?" he asked. "French Marylands. The steward didn't find my last package, although in the way of smelling out tobacco he's a better detective than I am."

He laughed a little, and his bright, deep-set eyes studied my face over the flame of the match he held. "I've brought you a quart of Scotch," he said, "in defiance of the law whose servants we are, and your sixteenth Dunhill pipe, which you need never smoke. It's a poor exchange, I admit," his Yankee lips twisted into a grin, "for what you have for me."

"Do you want me to start now, or——"

"No, not now," he interrupted. "Dinner first, and then you must tell me the story without stopping."

I cannot remember what we talked about during dinner, if we talked at all. I was too highly charged with excitement, too preoccupied even to listen intelligently. Kane, sitting opposite me, seemed calmer, but I knew that his self-control was a mask that hid nervous force, as his harsh, ugly features concealed his delicately balanced and sensitive imagination.

We were back in my living room again before he gave me the signal to begin. Everything that he might want in the course of the evening—it turned out to be the course of the whole night—was arranged beside him, a huge ash tray, his pipe cleaners, his tobacco pouch, his pipe.

He settled himself comfortably and looked over at me. "Now," he asked simply, "what have you been able to find out?"

"Almost everything," I answered, "except the solution of the crime. Things I know from my own observation, or that Moran and I found out through exhaustive inquiry—details only hinted at in the evidence, a shade of expression, the intonation of a voice. Together they form the plot. I'll reconstruct the situation and the story for you chronologically, if you like."

"Good," Kane said quickly. "Start at the beginning." He leaned back in his chair to listen.

"It's quiet enough, the beginning," I remarked, "even though it leads to murder." Then I took up my story.

PART I. THE EVIDENCE

(As I gave it to Kane on the night of June 19th, including in my relation everything that might be necessary to his consideration of the case, and everything that might serve to indicate to him which one of eight persons was guilty of murder)

CHAPTER II

THE SHADOW OF THE UNEXPECTED

ALONG WHAT is now the Fenway, Martin Greenough built his house, or rather his mansion, his castle. At the time when he bought the land, thirty flat, uninteresting acres of it, the Fenway was not a boulevard or a park. The ground itself was within the city limits of Boston, but neither the real-estate dealers, nor the contractors, nor the politicians had as yet conceived the idea of developing it, as they did later, of course for the benefit of the people. When Martin Greenough anticipated them and their plans, he did so, frankly and firmly, for his own pleasure and use. He built his huge Gothic house, laid out his land, surrounded it by a high stone wall, and topped that wall with threatening spikes of broken glass for his own purposes and his own glory. Later, when his place obstructed the course of the public parkway, and so might have been condemned by the city, he was able, in an underground but no less efficacious manner to prevent its condemnation. The interests of the people bowed graciously to the power of wealth, and the park merely skirted his wall, made a loop, and left Martin Greenough's domain untouched.

Someone might have made a good deal of that simple matter. In the first place, he might have said to himself, it is not for everyone that a great highway changes its course; in the second place, it is not everyone who has the obstinate and somewhat perverse desire to see that course altered. Proceeding thus, he might have gained for himself an accurate and exhaustive idea of Martin's character.

A great deal was said of Martin, although perhaps as little was generally known of him as of his place. No one questioned his wealth. As to the means by which he had made it—for he and he alone had amassed it—that was a more fertile field for speculation. He had organized and established a world-wide trade in white slaves, it was whispered. He had been the first of the bootleggers (those who advanced this opinion had, of course, to pass hastily over the fact that his millions were made long before the necessity for that profession arose). He had been the bull, bear, and wolf of Wall Street—this although Martin had never willingly gone to New York, nor stayed there longer than he was forced to. He had emigrated to South Africa in his youth and there dug for and found bushels of diamonds. But sadly enough for this theory, Martin had, since early childhood, loathed and abhorred manual labor, and it is doubtful that he would have dug for anything.

None of these rumors, however, was without its adherents, and none without its opponents. The most plausible was that of the white-slave trade. There could be no anachronism there, and it might be governed as easily from Boston as from New York. This fancy never came to Martin's ears, and if it had he would only have chuckled a little. It would have pleased him more than the dull truth: that he had made a great deal of money in the textile business; dropped that branch of industry in the nick of time to favor oil, steel, copper, and other minerals; invested cautiously in sound stocks which thereupon soared beyond the wildest of wildcat ventures, and so forth.

But the gossip about him held, philosophically speaking, a few elements of truth. Martin had never been burdened by scruples. In the place of them he cherished caution. But he was also endowed with a contradictory adventurous quality that was hard for his business associates to define. It was this bright audacity of his that had made them shy off from his schemes, so that he alone profited by them, and profited the more largely. He had too clear an air of originality, too unusual a distinction, to be trusted. As an older man, he embodied this quality of his, this uniqueness, in the home to which he retired.

In every way, his estate was a perverse gesture. The city clamored at his gates for the land which he held for no purpose beyond the gratification of his egoism. That part of it which would not have been included in the park should have been used for building lots, for houses and apartments. It was entirely unsuitable to Martin's taste in natural beauty, for it was as flat as a floor. Not a tree grew on it. The ground was poor and infertile. For such a house as he planned to build artificial foundations had to be provided. His builders, his architects, all his agents told him these things, and recommended more favorable sites beyond the city limits, but Martin had made up his mind, and no one could change it. Under his domineering perseverance, the lay of the land was changed. Little hills and slopes were built to satisfy his liking for rolling country. Trees and shrubs were transplanted to cover its bareness, and new soil brought in so that they would find something to feed on and continue to grow.

But not even Martin could entirely outwit natural laws. For

perhaps five years the place looked raw and artificial. A few of the transplanted trees died, a few of the shrubs refused to draw their nourishment from this doubly alien soil. But at the end of the five years Martin's perversity was in part justified. He had brought the country to the city at no matter what expense. As for the expense, at the end of twenty years that too was justified, for the land rose in value, and kept on rising until the money that Martin had put into it was less by a good deal than the money he could have got out of it if he had chosen to sell.

But he did not choose to sell. Now that he had established for himself a home in accordance with his personal taste, he could see no point in spending time in less pleasant surroundings. He rarely left his study, almost never left his house. Once or twice a year he would order his car, and in it drive down the winding avenue of trees that led to the gate, and through the gate onto the public streets of Boston. Like Wolsey, he might have been holding an orange to his nose meanwhile. In the city he would visit the two or three stores which he always patronized, and since he ordinarily slept in the daytime and would not rise before evening, these stores were kept open for him after business hours. Wisely so, for Martin, on these infrequent excursions, could be counted on to spend a great deal of money.

When he had finished his orgy of shopping he would return gratefully to his lawned and wooded estate, and to the gray-stone mansion, couchant among the foliage. In style, as his nephew George, with unaccustomed wit, later said, Martin had anticipated the collegiate Gothic, anticipated and outdone it, with his battlements, towers, ivy, and gloom. It was enormous, this house of his, and this too was incongruous, for Martin was not married, and planned to live, as far as anyone could guess, alone.

But when he was in his fifties, Fate, with his always sardonic acquiescence, managed to furnish him with a family—a family which only rarely inhabited the gray-stone house with him, it is true, but a responsibility in every other sense. Martin himself had been the youngest of five children. All the ability to succeed, to make money, which ran in his parents' veins he seemed to have absorbed. The other four lived inconspicuous lives and as inconspicuously faded out of existence, leaving their children poorly off. Naturally and wisely they left their children to the wealthier Martin as guardian and trustee. He accepted the legacies, as they came along, with the same satiric smile. He knew very well, he was fond of saying, what he had to guard—there were five of the children—but he hardly knew what he had in trust. And indeed, the only one of them who had any property at all, young Hutchinson Greenough, soon put himself on a level with the rest by an early and extravagant marriage and various unwise speculations.

"Cousin Mart," as they all called him, had done a great deal more than his duty by them, although while they were young he seemed to take little personal interest in them. He knew George as the one who avoided him, Anne, George's sister, as the one who ignored him, Blackstone as the one who fought back at him with his own weapons. Francis and Hutchinson he did not remember as children at all. They had come into his charge only as young men.

He showed more predilection for them as they grew older. It was for their amusement and pleasure that he kept a stable full of horses and had bridle paths built through his grounds. On one part of his property he had had a golf course constructed. There was a garage full of cars, always in perfect condition and ready for them to use when they stayed with him. When they went away they left the cars behind to wait for their next visit.

Martin was fond of thinking of new and expensive surprises for them, and not least of these surprises were his separate selves. With apparently the same keen attention which governed his choice of clothes, he was likely to choose a character part for a certain period of time. Sometimes, for weeks on end, he was cool, urbane, sardonic, controlled. His wit was then smooth and subtle, flavored for a discriminating and delicate palate. Again, bored perhaps by too monotonous a personality, he would switch his manner and his way of speech, becoming irascible, rudely blunt, subject to fits of angry temper. Behind these two manifestations there lay always a third Martin Greenough, coldly and cruelly inquisitive, watchful, aloof, sadistic. No one of his dependents, servants or relatives, not even Mrs. Warden, who understood him better than anyone else, could predict from moment to moment with which of the three Martins he would have to deal.

Although his nephews and nieces did not live with him, they were always free to come to his house and stay there as long as they liked. Each one had his own rooms, just as he had his own car, while he visited Cousin Mart. Martin never interfered with their actions outside his house, except in one way: he was very decidedly opposed to any attempt of theirs to make an independent living. As for their friends, they might have as many as they liked, but they could not bring them to intrude on his privacy. He was always, he said, delighted to have the members of his family there, but after their visits had lasted a certain length of time, he was likely to present each of them with a little check. It was a good idea, he remarked on these occasions, now that they were all mature, in mind as well as in body, that they should see the world and its vices while he himself could limit the pay of the piper. Very shortly after this speech and the presentation of the checks, he would have the house to himself again.

On the thirteenth of June, nineteen thirty-one, Martin Greenough sat in his usual chair by the window of his study. This room, in which he had spent most of his waking hours in the past twenty years, was one of eclectic taste. It amused him to put side by side a Græco-Aryan mask, with its cool perfection, and a contorted little mediæval devil; a delicately obscene Bacchus, and an ethereal Madonna. When he spoke of his possessions he liked to point out their contrasts.

His books had been chosen by the same plan. In the field of philosophy he read now the lectures of the schoolmen, now the works of Eddington and Whitehead. All ranked equally high, he liked to say, by the measures of eternal truth. He read indifferently the works of Æschylus and those of Walter Pater. In fiction he was interested only in the novels of Meredith, and in those of Henry James. Life, subjected to a directing intelligence, was so simple, he pronounced, that it was the duty of that literature which aped life to make it seem more complicated.

Cousin Mart was reading now, but with no great concentration. The book which lay in his lap was a Life of the Duke of Wellington which his bookseller had recently sent him. The Duke of Wellington was his only interest as a collector. It pleased him to glance from the framed engraving of that personage, which hung above his mantelpiece, to his mirror and see very much the same set of features. His mirror, incidentally, reflected only his image from the waist up, and this pleased him. For it had been one of the motivating forces behind his career that he was a small man and hated to be thought so. Sitting, Cousin Mart was a more impressive figure than standing. So he made a point of not entering a room in which other people were already gathered. He preferred to receive them when he had settled himself in a comfortable chair.

The curtains of the window by which he now sat were drawn to shut out the lingering daylight of the mild summer evening. The lamp by his chair was already lighted. It illuminated his aquiline face, the thin hair brushed away from his high forehead, the bushy eyebrows above his small, deep-set, glittering green eyes, his thin-nostrilled, salient nose, his thin lips that even in repose curled with more than a suggestion of malicious humor, and his high lean cheeks framed by closely trimmed side whiskers.

On his lap, pushing aside the Duke of Wellington, sat Lucy, his cat. For her, or rather for him, since Lucy was a male, however named, Martin cherished a deep affection. It pleased him to fondle his veteran of back-yard wars, to give the battered Lucy, one of whose ears had withered away, whose amiable face was scarred by conflict, silk cushions to sit on and the richest of cream to drink. Lucy's name had originally arisen from a mistake in his sex, but Cousin Mart had clung to it, finding amusement in his pet's departure from the behavior of the lady for whom he was called. His Lucy, he liked to point out, had neither dwelt among ways entirely untrodden, nor obviously had he lived alone.

Now Cousin Mart's delicate white hand stroked the cat's blemished head, now fell idly in his lap. His indifferent gaze rested on a chair that stood opposite him, the pair of his, and as consecrated to its position. Blinded by long habit, he saw it as little as he saw his silvery, tea-papered walls, his bookcases, or the fire which burned in his fireplace winter and summer. In a dusky corner of the room, his valet was quietly removing the tea things. From the table near his master he fetched two empty cups. He moved without a sound, a powerful, swarthy man, trained as a tiger might be trained to the motions of fastidiousness. In the shadows, his brilliant scarlet sash, which Cousin Mart, with a conscious pleasure in the picturesque, had him always wear, glowed and darkened to a ruby red.

The door that led into the hall opened quietly, letting in a path of light. Cousin Mart stirred a little.

"My dear?" he said. His voice rose, less to frame a question than to deny the sentimental connotation of the words.

"Am I disturbing you?" The woman's voice that answered him was as delicate in its implications, as nice in its tones, as his.

"No." Cousin Mart closed his book. "I have been wanting to talk to you." He smiled mockingly at some thought that flashed through his mind.

"Francis has just come," she told him.

"Francis?" Cousin Mart was mildly surprised. "I had thought," he said, "that the last little gift I gave him would last a day or so longer."

"Perhaps," she replied indifferently, "you do him an injustice. I wrote him that you had not been well, and he seemed concerned about you."

He chuckled. "Francis is very apt at arousing feminine sympathy. How does he do it?"

"In general," she answered, "I could hardly say. Personally, I find him always agreeable."

"And my other heirs, perhaps not always."

"Oh, they are very pleasant to me—" she raised her eyebrows with faint irony—"even considerate—lately."

Cousin Mart laughed aloud. "They're learning, you see. I told you they would learn, they must learn to accept things as they are. Well, I have a little plan." He changed his tone abruptly. "To come back to Francis and my health. It seems to me that my young relatives have been unusually concerned about me lately. An attack of grippe is nothing, of course, but with an old man . . . I think I see the connection they are making. I've received several little presents in the past week. You haven't seen them. Giulio!"

Without waiting for further instructions the black Italian carried a little table to his master's side. "This cigarette case from Hutchinson." Cousin Mart picked it up with a mincing gesture. "He shows an amazing lack of imagination. An expensive and odorous bottle of toilet water from Francis. His tastes are always feminine and florid. A thousand of my favorite cigarettes from George. Very carelessly he forgot to pay for them. I had the bill to-day. Nothing from Anne—as yet. And a rather rude letter from Blackstone." The old man's voice lingered over the last name with a trace of affection. He was so sure that she thoroughly understood him and his comments that he did not even glance up at her as he waved to the valet to take the table and its collection of objects away.

"You find their attentions surprising?"

"My dear Edith, yes and no. Yes and no. But in return I am going to make, with your help, some preparations which will surprise them."

For the first time she looked at him without comprehension, but she did not question him. She was too wise in his ways, too intelligent and too aloof. It was these attributes, more than any physical beauty, that formed the basis of her essential quality. Her face was plain, if not ugly, with its melancholy eyes and full lips. Her heavy features, which, framed in another face, might have seemed sensual, in hers expressed a dominant intelligence. Her broad white forehead and luxuriant hair were her only claims to comeliness. She advanced no artificial ones and tacitly admitted her age, close to forty, being entirely and justly content to rely upon her undeniable distinction.

The valet had come near to Cousin Mart. His intent black eyes studied the old man's face. "Mr. Francis Greenough," he said, "wish to know if you will see him now. He will understand, however, if——"

Cousin Mart made an impatient motion of his hand. "We will have our conversation another time, my dear," he said. And to the valet, "Ask Mr. Francis to come in."

"Perhaps you would like to talk to him alone," she suggested.

"No." Cousin Mart's voice had an edge of acidity. "Francis is always so pleasant that I enjoy his company more somewhat diluted."

Francis came in with a springing step. As he walked he rubbed his short-fingered hands together a little before he thrust them into his pockets. He embraced his elderly relative and Mrs. Warden with his wide, singularly charming smile.

"How are you, sir?" he said to Cousin Mart. "I'm delighted to see you again."

He shook hands warmly with Mrs. Warden, while Cousin Mart replied to his greeting with, "Extremely well—sir," and a slight grimace.

For a moment Francis stood between them, balancing his stocky figure easily, then he said with quick enthusiasm, "I *am* glad to be back. There really is no place like this." The tone of his voice implied "and no people like the two of you."

"Sit down, sit down," Cousin Mart replied drily. "Giulio, bring Mr. Francis a chair."

"Let me get it for myself." Francis waved the valet away with an almost placating good-humor. Mrs. Warden had, as a matter of course, taken the chair that stood opposite Cousin Mart's. The habitually enigmatic expression of her face had given way, as she greeted Francis, to one of pleasure at seeing him. A little color stayed in her pale cheeks.

Francis began to talk to them easily. His nice voice almost cast a spell over both of them as it flowed steadily on. He spoke to neither the one nor the other, but with quick glances included them both in a charmed circle of familiarity. He had been, he said, to such and such places and seen so and so. Quickly and amusingly he sketched in the people he brought before them, and then hurried on with an instinctive fear of silence, and the penetration of Cousin Mart's sharp eyes. Lightly he skipped from Bermuda to Palm Beach to Aiken. "And then a week ago," he began to conclude . . .

"Your allowance ran out," Cousin Mart finished for him.

"Martin! Martin!" Mrs. Warden expostulated with him tranquilly, using his name in the gently humorous tone in which she always spoke it.

"I *was* cleaned out," Francis admitted apologetically, "but it was on the train coming here. I haven't George's luck at cards."

No one spoke for a moment. Francis stirred a little uneasily in his chair and then started another topic. "Where is George?" he asked.

"In Boston, I think. I haven't seen him for a month. But you will see him soon enough." Cousin Mart's fragile, feminine hand dismissed him. "Hutchinson and Amelia I have seen frequently, almost as frequently as there have been breaks in the stock market. But you will see them too. In fact," Cousin Mart smiled at some fantasy of his own, "I am going to invite all the members of my," he hesitated, "of my adopted family here for a little party."

His shrewd gaze studied Francis's face, passed over his thick, waving black hair, his low broad forehead, and rested on his warm, liquid brown eyes, around which little wrinkles were beginning to gather.

"I believe, Francis," he remarked suddenly, "that you are getting stout."

Francis stroked his somewhat heavy cheek self-consciously, and glanced down his stocky figure. "I am a little heavier," he admitted.

"But," Cousin Mart's precise voice went back to his original subject, "as I was saying, I was planning a little party. I want to see you all together and to make a decision . . . As you know my ultimate provision for you is always in my mind . . . Perhaps I have not been entirely wise . . . However, my birthday comes on the seventeenth and affords me an occasion. I may have a surprise to offer you . . . in addition to what I hope will be a very pleasant evening."

There was an air of gentle malice about him that upset Francis. "A surprise?" he repeated. "Well, I'm sure it will be pleasant." But his brown eyes clouded with a faint dread of the unexpected.

CHAPTER III

HEIRS' ARRIVAL

At a precise four o'clock of the next afternoon, the butler hastened along the lower hall to answer a particularly heavy-handed ring at the bell. As he swung open the door he barely glanced at the somewhat imposing figure that stepped past him without a word, and his voice became more than usually mechanical.

"Good-afternoon, sir. Any bags, sir?"

Mr. Hutchinson Greenough removed his pigskin gloves and threw them on the table, together with his hat. He pulled one large shoulder and arm out of his topcoat, and finally turned to the servant behind him. "Here," he said, thrusting it at him. "Mr. Greenough upstairs?"

"Yes. In his study, sir."

Instead of mounting the stairs, the other turned and made his way down the carpeted hall as if he were perfectly familiar with the house. He was a large man, well tailored and well groomed, who left in his wake the faint and inoffensive odor of the best barber shops. His hair was straight and neat and iron gray. His mustache was darker than his hair and was divided, perhaps waxed, into two equal halves, which lay nicely along his upper lip. Above it was a nose with thin nostrils and a tendency to be hooked. It was a distinguished nose, a distinguished face, but handsomer and more appealing in profile, because from that angle the small, steadily cold eyes and the pallid skin of the cheeks were less noticeable. It was an almost wooden face, seen from the front, with a wooden expression about the mouth. And the man moved woodenly, as if his slightest actions were firmly purposed.

He turned from the hall into a room furnished with heavy, comfortable furniture, walled with bookcases, and dominated by a portrait of Martin Greenough, which hung over the mantelpiece. There was another occupant of the room—but of this Hutchinson was not instantly aware—a younger man whose face was dark with a look of perpetual fretfulness and nervous anxiety, who lay sunk in a corner of the couch.

Hutchinson had stopped before a table on which several newspapers were lying. He flipped through a number of sheets and then took a step or two toward the door. "Griggs!" he called.

The butler entered, light-footed.

"I don't find the financial section of the *Transcript.*"

"Let's see, sir. It was here a minute ago. Perhaps Mr. Pickering he——"

"Hello, Hutchinson," George Pickering, still lying on the couch, spoke up pleasantly, raising his head a little from the pillows. Hutchinson surveyed him without surprise, coolly, taking in at a glance the other's attitude, the long amber drink on the table beside him, the cigarette smoke that swirled about his head. "It's over by the window, maybe. Had it there, I remember. How are you, Hutchinson? Haven't seen you for months." George stretched a hand over the back of the couch, but Hutchinson had gone for the paper, and when he came back the hand had returned to its owner, and George's clouded eyes were occupied with the scrutiny of his own slender, nicotine-stained fingers.

"Did you find the right section, sir?"

"Yes."

The butler turned to go. "Just a minute. I'm in the habit of reading the *Herald* and the *Times*. I don't see them here. That's all right, to-day. Tomorrow, however, I'll want them. And of course as long as I stay."

"Yes, sir."

Hutchinson bent over the table, passing a white, well kept finger down the newspaper column.

George Pickering assisted his loose-limbed, loosely clothed body to a more erect position. But he still rested on his spine. "Still doing stocks, Hutchinson?" he asked politely.

The other's finger continued carefully down the page, and he did not look up. George waited for a moment, and then with a slight shrug turned away and picked up the glass beside him. Holding it between his thumb and his two first fingers, he shook it gently and watched the swirling amber liquid. Finally he raised it to his lips, tilted it slowly, and took a long swallow. The glass clicked softly against the table as he set it down again.

Hutchinson folded his paper and threw it on the pile. Abruptly he walked around to the other side of the couch and stood looking down at George. He considered the tall glass and George's fingers still encircling it.

"You look familiar," he said.

The younger man's eyebrows went up mockingly, but he did

not bother to answer or to change his position. "Better sit down, Hutchinson. You must be tired."

Hutchinson thrust his hands deep into his pockets. "You're still at it, I see."

George listened for a minute to the coins jingling in Hutchinson's pockets. Then he took another swallow of his drink and set it down painstakingly. "Resting, you mean?" he queried, smiling.

"Resting!" Hutchinson walked away.

For a moment George looked bored. He yawned, passed his languid hand through his dark hair, and reached for another cigarette. Before his hand touched the package, however, a sudden violent spasm of irritation crossed his face. He twisted sharply to stare at Hutchinson's impassive, well tailored back.

"What's the use of doing anything else?" he demanded. "What's the sense of my trying?" He laughed a cracked, nervous laugh. "I'll rest and drink my head off for a while longer, till I get money enough to enjoy other things!"

Hutchinson was unmoved by the outburst. "*Is* there anything else you enjoy?" he asked coolly.

George's excitement had already ebbed away. The flush had faded from his sallow cheeks as quickly as it had come. "Perhaps not," he agreed dully. "You may be right." He sighed and leaned back against the cushions. "Have a drink."

"Very well."

"I'm ready for another." George drained his glass and stood up. He walked steadily to the bell cord and pulled it. The butler had evidently anticipated his desire, for in a moment he entered with a decanter and a siphon.

"You may as well leave those things," George directed him, "and fetch another glass."

"Yes, sir." The butler obeyed him. Returning, the man said to Hutchinson, "The taxi is still waiting, Mr. Greenough."

"What taxi?"

"The taxi you came in, sir."

Hutchinson frowned. "I didn't instruct him to wait. He's made a mistake. You may tell him to go."

"But Mrs. Greenough, your wife, is sitting in the taxi, sir."

Hutchinson's glass was halfway to his lips. At this announcement he set it down on the table with a sharp rap and got up from his chair. He took several steps toward the door, then changed his mind and came back. "Tell her to come in," he said curtly.

"Amelia come alone?" George asked, as the butler left the room on his errand.

"No. We came together." Hutchinson looked toward the door as the sound of apologetic thanks was heard in the hall.

In a moment a small plump woman, encumbered with several paper parcels, peered into the room and, reassured by the sight of Hutchinson, made a nervous entry. Though her hat lay stylishly far back on her forehead, it could only be supposed after one glance at her that it had climbed there since the time when she had put it on. From under the hat there escaped in a brown fringe the wooly ends of a bad permanent wave, and at these she made ineffectual dabs from time to time with her fat little hands. In walking she skimmed along the floor without using her heels, as if a continual state of faint agitation kept her always up on her toes.

She took a series of these birdlike steps across the room toward her husband. "Hutchinson," she breathed, "I didn't understand. I thought you said—I thought you were coming back."

Hutchinson looked at her from a distance, as if he saw her for the first time. "What on earth, Amelia," he asked coldly, "kept you sitting in that taxi?"

"Hello, Amelia," George interrupted, coming around the table toward her with outstretched hand. "You've got thinner since I saw you—I swear you have."

Flustered by Hutchinson, flattered by George, Amelia became lost in uncertainty. "I don't know—have I?" she murmured while George shook her hand and bent down to pick up a package dislodged in the greetings. "The suitcases were all in the taxi—I thought you were coming back to pay for them—the taxi fare, I mean. Thank you, George. I haven't really been dieting. I was sick, though—last month it was. We thought about going to Florida——"

"Didn't you have your purse with you?" Hutchinson brought her back to the point. "I fully expected you to pay the man."

Amelia turned her large eyes—too large and swimming for beauty—on his face. "I didn't know that. Yes, I had my purse. But there wasn't enough money. You know that three dollars you gave me yesterday? Well, there was lunch and——"

"Better sit down with us, Amelia." George propped himself against the table. "Griggs will fix you up a nice pink claret."

"No-ooo . . ."

"Then who did pay the man?"

"The truth is, George," Amelia was more than ever caught between the tides, "I hardly ever drink—even a claret." She giggled and went on without stopping. "Griggs paid him—so it's all right. But I'm sorry . . ."

"You'd better go up now and attend to your unpacking." Hutchinson's even words broke into her chatter and set her on her path. Smiling amiably at them both, she departed.

George sat down again and stretched out his long legs before him, but Hutchinson remained standing. He picked up his glass and drank off half its contents at one swallow.

"Where's your sister?" he asked, wiping his lips with a folded handkerchief, which he replaced carefully in his pocket.

"Not here."

"Coming to-morrow?"

"No, not coming to-morrow. Not coming at all." George gave his cigarette a vicious punch into the side of the ash tray. "Anne's fed up with Cousin Mart and his dictates. Absolutely. Told him so."

"You mean they quarreled?" Hutchinson's tone was interested.

"Yes. Cousin Mart has told her what to do and how to do it for just long enough. Now she's through. She has courage." George spoke with pride.

"I should say she's been rather foolish."

"Well, that's her business. If she chooses to fight with an arrogant old tightwad who won't leave her money unless she licks his boots, I say more power to her. God knows she shows more guts than the rest of us. We come to heel all right—whenever he cracks the whip. We always will. *We* know the buttered side of our bread. Eh?"

Hutchinson looked him over with icy disapproval. "Frankly, it hadn't appeared to me in that light."

George drew a long, enraged breath and let it out explosively. "Bah!" he said.

Apparently the other was untouched by this exhibition of

bad manners. "Perhaps we'd better leave this discussion for another day—when you are, let us say, more yourself. In the meantime, I'll go up. I haven't paid my respects to Mrs. Warden." He walked heavily toward the door.

George poked a mocking face over the edge of the couch. "Oh, that's good—that's awfully good! You'll pay your respects to Mrs. Warden!" he minced. "And you're the fellow who doesn't butter his bread!"

Five minutes later, dispirited, he spoke to the butler. "Griggs, that decanter's empty. Let me have another drink."

CHAPTER IV

THE SHADOW AGAIN

GEORGE WAS among the first to make an appearance in the library, dressed for dinner and controlling his movements with the ease of long practice. His salutation to his cousin Francis was morose.

"This is going to be stupid," he said.

"I don't know," Francis tried to reassure him. "You aren't stupid, and some of the others aren't, and I think I'm an entertaining fellow, myself."

"You are," George admitted, "but—" he turned to accuse his cousin—"you're too damned pleasant for my taste. There you are now, all set to be agreeable to everybody!"

Francis leaned back in his chair and laughed good-humoredly. "You aren't," he retorted.

George went on with his complaint. "I've seen you listening for hours to the *worst* bores as if they fascinated you, and you make them think they have by the time you're through with them. And what I want to know is—how do you do it? You don't say much."

Francis turned a wicked brown eye toward his cousin. "It's charm, George, charm."

"It's disgusting," George corrected him. "You're thirty-five years old——"

"Thirty-eight."

"—and you spend your life pleasing people." He paused. "Especially women. It beats me what they see in you."

"Yet you admit they see something." Francis crossed his legs contentedly, a broad smile on his heavy, amiable face.

"I wouldn't like to have you try to take a girl of mine away from me," George grumbled. "You've got the moral sense of a chicken hawk, anyway."

"Thanks!"

The two men smoked in comfortable silence for a few moments. Then George, suddenly serious, turned to Francis again, "Don't you ever get sick and tired of it?" he asked.

"Tired of what?"

"Tired of being Martin's plaything." George's voice was deeply melancholy. "Look at us. We have money to spend, always, and not one of us has a cent of his own. He's seen to that. We can go anywhere we like—I mean with what they call the 'best people'—but we're utterly detached from them. Look at you, Francis. You have a great voice, and he hasn't let you use it, except for a parlor trick."

"Are you trying to put me on the stage, willy-nilly?" Francis protested. "I don't want to sing for my living. I'd rather be pleasant for mine. You can work if you want to, George. Anyhow, aren't you getting a little cosmic in your thinking?"

"I suppose so." George shrugged his thin shoulders. "Something gets me occasionally—the way he gives us everything with one hand and takes it away with the other. However——" He fell silent, and then asked suddenly, "What's happened to Blackstone?"

"Oh, he's coming to-morrow. And have you heard the news?"

"What news?"

"He's bringing a girl with him. Called up Cousin Mart to ask if he could."

"What girl?"

"*His* girl, apparently. I don't know anything more about it, except that she's to have Anne's old rooms."

"But that's serious." George leaned forward. "That sounds— definite. Introducing her under the parental roof, as you might say."

"Cousin Mart has the idea it's serious. He's all for it."

George frowned a little. "I suppose so. He likes Blackstone better than he does the rest of us. Don't blame him, myself." He spoke jerkily, as if he were ashamed of the tinge of envy that had crept into his voice. "So he wants him to marry."

"Apparently."

"Well, that's settled, then." He cast a sly look at Francis. "This affair of Blackstone's isn't likely to turn out as *your* attempt at matrimony did."

Francis shrugged his shoulders.

"You pulled a prize boner," George went on, "picking the daughter of the family feud."

"Good Lord, I didn't know that at the time, or—" Francis smiled faintly—"I shouldn't have been so tactless."

"I'm sure you wouldn't."

He spoke pointedly, but Francis chose to ignore both his

meaning and his words. "She was very attractive," he said reminiscently.

George regarded him with an air of skepticism. "She didn't break your heart."

"But she wouldn't take me penniless," Francis concluded tranquilly.

George gave a short laugh of derision. "You mean you dropped her like a hot coal when you found out you'd be penniless if you married her."

"Even if that were so," Francis said coolly, "I fancy, George, that the lady would prefer my phrasing. In the best circles, one takes it for granted that the lady bids adieu. Chivalry, you know!" As he spoke he gave his companion a mocking clap on the shoulder and got to his feet. Cousin Mart and Mrs. Warden were coming into the room.

"A victim for your chivalry!" George muttered *sotto voce*.

"And an attractive one, too," Francis retorted out of the corner of his mouth, "which you would see if you had more observation and less morality."

He took a few steps forward. "Good-evening."

Cousin Mart was testy. "Didn't know you were downstairs yet. Giulio, why didn't you tell me? Never mind, now." His irascibility glinted out of his sharp green eyes.

Francis had turned to Mrs. Warden. "That's a most becoming dress," he said. "I like that electric blue."

"Electric blue!" Cousin Mart snorted, and examined his companion's gown with a belligerent eye. "Blue, I call it. What makes your generation talk like men milliners? In my day, the man who knew the difference between sun-tan and flesh pink would keep still about it."

"And he wouldn't admit in so many words that he read the silk-stocking advertisements, would he, Martin?" Mrs. Warden answered him, a glint of amusement in her eye. He acknowledged the touch with a slight grimace. "Thank you, Francis," she went on. "There's nothing nicer than a new compliment on an old dress."

Francis met her with silence and a smile, pleasantly intimate, while Cousin Mart settled himself in his favorite chair, grumbling. "Women!" he snapped at the world in general. "Women always like flattery and flatterers. They want to be smoothed over. Some are worse than others, though, there's that much to be said. What's the matter with your sister?" and so speaking he swung on George.

The attack was unexpected. "What? Oh, Anne. Why, nothing," George answered nervously. "She's not coming. She wrote you."

"Perhaps she did. *I* don't know."

George stood his ground for a minute, his pale face flushing with anger. "Well, I know she wrote you."

"I didn't say she didn't." Cousin Mart swept him aside. "But when you next see your sister you may give her a message from me—that I have nothing more to say to her until she comes to her senses."

"Anne isn't going to——" George began, glaring at the old man. Then, under the other's acid scrutiny, he faltered.

"What were you about to say?"

George's eyes grew dull. He looked away. "Nothing," he said.

The coming of the butler with the cocktails was an opportune distraction. On his heels came the Hutchinson Greenoughs, Hutchinson more than ever perfect in dinner clothes, his wife flaunting an unbecoming décolletage. From moment to moment she peered at her costume, painfully and surreptitiously, to make sure that nothing had shifted from its proper place.

Cocktails were drunk in a buzz of family gossip. Occasionally Mrs. Warden, who sat somewhat isolated from the rest, put in a comment. When this happened the others looked at her, gave her polite attention, nodded, smiled, and returned to their cocktails. The subject on which she had spoken was likely to be dropped soon after. Then Cousin Mart looked sharply around the group, his eyebrows raised in annoyance, and a moment later smiled to himself, secretly and contemptuously.

"What's in the cocktail?" Francis asked him.

"Bourbon. A good quality. Almost as old as I am. You like it?"

"Very much."

"Then," Cousin Mart made a swift return to his favorite type of humor, "you'll be glad to know there's a fair amount left, so that on the day of my funeral you can assuage your grief. It will distract you from the thought of death."

Amelia laughed hastily. "What a morbid idea!" she twittered.

Cousin Mart fixed her with a mocking eye. "The thought of death? Oh, yes. I use it sparingly, like the Bourbon."

Francis, George, and even Hutchinson, made perfunctory gestures of amusement. Mrs. Warden looked at Cousin Mart with mild disapproval, and, having satisfied his temporary ill temper, he acknowledged her reproof by mollifying his attitude slightly. There ensued a flutter of small remarks calculated to change the subject. Amelia excused herself and left the room for a moment.

When she came down again her bare shoulders and neck were wrapped in the folds of a long green chiffon scarf.

Cousin Mart looked at her with surprise. "Were you cold, Amelia?" he asked. "I'll ring for Griggs to mend the fire, if you——"

"Oh, no." Amelia hurried to her chair. "I meant to wear this and forgot to. That's all."

When the men had started to talk together again she got up and walked over to Mrs. Warden.

"Do you like it?" she asked breathlessly.

"You mean the scarf? Oh, yes, indeed. It's almost the color of a fine emerald, isn't it?"

Amelia pulled the silk fringe through her fingers with a childish pleasure. "That's just what I thought," she said contentedly. "Yes, I like it."

"Is it new?"

"I got it to-day. Only this afternoon. You know," she went on confidingly, "I was walking through Jordan's, and I just happened to see this lying on a counter. I couldn't resist it."

The excited note in her voice carried beyond Mrs. Warden to her husband's ears. Hutchinson, a few feet away, turned his head to look at her. Suddenly his eyes narrowed suspiciously. He moved over and stood quietly behind her.

"I wasn't really looking for a scarf," his wife was saying, "but the color of this one . . . I couldn't keep my eyes off it. So I got it. See how far it comes down over my shoulders. Just look!" She turned and caught sight of her husband. The pleased excitement faded from her face. She stared at him with a vacant expression.

Hutchinson stood like a rock before her and searched her face with cold eyes. All conversation in the room had died away. The other three men were watching the scene with ill concealed amusement. Only Mrs. Warden made an attempt to behave as if nothing were happening.

"Amelia," she said quietly, "the ticket is still on your scarf. I'll pull it off. Here——"

"Thank you." At last able to shift her overlarge brown eyes from Hutchinson's face, Amelia half turned and took the price tag from Mrs. Warden's hand. She laughed nervously. "Isn't that funny!" she said. "I thought I'd taken it off." She took a step toward the fireplace. "I'll just throw it——"

"I'll take it, Amelia." Without waiting for her consent or paying any attention to her little gasp, Hutchinson took the square of cardboard from her yielding fingers. He glanced at it, put it in his wallet, and motioned Amelia to the far end of the room. Unwilling, but unable to escape him, she was propelled out of earshot.

"And what do you make of that, sir?" Francis asked, smiling broadly.

Cousin Mart's sharp green eyes twinkled with amusement. "A reappearance of the family skeleton," he said.

Mrs. Warden frowned at him reproachfully. "That skeleton wouldn't be so laughable, Martin, if it displayed itself in your particular branch of the family. Isn't there any way of curing her?"

Cousin Mart shrugged his shoulders. "I wonder if she wants to be cured." He chuckled. "I imagine Hutchinson has tried all the remedies, my dear. I've rarely entertained such a celebrity as Amelia. There's not a clerk from Boylston to Hanover Street who doesn't jump to attention when she comes to his counter. No other wife in Boston gets so much attention as Hutchinson's."

"But, Martin," Mrs. Warden tried again to soften him, "you know it's really an affliction."

"I'm not sure." Cousin Mart stole a glance at the couple at the other end of the room. "It may be kleptomania; it may simply be an easy way of gratifying small desires—in other words, a habit. Of course," he went on after a moment, "the really tragic thing is that she never gets away with it." He gave a snort of contempt. "She bungles and drops. There's no word to describe her lack of skill! In sight of everyone! She's always caught, and Hutchinson always gets a little bill, and Amelia can only weep and make vain denials. Very vain, after a polite clerk tells Hutchinson that of course his wife intended to charge the object, but in the hurry of the moment, she forgot." His precise voice took on the suave accents of a salesman.

Francis laughed appreciatively. "I'm glad the bills don't come to me," he said.

"Oh, well," Cousin Mart dismissed the subject, "they don't amount to much. Amelia's tastes are simple, fortunately. Handkerchiefs, scarves, powder boxes. Hutchinson can afford——"

Francis got up quickly and began to shake the cocktails again. Amelia and Hutchinson were about to join the rest of the family.

"Enough for a small one all around," Francis announced. "Hutchinson, where's your glass?"

"Here." Hutchinson held it steadily while Francis filled it.

"And where's yours, Amelia?" Francis turned to her gayly.

Amelia looked up at him with abject eyes and then hurriedly looked away. "I don't believe I want one," she said. "I hardly ever drink."

Cousin Mart had already finished his cocktail. "We'll let you off this time, Amelia," he said briskly. "However, there may be an occasion, in a day or so, when even you must drink one toast. Only one. I think I shall have a surprise for you, then." He put his glass on the table and stood up.

"Do you think we've forgotten, sir?" Francis caught him up

with quick enthusiasm. "Do you think we've forgotten your birthday?"

Cousin Mart hesitated. "My birthday? Oh, yes. But I wasn't speaking of that. My surprise is—er—of a more serious nature." He made a stiff little bow before Mrs. Warden and held out his arm to her. "Shall we go in to dinner, Edith?" he asked in quite another voice, and smiled down at her.

CHAPTER V

HEIRS IN WAITING

GEORGE WAS pacing sullenly up and down the library. His way of walking was erratic. Sometimes he stepped with belligerent decision; then again his tread became uncertain in its fall. Now and again he paused to look out the mullioned windows and across the sweep of close-cropped lawn, only to turn back to the paneled room, heavy with its dark English oak. His long pointed fingers fiddled with the books in the bookcases (all of them—they ranged narrowly from Dickens and Scott to Cooper and Bulwer-Lytton—had been selected, as Cousin Mart had explained, to suit the tastes of the, by implication, still adolescent Greenoughs). Restlessly he stared from Sargent's vulpine image of Cousin Mart which hung over the mantelpiece to the table which supported his decanter and siphon, to the grand piano, lost, except for its gleaming, polished blackness, in the far corner of the room. Unsatisfied, he resumed his irregular pace, up and down, up and down.

Sometimes he altered his course and made a complete circle of the library. Whenever he did so, he passed between Hutchinson and the window, and his long shadow fell across his cousin's newspaper. Near the fireplace Francis sat, indifferent to both of them. There was a little line of worry between his eyebrows. It contrasted strangely with the other lines on his forehead that had certainly not been etched there by anxiety.

For a while Hutchinson endured George's perambulations, but finally he could stand them no longer. "Would you mind keeping out of my light, George?" he asked coldly.

George looked at him with a quick flare of irritation which died impotent.

"Oh, very well," he said, and flung himself into a chair. He reached for the decanter and poured himself a drink. "Have one?" he said to Francis.

"No, thanks. I think I'll wait for tea."

"Tea?" Hutchinson, reminded of the time of day, dropped his paper and looked at his watch. "Almost five," he said. "They should be back. I can't see what pleasure women can take in dawdling about shops."

"Who's dawdling about shops?" Francis yawned a little.

"Amelia and Mrs. Warden." Hutchinson, as did all the rest, pronounced the name of the latter stiffly. "I can't see what they find to do." Like many men whose time was utterly unproductive, he was annoyed at the waste of it on the part of other people.

"They must have gone to do something," Francis suggested, yawning again.

"Two errands for me. That's what Amelia went for," Hutchinson retorted. "She went to order a birthday present for Cousin Mart and to leave my dress studs to be repaired. She didn't even have to tell the jeweler what to do. He is to call me."

"She may be getting you a whole new set," Francis said slyly. With his cousins he left off as much of his affability as he ever dispensed with.

Hutchinson did not answer him. It was George who spoke up from the depths of his chair. "Blackstone's here," he said, in a strained voice. "He's brought his girl with him."

Francis was interested. "What's she look like?"

George's eyes dropped. "This is going to be a mess," he said harshly, and refused to go on.

The others, used to his moodiness, ignored him. Francis seized the opportunity for a little idle gossip. "Know anything about her, Hutchinson?"

"I haven't even seen her," Hutchinson replied briefly, "and I don't so much as know her name."

"She's the first person outside the family who's been here, to my knowledge, in the last ten years," Francis wandered on. "The first one, that is, except Mrs.—Mrs. Warden. And I've got used to her."

"I shall never get used to her," Hutchinson answered. "Not in another ten years."

"You may as well." Francis shrugged his shoulders. "I imagine she'll be here as long as Cousin Mart——" He checked his speech.

George roused himself. He looked at the others with a queer intentness. "What did Cousin Mart say in his note to you, Francis?" he asked.

"He didn't write me a note," Francis replied. "I was here when he wrote the rest of you. Why?"

"He wrote me," George seemed a little on the defensive, "that he had not only the party to offer as an inducement, but a piece of news that he hoped would give us all pleasure. Pleasure—that's what he said," George repeated obstinately.

"What of it?" Hutchinson was matter of fact. "He's probably built a squash court in the cellar or a garden on the roof."

"I can't think so." George gazed unhappily into space. "That wouldn't be news, exactly. And when he talks about pleasure, I, for one, don't trust him." For an instant George was defiant: he defied Cousin Mart, he defied Hutchinson and Francis. Then he fell into lassitude again. "Did he say the same thing to you?"

"Certainly." Hutchinson's matter-of-factness made ghosts of George's fears. Francis was hardly more impressed, but certainly more curious.

"What's the matter with you, George?" he inquired. "You look as if someone had put you through a wringer. You must have more on your mind than that note. What is it?"

George was still defensive. "He said to Anne—when he was scrapping with her, you know—that he thought we all took too much for granted and perhaps needed a little lesson."

Even Hutchinson pricked up his ears. "A little lesson?" he repeated. "Do you suppose," he looked at his cousins with cold blue eyes, "that he intends to change his will?"

Francis whistled a little through lips suddenly stiff. "That reminds me," he said softly, "of what he said to me. Something about having his ultimate provision for us always in his mind."

Hutchinson's face hardened. "Why should he want to change it now?" he asked in a harsh voice. "It's impossible!"

Francis's expression changed rapidly with his changing calculations. "It isn't impossible, Hutchinson," he said finally. "I agree with George there. But I agree with you that it isn't likely."

"Why not?" George's voice rose in a protest against fate. "Why can't he? He can cut us out of it entirely, if he wants to."

"He can," Francis acknowledged, "but he won't."

"Your imagination is running away with you, George." Hutchinson brushed him aside.

"Well, now, look here"—George persisted in his self-afflicted misery—"we're absolutely dependent on him, aren't we? I haven't got a cent to call my own, have you, Francis? Hutchinson?"

"Not a one," Francis admitted calmly. Hutchinson refused to answer, but his silence was enough.

"Then," George went on, "instead of money we have a fine lot of expensive tastes. And not one of us could earn a nickel if we had to!"

"I hope I never have to," Francis put him off gayly. "Forget it, George. You've only got a hangover."

"I wish I had," George answered him bitterly. "But I know he's got something up his sleeve! And Anne——"

"What did Anne fight with him for?" Francis interrupted him.

George turned on him viciously. "She fought with him because she's got some spirit, some decent independence!"

"All right." Francis tried to soothe him. "What I meant to ask was this—what was the immediate cause of the battle?"

"He found out somehow that she'd saved some money he'd given her and used sense in investing it. She didn't even get caught in the break." George was proud of his sister's ability. "So he turned on her. He wants every one of us at his mercy all the time! If he says anything to me against her——"

"You let Anne fight her own battles," Francis advised him. "She's much better able to take care of herself than you are to take care of her."

George was silent, his weak, melancholy face shadowed by his thoughts. There were quick footsteps in the hall. All three looked up. In the doorway stood a slim, somehow haughty figure, the small, finely shaped head thrown a little back. The man's hair was reddish and crinkled, although it was cropped close to his head. Like Cousin Mart's, it grew down a little on his cheeks. He too had a long aquiline face. His eyebrows were finely curved over his keen amber eyes. His thin, delicately carved nose and his cynical mouth were Cousin Mart's own.

"Hello," he said coolly. "Am I interrupting something?"

Francis returned the greeting equably. "Hello, Blackstone," he said. "Nothing that doesn't concern you. Come on in." A question seemed to hover on his lips, but he did not put it into words. No one of them cared to interfere with Blackstone's jealously guarded personal affairs.

Blackstone accepted the invitation and crossed the room to the fireplace. He stood with his back to the mantel. His body was beautifully symmetrical. He moved easily and looked, as he was, a horseman born. Standing under Cousin Mart's portrait, he unconsciously put himself in contrast to the old man. Their likeness was obvious. They showed the same directness of mind, the same acuteness, in the same chiseled features. But their coloring was different. Where Cousin Mart's green eyes looked out on the world coldly, skeptically, Blackstone's amber ones glowed in their hot defiance of everything that might oppose him.

"What were you talking about?" he asked. His voice was quick and pointed.

"About Anne," George answered dully, his fitful emotions wiped out. He told Blackstone of his distrust of Cousin Mart, of his sister's quarrel with their uncle. When he came to the end of his story he glanced at Blackstone appealingly. There was some affection between them, even though it was contemptuous on Blackstone's part.

"Too bad," he commented, when George had finished. "If you like I'll speak to him."

Francis laughed. "I shouldn't if I were you, Blackstone," he said. "Even you might get your fingers burned. Take my advice, George, and seek out Mrs. Warden. She's the only one who can speak for Anne successfully."

"I won't do it!" George attacked his easy-going cousin. "Not even for Anne. She'd hate it if I did! I admit I lick Cousin Mart's boots, but I draw the line at Mrs. Warden!"

Francis shrugged his shoulders. "It makes no difference to me," he said. "Do as you like. But we may all as well learn that lesson." He caught Blackstone's angrily sparkling eye. "Even you may have to some day, Blackstone."

Blackstone turned on him with the speed and accuracy of a snake about to strike. "I'll see myself damned first," he said.

Again Francis raised and lowered his heavy shoulders. "Also, George," he went on imperturbably, "if I were worried, as you seem to be, about Cousin Mart's changing his will, I should go to Mrs. Warden for advice and help."

"Why should she help us?" George sneered at him. "She might find herself better off if he did."

Francis was reasonable with him. "You're making a big mistake, George," he said. "In the first place, Mrs. Warden is not mercenary. If she had been, we'd have been ditched long ago."

"I see no reason for your saying that, Francis." Hutchinson entered the conversation. "She has, after all, no legal claim whatever."

"Nor, I suppose you were about to add," Francis replied

slyly, "any standing in society. Don't talk like an old woman, Hutchinson."

"I'm simply stating facts." Hutchinson's answer was stilted. "And the fact is that she is merely his mistress."

"And has been for ten years," Francis reminded him. "We're lucky he's had a mistress. It's kept him from marrying."

"From marrying! At his age!"

It took all of Francis's trained patience and affability to answer Hutchinson calmly. "He hasn't always been his present age," he reminded his cousin. "Ten years ago, when he first encountered Mrs. Warden, he might have met and married someone else. That he did meet her, that she was married, that her husband at that time refused to divorce her (though he did later)—all those things, Hutchinson, you should give thanks for in your nightly prayers. Another woman might have made a great deal of trouble for us. Remember that if Cousin Mart were married we would not stand where we do now."

"Nothing could change the fact that we are his next of kin," Hutchinson replied exasperatingly.

Francis almost gave up the argument. Then he made one more effort. "Use your imagination." He emphasized the word mockingly. "*If* Cousin Mart had married, would we be his next of kin? Would we——"

"Would we stand to inherit the money he's always dangling in front of us?" George finished the sentence acridly.

Hutchinson was silenced. "All that I am saying," Francis continued, "is that we are very fortunate that the present situation exists. And also that we're lucky in another way—Mrs. Warden is not interested in Cousin Mart's money."

"What's the idea, Francis?" Blackstone broke in bluntly.

"Why this elaborate speech on—Mrs. Warden?" His lips curled over her name.

"Not a speech," Francis defended himself. "I'm trying to make you acknowledge what's true. You may dislike her, but I, for one, advise you not to show it. You might say, Hutchinson, that fine words butter no parsnips, but they do according to my experience. And the facts remain. We're useless without money, as George points out. With a few well chosen words to Cousin Mart, Mrs. Warden could do for us if she wanted to. And she hasn't, in these past ten years. She's kept him from marrying anybody else, and she hasn't tried to marry him herself. She's a very remarkable woman, when you consider the position she's been in, and for how long. I advise you all to treat her with tact and consideration, as I intend to. Besides," he smiled easily, "she's very attractive."

"I have no intention of offending her." Hutchinson stated his plan of campaign.

"No," George took him up, "we realize you haven't. It would be unnecessary, wouldn't it? Well, I'd like to be unnecessary, for once."

"But you won't, will you, George?"

"Oh, no!" George joined in Francis's sneer at himself. "I suppose not." His eyes burned with rebellion against his own weakness. He stared at Blackstone with envy. There was no indecision in Blackstone. He knew his own mind always and yielded to nothing.

Sitting in silence, each occupied with his own thoughts, they heard a car drive up to the door and Amelia's quavering voice answered by Mrs. Warden's warm, flexible accents. Nothing more was said between the four of them, except when George turned to Blackstone.

"What are you going to do about this business of yours, Blackstone—I mean, bringing that girl here?" he asked in a troubled voice. "You'll never be able to get away with it."

"I can get away with whatever I like," Blackstone answered him positively.

CHAPTER VI

WHO SHE IS

TEA WAS to be served in the library. The younger members of the family, remembering Cousin Mart's peculiarities, tactfully withdrew from the room while he made his entrance, and arranged himself to receive them. In honor of the young lady whom Blackstone was about to present to him, Cousin Mart had left off his usual costume, a deep-red brocade lounging robe, and substituted for it a more formal afternoon dress. His instinct for the picturesque led him to vary from convention in substituting a stock for collar and tie. Over his knees was thrown a robe of soft, glistening leopard skin, on which Lucy had made himself thoroughly comfortable. Both were in the best of moods.

Mrs. Warden had taken her place behind the tea table. She always made a ceremony of the pouring, and Cousin Mart always watched her, fascinated by her swift and graceful gestures. Only once had he allowed himself to suffer through a tea of Amelia's offering. If, as Blackstone had acutely remarked to Hutchinson, his wife had been more skillful in the performance of her social duties, Mrs. Warden might never have found a habitation in Cousin Mart's palace.

One by one the others made casual entrances, as if most of them had not recently left the room for that particular purpose. They had little to say to each other while they waited for the appearance of the unaccustomed guest. Tacitly they acknowledged the importance of the occasion, the significance of the impression she might make on Cousin Mart. Only Amelia was impervious to the general expectancy. She was preoccupied with her own activities, balancing a cup of tea with a great deal of cream in it and a plate dotted with small sweet cakes.

When Francis came to her assistance and placed a table by her side, she rewarded him with a grateful but abstracted smile. Volubly she plunged into an account of the adventures which she and Mrs. Warden had had that afternoon—a traffic jam, an insolent policeman, the curb on which she had stumbled, almost turning her ankle. Her voice meandered on cheerfully. No one listened to her or encouraged her. Now and then Mrs. Warden threw her a sympathetic smile, or Francis stooped to pick up her napkin. The various objects which they had seen in shops or shop windows gave her subject matter for endless comment. Hutchinson was the first to get tired of it.

"I hope you weren't too busy to attend to my errands," he interrupted her impatiently. "You may not remember it, but you went to town to do some things for me."

"Oh, yes, Hutchinson," she protested, "I did do your errands. Didn't I, Edith? I put in the order you wanted given, and I left your studs at Banks and Tiffany. And I didn't forget that you asked me not to give any instructions about fixing them. The repair clerk is going to call you. Isn't that so, Edith?" In spite of Amelia's shocked disapproval of Mrs. Warden's position in the household, the years had constructed a mild friendship between them, and Mrs. Hutchinson had arrived at acceptance of and dependence upon the lady whom she always euphemistically called Cousin Mart's "companion."

Now she waited for Mrs. Warden's confirmation, soon and silently given, as though she herself were in some doubt as to what they actually had done.

Blackstone was restless. Two or three times he glanced at his watch. His eye frequently turned toward the door. "I don't see what's keeping Stella." He threw the words into the midst of Mrs. Hutchinson's lucubrations.

"She's probably undergoing an emotion you've never experienced," Cousin Mart replied tartly. "If she is shy, go and fetch her."

"Very well." Blackstone moved with the speed of a released spring.

Amelia's voice followed him to the door with "Stella? Stella? There's something very familiar to me about that name!"

"Really?" Francis answered her. "Aren't you going to have another cake?" Charmed by his wide smile she accepted the offer, murmuring, "You are very thoughtful, Francis."

With the swiftness that had characterized his exit, Blackstone returned. Standing in the doorway, he said to someone in the hall, "We are all in here, anxious to see you." There was an undercurrent of gentleness in his exact voice.

A girl in her early thirties entered the room. In the dusk beyond the lamplight it was possible only to see that her hair was dark and her face pale. She was dressed in a soft deep red, against which her white hands showed, long-fingered and fine. As she came closer, her features were revealed, too irregular for beauty. Her eyebrows were heavy over her brown eyes. Her thin cheeks and the distinct lines of her chin gave her face definiteness and an implication of pride.

With a magnificent courtesy Cousin Mart put aside his robe and, holding Lucy under one arm, rose to greet her. "We are delighted to see you," he emended Blackstone's speech. "Delighted."

Blackstone made the introductions, and omitting all formalities, admitted her to the family. "Stella," he began and ran quickly through the names, nodding to indicate their owners, "Cousin Mart, Hutchinson, Amelia, George, Francis, and Mrs. Warden." He spoke the last name stiltedly, not bothering to conceal his brusqueness.

Stella acknowledged the introductions with an ingenuous self-possession. Her dark, shadowy eyes were a little frightened in their steadiness, but she kept them no less steady. Her cheeks retained their translucent pallor. "May I have a cup of tea?" she said to Cousin Mart. "I've been looking forward to one."

Cousin Mart satisfied her with alacrity and evident pleasure. He himself passed her the cup and motioned her to a chair by his side. Obviously he approved of her and liked her low voice, for he encouraged her to talk, and listened more to the sound than to her words. Meanwhile his astute eyes studied her face, finding there a combination of sophistication and candor that interested him. She was half a woman of the world and half a child that wished to please. Underneath her alternating currents of shyness and confidence ran an unmistakable depth of emotion and strength of purpose.

In the midst of the small talk she unpretentiously put before him, Cousin Mart broke in with an inward grace that excused his apparent rudeness. "I'm glad to see that you're not a ninny, my dear," he said. "I should never notice you in a crowd, but I shall never forget you now that we have talked together."

She was intelligent enough to be pleased. Still she was not

wholly assured, and timidity had not completely died out of her eyes. She glanced up at Blackstone in an appeal for confidence, and he returned the look with an understanding solicitude that was foreign to his nature. He seemed to be standing guard over her, and he watched Cousin Mart as a fencer does his opponent in the midst of a bout.

Suddenly Cousin Mart began to pay some regard to the rest of the group. Except for Mrs. Warden, whose equanimity was unshaken, they stood in a state very close to embarrassment. After a moment of cool contemplation he turned back to Stella. "My nephews don't seem to be at their best to-night," he remarked dryly. "I hope they'll manage soon to be more entertaining."

Francis sprang into the breach. "You've been keeping us off the stage, sir," he remarked smiling. "If you'll give us a chance———" He moved over and stood by Stella's side, his eyes bright with pleased excitement. Blackstone did not seem to care for his intervention, but said nothing.

From the other side of the room Amelia piped up suddenly: "I *cannot* seem to think"—she worried her words—"*why* the name 'Stella' is *so* familiar to me. I don't think I ever *knew* anyone of that name, but—"

It was George who, in a cracked voice, answered her, "You're probably thinking of Stella Maris," he said, "or 'Bright star, would I were steadfast as thou art,' or—or Sonnets to Stella," he concluded lamely.

"I never heard of any of them," Amelia retorted with unwonted firmness.

It was Stella herself who laughed a little at this interchange, and relieved the atmosphere. "It's not an unusual name," she said gently, and turned back to continue her conversation with

Francis, who bent over her eagerly. Blackstone refused to give up his place by her side, however, until Cousin Mart preempted him, beckoning him to a chair. If there was one thing the sharp old man disliked more than another it was to have someone towering over him.

Blackstone did not want to abandon Stella to Francis's graces, but he submitted, pressing his thin, well shaped lips together a little. Cousin Mart noticed his reluctance. "You seem entirely devoted," he remarked smoothly.

"Entirely." There was a note of real antagonism in Blackstone's voice, out of place in the mimic warfare usually carried on between them.

Cousin Mart frowned a little, the acuteness of his perceptions heightened by Blackstone's manner. For the moment, however, he did not pursue his intuition. There was a genuine basis of affection between him and his young prototype, and they had always dealt with each other in mutual respect and understanding.

It was with warmth that Cousin Mart voiced his approval of Blackstone's choice. "I wanted you to marry," he said, and then, with a rare admission of his preference, "you more than any of the others. But I'd have been bitterly disappointed if you had chosen an unsuitable wife. We already have an example of that sort of stupidity in the family. I need not tell you how strongly and actively I should have opposed another such misstep. As it is——" He was content to express his satisfaction with a gesture.

Somehow Blackstone did not rise to a full appreciation of his words. "Thanks," he said shortly.

"We seem to have the same propensities," Cousin Mart continued after a momentary pause. "The same qualities seem to attract us both. Certainly I have no interest in the ordinary types of beauty, and neither, apparently, have you. I demand a certain distinction of mind and bearing, and this, I am very glad to say, I find in your Stella." He glanced toward her with undisguised approval.

Again, from the other side of the room, came Amelia's murmur, "Stella—very familiar."

A sudden look of wariness came over Cousin Mart's face, "Stella," he repeated, considering the name. He turned to the girl herself, speaking with a rising inflection, "Your name is Stella———?"

Before she could answer, Blackstone stepped in. "Yes, Stella," he said flatly.

Cousin Mart studied him coldly. "Thank you, Blackstone," he said. "My question may have been unnecessary." His glance traveled over the room. "A little while ago," he said almost to himself, "I was amazed at the awkward behavior of the members of my family. It never occurred to me, from what I know and have heard, that any of us might not be competent and finished—socially speaking. Now I think I . . . understand." He sank back in his chair and became less active in the conversation. His abstracted gaze centered frequently on Stella and Francis, still talking by his side. A few words of theirs caught and held his attention.

"You play the piano?" Francis said as though he were feeling his way to a common ground of interest.

"Yes," she answered him unwaveringly. "Yes. I still play a great deal. And—" she caught her breath, but went on—"do you still sing?"

Francis took the cue from her. "My voice isn't even as good as it was when you first heard it," he said, "but I still sing."

Cousin Mart's nostrils twitched a little. His mind seemed suddenly to have focused on a doubtful point. "You two have met before, then?" he asked.

"Oh, yes," Francis admitted airily. "A number of times."

Again Cousin Mart relaxed into one of his dangerous calms. He watched the two of them as they rose and walked over to the cabinet which held the sheet music. In a moment he beckoned Blackstone to him.

"Who is this young lady?" he asked.

"Your guest," Blackstone answered him.

"I don't need to be reminded of that fact," Cousin Mart replied, "or of the privileges to which it entitles her. You have brought her to my house, and you shall answer for her. At the present moment, I intend to find out one thing. What is her last name?"

Blackstone told him. "Irwin," he said overemphatically.

Cousin Mart looked at him almost with admiration. "And so you," he said softly, "have had the audacity to bring into my house the girl whom I forbade Francis to marry."

CHAPTER VII

THE CONSTRUCTION OF AN INTRIGUE

THE NEXT day Cousin Mart went so far as to vary his invariable habits. Somewhat to the discomfort of his relatives, he made his appearance at lunch time. He ordered the impassive butler, Griggs, to have the curtains in the dining room drawn to, and the huge silver candelabra lighted, so that, seated in his high-backed, ornately carved chair at the head of the table, with Giulio at his elbow, he should feel less the change in his routine. If he made himself happier by that procedure, he did not perceptibly improve the spirits of his guests. In spite of their efforts they could not dispel the depression that had come over them with their entry into the huge, shadowy room with its somber magnificence and twinkling, ineffectual illumination.

All of them knew by this time that Blackstone had told Cousin Mart the truth of Stella's identity. All of them knew too that his manner, superficially at least, had not altered toward her, but they were uneasy at his very tolerance, and at his smooth ignoring of their awkwardness. Only Hutchinson seemed to think that Blackstone's mistake had its advantages. He glanced at his younger cousin with a wooden complacence and stroked his mustache with his square-tipped fingers. He was sure, for once, that neither he nor Amelia had put Cousin Mart out, but his wife, for her part, was so accustomed to a sense of guilt that even her chatter was utterly subdued. Blackstone himself fingered the delicate stem of his wineglass with accentuated haughtiness, while George demanded whisky and soda with undisguised nervous wretchedness.

The meal ran through its courses while Cousin Mart chatted pointedly with a pale but composed Stella. Once or twice she looked at Blackstone, but it was Francis and not he who unbent to help her. Her eyes were fleetingly perplexed at the turn of events, but she had no choice but to accept the substitution. He made every effort for her, encouraged by Cousin Mart's sardonic approval.

In the middle of lunch the butler went to Hutchinson's side and murmured something to him. He rose with alacrity. "If I may be excused," he said to Cousin Mart, "I'll answer a telephone call."

"You can't have the call repeated later?" Cousin Mart hated to have his meals interrupted.

"I'd rather not. It's from Banks about my studs." Hutchinson, reminded of something, turned to Griggs. "Did some large packages come for me this morning?"

"I think so, sir. Several packing boxes, though, rather than packages."

"That's all right, then." Hutchinson dismissed him brusquely and went to answer the telephone.

He was gone a long time. When he made his reentry everyone looked up at him and looked quickly away again. His heavy, usually unimpassioned face was contorted with violent anger. It was a clear and nakedly embarrassing revelation of Hutchinson's inner temper. They were startled—all except Cousin Mart, who asked with a facetious curiosity, "Has something put you out, Hutchinson?"

"No, no," Hutchinson spoke with difficulty. "Nothing at all."

As he took his place again he glanced across the table at the flustered Amelia. His eyes were stony with latent dislike. When Mrs. Warden gave the signal and they left the dining room for the library he singled her out from the others.

"You've outdone yourself this time," they heard him say to her brutally, and her wailing answer, "Oh, Hutchinson, I never——" The rest of her speech he must have cut off. His own low menacing tones went on, until he left her abruptly and, still shaken with anger, entered the library. She followed him hurriedly, seeking protection in the group.

Their appearance seemed to be a signal for Cousin Mart's departure. To Giulio he gave his leopard-skin robe, which the valet folded neatly over his arm. Casting a derisive eye on the Hutchinson Greenoughs, he excused himself, saying, "I think you will be able to amuse yourselves this afternoon. I myself have a little work to do."

George watched his slow exit with a rebellious eye. "He means he's going to take a nap," he muttered, "but he won't admit it. I'll do the same, I guess." He extricated himself from the group around the fireplace. No one needed to explain to him the symptoms of coming trouble.

Amelia had drawn Mrs. Warden into a corner, distressful confidences in her very gestures. Her voice went on and on, interrupted at rare moments by Mrs. Warden's aloof, slightly weary tones. The others, Hutchinson, Francis, Stella, and Blackstone grouped themselves about the fireplace, staring into the flames. Francis occupied himself with putting wood on the fire, until Blackstone could stand it no longer. "God in heaven, Francis!" he said. "It's almost eighty outside."

Francis looked at him obliquely and murmured an apology. "I thought it seemed a little chilly in here," he explained.

There was a short silence. "I'm going out," Blackstone said decisively. "Will you ride, Stella?" He half demanded it of her, half excused himself for ignoring her during lunch.

She brightened a little. "I'd like to," she said. There was a maternal tolerance in her tone which he was too impatient to detect.

"Very well." He rang, and, when Griggs appeared, gave his orders. "Have Gemini and Jemima brought around in a half hour." With a characteristic scorn for half measures he had chosen the two best horses in Cousin Mart's stables. "That will give you plenty of time to change, won't it?"

This time she showed her amusement. "It usually takes me ten minutes less than you," she said smiling. "No fussing, now."

Blackstone was unwillingly restored to good-humor. She was the only person to whom he yielded one jot or tittle of his touchy pride.

"I wish we could go cross-country," he said, "but we'll follow the bridle paths as long as we can before we go out on the Fenway. He's built some fair jumps for us, and then, too, you can get a good look at the whole place. Come along!" He held out a hand to her and half turned to see Giulio standing by his side.

"Well, what is it?" he said to the silent valet.

"Mr. Greenough send his compliments to Mr. Blackstone Greenough and would like to see him at half-past three this afternoon." He spoke like a ventriloquist's dummy, his glittering eyes the only lively feature of his face. Impassively he watched Blackstone's gathering irritation.

"He can see me some other time." Blackstone spoke rapidly. "I'm fixed for this afternoon. Tell him that—or tell him that I'm going riding and I'll see him at five—no, that won't do! Tell him—— Damnation!" His emotions passed kaleidoscopically across his face. He thought for a moment and turned on the waiting, stolid servant as if to stare him out of existence. "Very well," he said. "I'll come to his rooms at three-thirty." To Stella he said, "I'll have to see him. I really don't want to offend him."

"Especially not now," Francis put in for him helpfully.

"Now or any other time," Blackstone snapped back at him. He thought again of Stella. "There's no sense in our waiting till later," he said. "It'll be tea and then dinner, and he's up and will expect us to be there. Can you read or do something for a while?"

"Why can't I substitute for you, Blackstone?" Francis suggested. "I'd be glad to, if Stella would——"

"That'll do." Blackstone accepted for her grudgingly.

Stella was apparently tired of being a pawn in the game. "You are very nice, Francis," she said with gracious decision. "I'll go up and change."

Amelia, deserted by Mrs. Warden, advanced upon them. "You are going riding with Francis, Stella?" she asked vaguely. "So nice for you two to have an opportunity to renew your friendship."

She embraced them with a benedictory smile which faded suddenly as she looked away. Hutchinson was coming toward her from across the room.

"Come upstairs, Amelia," he said to her stiffly. "We haven't finished our—talk, you know." He spoke in a quiet tone, but there were mingled anxiety and anger in the insistent way he pushed her toward the door, one hand beneath her elbow. Amelia's face grew pale. She cast a helpless look around the room as she walked away.

CHAPTER VIII

WARNING

BLACKSTONE PARTED from Francis and Stella at the head of the stairs. For a moment he watched them as they walked down the wide hallway, and then he resumed his way toward Cousin Mart's rooms. Giulio stood outside his master's door. His chief duty was to spare Cousin Mart undesired interruptions, and, a suave, swarthy Cerberus, he carried out his orders to the letter. Now he bowed a little and let Blackstone pass unhindered.

From the light, airy hallway the other went into the artificially darkened room, pausing on the threshold in his quick stride. He peered into the obscurity, his near-sighted eyes strained in an attempt to see more clearly. Cousin Mart chuckled a little. "I wouldn't have you wear spectacles, my dear boy," he said, "but you might find a monocle effective."

Blackstone was too sensitive about his only physical defect to reply. "I don't share your taste for darkness," he said bluntly, a myopic frown between his brows.

"Draw the curtains," Cousin Mart suggested amiably.

Blackstone reached for the cord. As he pulled it, the curtains slid apart, the rings clinking against the brass rod. The afternoon sunlight flooded in, paling Cousin Mart's lamp to insignificance.

"So clear as to be uninteresting," Cousin Mart pronounced of the sudden daylight. "But if you like it, sit down." Blackstone took the chair already set for him, facing the light. He shifted it a little so that the sun did not shine directly in his eyes. "A cigarette?" Cousin Mart offered his nephew one of his own particular brand and took the light Blackstone held for him in exchange. Lucy, who lay on his lap, sneezed at the smoke. As his hand ceased to stroke the cat's gray flanks it reached up a long gray paw and patted him to attract his attention.

The two men smoked silently for a few minutes. Cousin Mart's face, like his lamp, had paled in the unaccustomed daylight, but not into insignificance. The distinctive outline of his pointed features did not alter. The sharp lines around his mouth and eyes were accentuated by the smoothness of his skin. He leaned back in his chair comfortably, but there was little relaxation of will in his posture. He did not permit any emotion he might have felt to alter the expression of his face, but his voice, when he spoke, held an unusual warmth.

"There has been very little conversation of an intimate nature between us, Blackstone," he said, a certain preciousness creeping into the words he chose. "I find it difficult to talk to you on that level now."

Blackstone helped him only with a gesture of reluctant understanding. The resemblance between them lay deeper than their physical likeness, but Blackstone had not lived long enough to be rid of the awkward embarrassments of youth.

"I dislike making invidious distinctions," Cousin Mart continued, "between you and my other nephews and nieces. As far as I know I have not indulged to any great extent in that luxury.

You all went to the same schools—very expensive ones—and colleges. None of your various educations"—Cousin Mart permitted himself a faintly malicious smile—"has been neglected. If I have been more indulgent to any one of you than to the others, it has been to Francis—I can hardly say why. He enjoys a definite allowance from me, and the rest of you do not. But that is of no importance at this moment. What I am trying to say to you, with great difficulty—" elaborately he tapped the ash from his cigarette—"is that I am personally fond of you, Blackstone. I regard you in some sense as a reappearance of myself in another generation. I can't force you to believe in the sincerity of my affection for you. But I hope you will believe me."

Blackstone fidgeted a little. "There's no need of saying that," he retorted antagonistically. "I know it. I feel the same way. We scrap——"

"Exactly," Cousin Mart finished for him. "We disagree with perfect understanding. But, you see, Blackstone, we are on the verge of a disagreement in which we must make an effort to understand each other."

Blackstone frowned. "There's no use of going into that," he said sharply. "You may do as you like. I know what I want."

"You can't dismiss me in that fashion," Cousin Mart reminded him. "I am not, please realize, speaking of financial complications, but of our mutual—affection."

Blackstone stirred restlessly again. His silence admitted the truth of what Cousin Mart had said. An unhappy look flashed across his face; then his habitual arrogance reasserted itself. "What is it you want to say to me?" he asked a little less abruptly.

Cousin Mart answered him with another question. "Why do you suppose I forbade Francis to marry Stella?"

"Because you like to keep him on the jump," Blackstone replied without hesitation.

"No." Cousin Mart was not offended at the statement. "That might have been the reason, but it wasn't. A great many years ago now, I was in business with her father. We were extremely successful for a time. Then, without warning or reason, our business dropped off. I had my lawyers look into it. They found that the late Mr. Irwin was guilty of an undoubted misuse of our common funds. We quarreled, and I forced him to make restitution. The moral of my story is briefly this—that figs do not grow on thistles."

"I've heard that story from another point of view," Blackstone answered remorselessly. "That you trapped and cheated your partner—legally, of course—so outrageously that you have hated the mention of his name ever since."

Sudden anger flushed Cousin Mart's cheeks, but he had a strong hand over himself. "Your version is not true," he said stiffly. "I suppose you had it from your fiancée."

"She has not mentioned the subject to me." Blackstone's amber eyes were beginning to glitter. He bit his under lip until it was crimson.

"We'll dismiss that part of it, then." Cousin Mart even attempted to soothe him. "There are certainly no two stories about her engagement to Francis?"

"No," Blackstone retorted. "I'll repeat for you the only one there is. She was in love with Francis and wanted to marry him. You threatened to cut him off if he married her, and he jilted her as gracefully as possible. After he did that, she knew him too well to have any regrets about him."

"Are you so sure of that?" Cousin Mart leaned forward to look out of the window. On the road beneath, Francis and Stella were mounting their horses. She was talking to him gayly, as if she felt with him a sense of release. Blackstone peered at them, frowning.

"I told Francis to take her riding," he said.

"Of course." Cousin Mart passed smoothly over the point. "What do you know of Francis's way of living, Blackstone?" he asked.

"More than I want to," Blackstone replied.

"I supposed so," the old man went on, "since rumors reach even me. And you still want to marry a lady he picked out, and one who wanted to marry him?"

Blackstone turned on him in a rage. "She had no idea of the kind he was. She never suspected anybody. She isn't even suspicious now of you. Yes, I do!"

Cousin Mart observed him through narrowed eyes, as if to judge the state of his temper. Blackstone's color had mounted to two red spots on his cheek bones. His thin, powerful hands were clenched on the arms of his chair. His breathing was fast. He was on the verge of an overpowering rage.

Cousin Mart did not press his point. "Very well, then," he said. "After all, it's for you to decide. Why should I care?" He was momentarily pettish, but his next words showed a change of feeling. He weighed them critically. "There's this about it, Blackstone," he said. "As I told you, I don't think she's the sort you should marry. I'd be sorry to see you involved in—— But never mind. Judge for yourself. I haven't any more to say. You had better go now, and incidentally—" he gave a mocking glance at the other's face—"I'd practise self-control, if I were you."

Blackstone got up and walked blindly toward the door. His hand felt for the knob. As he left the room he passed Mrs. Warden in the hall but did not seem to see her. She came into Cousin Mart's study quietly.

"You've been talking to him about——?"

"Yes. Blackstone is not what you might call amenable." Cousin Mart was tired and annoyed. "Why he should indulge in such a piece of stupidity——! I'd have expected it from the others, but from him——!"

He glanced irritably out the bright window, his hand creeping toward the curtain cord. "Ah!" he breathed. Blackstone was riding furiously by, bareback. He had not paused to change his clothes. Without hesitating he guided his horse down the path that Stella and Francis had taken.

★　　★　　★

That evening, after dinner, Cousin Mart and his guests assembled again in the library downstairs. As a group they were still uneasy. Cousin Mart himself was cranky and disagreeable, although Mrs. Warden exerted herself to smooth him down. George's weak, melancholy face was etched with nervous trouble, which he tried to drown and succeeded in magnifying with incessant doses of whisky. He took refuge in petulance and kept well away from his caustic host. Hutchinson still nursed his bottled-up, unexplained anger, his eyes as cold and as intent as a basilisk's. The unfortunate Amelia chattered on, avoiding Hutchinson's company and his glance. Francis could not combat the prevalent disease alone. His verve vanished, and only the enamel of his pleasantry remained. He became restless and glanced covertly at the clock.

Cousin Mart's sharp eyes caught him up. "You seem to find the evening unusually long, Francis," he remarked testily, "but I haven't noticed you doing anything to make it shorter or more enjoyable for us all."

"I don't know that I'm a very good entertainer, sir," Francis said ruefully, "but I'll do my best at whatever——"

"Why don't you sing for us, Francis?" Mrs. Warden suggested.

"Yes, do. I've heard you sing perhaps ten times, and each occasion," Cousin Mart lapsed into grumbling, "has, I calculate, cost me a thousand dollars. I'd like to bring the average down."

Francis gave him a genial smile. "I'll sing," he said, "and perhaps Stella will play for me?"

Stella nodded to him. It seemed to be a relief to her to move from the chair where Blackstone had established her. For the last hour he had stood by her side, saying nothing. She gave him a puzzling look as she rose and went with Francis to the piano.

For a minute or two they turned over the sheets of music. Then he picked out a score, and she began to play for him. He sang easily and naturally, without embarrassment or affectation. His voice was smooth and lovely in its effortlessness. The sound of it seemed to intoxicate him. They ran through the woes of Pagliacci and the lover of Manon, the wailing notes of Water Boy, the jovialities of the old bold mate of Henry Morgan.

As they came to the end of Francis's selections, Stella looked up to meet Blackstone's glowering eyes. She smiled a little. "I have a song for you, Francis," she said. "I noticed the music——" She ran through the pile again to find what she wanted. "Here it is." Her fingers touched the keys. A gleam of understanding came into Francis's face as she played the opening bars. Again effortlessly he began to sing, "*La donna è mobile . . .* "

Blackstone turned away scowling.

CHAPTER IX

STRANGE TACTICS

"Nothing's the matter with me. Nothing," Blackstone insisted, as if Stella had contradicted him. "Nothing at all."

She looked at him in silence. "I'm three years older than you," she said finally. "I suppose I should know how to deal with you, but I don't."

He stood by the mantelpiece facing her, but his eyes refused to meet hers. Instead they stared into angry, incomprehensible distance. "Three years!" he said. "What difference does that make?"

"A great deal happens in three years," she answered him lightly.

"That doesn't make any difference either," he retorted. "It makes no difference at all." His resentment cut him off from her.

"Something seems to," she replied.

He hesitated on the brink of speech. "Why—why did you——"

"Why did I what?" she prompted him.

He bit his thin, delicately curved lips. "Never mind," he said rapidly. "Nothing."

"Again nothing." She laughed, mocking him a little.

He looked at her as if he had never seen her before. With a sudden anxiety he scanned her pale, thin face, whose deceptive fragility was emphasized by the darkness and depth of her eyes. He seemed to be trying to read there the answer to the question he had not put.

"He's very fond of me, you know," Blackstone said at last.

"Your uncle?" Her low voice was full of bitterness.

"Yes. Who else?"

"It's too bad he isn't equally fond of me."

Blackstone resented her words. "You might have a little patience," he said. "You might try to understand the situation."

"Patience!" She laughed again. "What a strange attitude for you to recommend, Blackstone. As for understanding, you must give it to me. I haven't the humility to ask questions."

"You don't need to ask anything. You ought to know," he said. "He's acting for my sake. I'm fond of him. I can't go against him."

"Neither could Francis."

Blackstone threw his head back as if he had had a blow in the face. "Francis," he said. "Always Francis!" His eyes glittered with anger.

"Don't press me too far," she warned him. "After a certain point I might not—have patience."

"Stella!" His voice had lost its sharpness. He almost appealed to her. "Don't be too hard on me. All this doesn't make any difference. I——" He checked himself. There was a queer, muffled sound in the hall that by its very slightness caught his attention and hers. They both listened, but heard nothing else.

When Blackstone spoke again his gentleness was gone. "There's no sense in talking," he said rudely. "Cousin Mart's right. He told me long ago that I'd have a happy life if I could keep from too great a liking for anything." He laughed. "Or anyone," he added.

"Yet he cherishes a certain affection for Mrs. Warden," she reminded him.

"Mrs. Warden!" Blackstone's attention focused on the name. "Leave her out of it! I——"

Stella interrupted him coolly. "Perhaps, if you are going to put yourself in Cousin Mart's hands, I might go to her for advice."

Blackstone took a quick step towards her, his fists clenched at his sides. Again the strange sound came from the hall, as if someone, anxious to disguise his presence, were treading softly on its thick carpet. With a quick change of purpose, Blackstone stepped towards the library door and threw it open. He stared in amazement at the person who confronted him.

"What in God's name are you doing, Hutchinson?" he asked.

"None of your business," Hutchinson's steely voice answered.

He walked away, his heavy footsteps thudding dully now that he had nothing to conceal.

From the other direction Francis sauntered towards the library.

"Question and answer," he said, smiling at Stella as he entered the room. "What was he doing, Blackstone? People who ask usually know anyway."

"I don't know." Blackstone's reply was curt.

"What made you think he was doing anything, then?"

"He was creeping around the hall as if he didn't want to be caught at it. When I opened the door he was peering into that cabinet out there—where Mart keeps the chessmen."

Francis laughed. "Perhaps he was overcome by a sudden passion for chess," he said, "though it doesn't sound characteristic. But—" he looked from Blackstone to Stella with a charming understanding—"I didn't come here merely to interrupt your tête-à-tête. You know that this is the great day—Mart's birthday," he explained more clearly to Stella. "For a second time in succession he is lunching with us. I thought you'd better know."

"You mean he is coming down now?" Blackstone was slightly exasperated.

"So Giulio whispered to me. I took it that it was my duty to clear the field for him."

"All right. Come along, Stella. We'll talk somewhere else." He ignored Francis.

"I thought we'd finished," Stella said in a tone that startled her fiancé. "I had finished."

"Very well, then." He stared at her hard. "But I warn you don't get *her* to interfere in my affairs."

She laughed a little. "I'll give you a warning in exchange," she said proudly. "Don't let *him* interfere too much in mine."

Francis looked at them curiously. He was puzzled. A question was on the tip of his tongue, but he kept a tactful silence. "See you later," he said and vanished. Blackstone and Stella parted at the library door.

Cousin Mart was already on his way downstairs, attended by Giulio. The old man stepped spryly enough when he wanted, and he seemed in good spirits now, in spite or because of the advent of his seventy-fifth birthday. Age had not dulled his vitality or his perverse humor. Midway in his brisk descent he paused and turned to the valet. There was a brightening spark of anger in his eye.

"Tell Mr. Hutchinson Greenough that I want to speak to him, here, now."

"Yes, sir." The valet turned and softly mounted the stairs, the dark mask of his face showing neither curiosity nor surprise at the summons he was so unexpectedly commanded to deliver.

Cousin Mart stood erect at the turn of the staircase, waiting for the appearance of his eldest nephew. He had some sixty seconds to stand there. When Giulio left him he was motionless, his eyes as indefinite as they ever were. When the valet returned, with Hutchinson in his wake, Cousin Mart's mood had crystallized. There was a little frown between his eyebrows, and his foot tapped impatiently on the stair.

Hutchinson was sullen, although he tried to assume a certain amount of urbanity. "It didn't occur to me," he said in his stiff voice, "that you might want to speak to me. If it had, I should not have passed you by so quickly a moment ago."

"I didn't want to speak to you until you passed me by so quickly a moment ago," Cousin Mart answered him pointedly. "What I have to say now can be said in very short order. You are, of course, at liberty to behave as you think best. I should *recommend*, however"—as he emphasized the word, his sharp glance suddenly focused on the other's face—"that you confine yourself to less peculiar activities than some I've seen you at this morning."

Hutchinson, stung by the words, hid his anger with an effort. Swallowing hard, he tried to say something to the neat back that Cousin Mart presented, once again agilely stepping down the stairs. His muttered attempt at an apology ignored, he swung on the impassive Giulio.

"Get out of my way!" he said.

Smoothly the valet stepped aside, and with unalterable discretion followed his master to the library.

Cousin Mart lowered himself easily into his favorite chair and watched Giulio advancing toward him, the leopard-skin robe over his arm. The valet unfolded it expertly and threw it over Cousin Mart's lap. He regarded it with sudden distaste.

"Take it away!" he snapped. "Get something else! I can't look at the same thing day after day!" As Giulio left the room with the offending article, Cousin Mart called after him. "Tell Griggs to come here!"

A minute later the butler appeared and approached the old man with a propitiatory smile. Cousin Mart ignored his timid good-morning. "You may tell your staff that if this house is not better run in the next twenty-four hours than it has been in the past, you will pay them off to-morrow."

"Yes, sir." The butler's obsequious assent only served to increase Cousin Mart's ill temper.

"In the meantime, get half a dozen men here."

"Yes, sir."

Again Cousin Mart's foot began to beat on the floor. It had a magical effect. The six men sprang up like mushrooms, and under his orders set to work feverishly. In ten minutes every piece of furniture except Cousin Mart's chair was moved out of the room. In ten more a new set was arranged. Nothing remained the same except the portrait over the mantelpiece, out of which a second Cousin Mart watched sardonically the creation of a new kingdom.

In the midst of the storm Amelia blundered in.

"Where's your husband?" Cousin Mart barked at her. "What's the matter with him?"

She cowered under the tone of his voice. "I—I really don't know," she said, and then, taking refuge in further vagueness, "I simply can't understand Hutchinson and the things he's been saying."

"Then if you will get out of the way," Cousin Mart cut her off, "I think that desk may get into the room."

Amelia cast a glance at the massive object that had come to a halt behind her, and another at Cousin Mart. Wordlessly she fled, stumbling into George, who stepped aside to avoid her. In her haste she did not see Francis watching the reorganization, his lips puckered in a soundless whistle. For a moment or two he looked on and listened. Then he wandered down the hall to meet Mrs. Warden. He paused by her side.

"Martin is not behaving like a birthday child," he said to her.

He was so obviously not joking that she was startled. "What is it?" she asked. "What is the matter?"

"I don't know," he answered her. Absently he rubbed his clean-shaven cheek. "He's ordered a new lot of furniture and a new set of servants. The next step may very well be a new deal in relatives." He turned to her with his sweet supplicating smile. "Try to smooth him down, will you? You're the only one who can do it."

She was pleased by his flattery. "Of course," she said. "I shouldn't worry if I were you. He has his whims, you know."

"Yes," Francis remarked with a certain dryness. "I have reason to know that. But, in this case, I'll count on you." He put into his words a warmth of feeling that touched her. She nodded to him and walked on toward the library. He heard her smooth voice speaking to Cousin Mart and watched the servants, released from their task, make their hurried exits from the room. He nodded a little with satisfaction and turned to go to his own rooms. On the way he met George and warned him.

"Wait a half hour," he said, "before you beard our lion tamer." He did not bother to see whether or not George took the hint, but went on, his springing step carrying him quickly and quietly up the stairs and along the second-story hall. There a slight sound brought him to an abrupt halt. Hutchinson, some fifty feet away from him, was bending over a desk, feeling with clumsy hands in its gaping pigeonholes, opening its drawers. He had not heard Francis, nor did he see Giulio silently watching him.

CHAPTER X

DISCLOSURE

THE FAMILY, except for Hutchinson and his wife, had assembled again in the altered library. One by one they had offered their congratulations, from George's mumbled, tactless speech to Blackstone's clear, curt one. Since Cousin Mart had asked them not to give birthday presents, they had nothing to offer him. With more than his usual contrariness he told them that it was "pleasant at least to *hear*" that his anniversary had not been forgotten. The emphasis smote them disagreeably.

No one mentioned the change in the room, until he himself brought up the subject. With a swift return to ostensible suavity he said, "I hope you approve of my new arrangements," waving his hand to take in the surrounding objects.

"Oh, yes," Francis supported him helpfully, "I like the way you've grouped those things over there."

"It hadn't occurred to me that they were grouped," Cousin Mart came back at him. "Don't talk like an interior decorator, Francis." He turned to Blackstone. "Let me have your ideas on the subject, Blackstone."

"I haven't any ideas," Blackstone said rudely, as he peered

near-sightedly about him. "Personally, I can't see why you didn't leave things as they were."

"For a very simple though comprehensive reason, Blackstone." Cousin Mart included them all in his audience. "For the past ten years," he said clearly, "I have been content to live in a distressing monotony. I am not content to do so any longer. In the next decade you will see many changes in my manner of living."

A wave of uneasiness passed through the room. George drew himself farther back in his chair, as if he sought support and protection from it. The deep lines that stretched down his gaunt cheeks deepened against the pallor of his face.

"I hope you aren't going to make too many changes, Martin." Mrs. Warden humored him with easy good-temper. "I'm afraid I've come to the point of being comfortable in an old shoe."

"My dear," he turned to her gallantly, "I cannot continue the metaphor in footgear, but I have learned very well that certain wines can only improve with age. Others"—he glanced at Blackstone, Francis, and George—"acquire an unpleasant acidity." His green eyes became frosty. "The young," he said meditatively, "take everything for granted."

Francis gave a somewhat forced laugh. "Well," he remarked, "I wish I could think of myself as young still, even in the face of your aspersions. I'm thirty-eight, and getting gray."

"To me, Francis," Cousin Mart answered him, "you still seem to have at least some of the qualities of youth."

Mrs. Warden interrupted the disquisition that hovered on his lips. "How would you like it, Martin," she said, "if I were to make you a special cocktail in honor of your birthday? I think we might all enjoy one." She might have been setting herself to please a small child.

"You are very thoughtful, Edith." Again he softened his mood for her sake, and looked after her with approval as she left the room.

"Where is Hutchinson?" He turned back sharply to the others.

"Upstairs, I think," Francis murmured vaguely. Cousin Mart's foot began to tap on the floor.

"Giulio!" he called suddenly.

As if by magic the powerful figure of the valet materialized in the doorway. Cousin Mart beckoned him to come in, and when the man stood close to his chair murmured a question to him. The Italian bent down to answer it. Francis watched the two of them with a sudden intensity, which came to its height when Cousin Mart cast his robe aside, got up rapidly, and left the room.

"Damn Hutchinson!" he said.

"Damn everything!" George echoed him savagely. "Damn the slavish, miserable life I've led! I told you! We're ditched!" He beat his fist against the palm of his hand. "We get our just reward for all our bootlicking!" He laughed wildly. "And I thought I might spend some of my days in decency and peace!"

"Be quiet, George." Francis turned on him brutally. "Listen! Hutchinson's been sneaking around like a thief, and Cousin Mart got suspicious and had Giulio watch him. Now he's caught him in the act. Listen!"

He had hardly spoken when they heard Cousin Mart's mordant voice upstairs. "Hutchinson! May I ask what you're about?"

They heard the quick sound of a drawer being pushed shut. "Hutchinson covering up his tracks," Francis whispered.

"I—I was just looking through this table," Hutchinson's ponderous voice was tinged with nervousness.

"Why must you, this morning, spend your time looking through tables, desks, bureaus, and so forth?"

There was a moment of silence. "I was—looking for something."

"Looking for something!" Cousin Mart's voice cracked with anger. "Looking for *what?*"

Hutchinson did not answer, and Cousin Mart went on. "You seem to forget that you are a guest in my house. This 'looking' business of yours is the last straw. What are you looking for?"

"I can't tell you." Hutchinson's voice grated in his throat.

"I'd advise you to."

"Very well, then." Hutchinson turned to recklessness. "It doesn't make any difference one way or the other now. Remember I tried to find it. I tried not to let you know about it."

"Whatever you are trying to conceal," Cousin Mart cut in on him, "you're not being very successful about it."

"This is Amelia's fault," Hutchinson said bitterly. "She's done for me this time."

"What do you mean?"

Again there was no answer. The three men in the living room strained their ears. They were startled when they heard Cousin Mart's high laugh.

"You mean she has picked up something else?" he asked incredulously. "And you are putting on this entertainment for us merely on that account?"

"You don't understand." Hutchinson's words were muffled in wretchedness. "It's not just something else. I've stood it so far, but I can't stand this. I've *got* to find it."

"Why don't you advertise that you're not responsible for her debts?" Cousin Mart was becoming more and more amused.

"I have my position to think of."

"Your position!" Cousin Mart scoffed at him. "Let people say what they like. Divorce her!"

"I can't get a divorce on the grounds of kleptomania," Hutchinson replied stiffly. "I looked it up."

"Well," Cousin Mart dismissed him contemptuously, "if you can't pay for her scarfs and handkerchiefs——"

"Scarfs and handkerchiefs!" Hutchinson's voice rose in protest. "I can't make you understand. It isn't anything of the sort she's taken! She went to Banks and Tiffany the other day, and they saw her make off with it."

"Make off with what?"

There was a pause. Hutchinson was evidently summoning up his courage. "With a necklace," he said finally, "a necklace that they value at five thousand dollars." He stopped, and then went on hopelessly. "They saw her take it. Called me up yesterday and told me—very politely—that she had forgotten to give them instructions about it and so they had put it on my bill. My God! Where am I to get five thousand dollars to pay for a necklace?"

"Pay for it? Take it back!"

Hutchinson was desperate enough to fight. "Take it back?" He laughed scornfully. "Do you think I wouldn't if I could? I can't *find* it. I can't do anything with Amelia. She denies the whole business. Starts crying. I've kept at her steadily, and it does no good. She's like a squirrel. She's hidden it somewhere— God knows where. That's what I've been trying to find."

Francis stepped out into the downstairs hall as Mrs. Warden came from the pantry. "Do you hear what's going on upstairs?" He could not keep his amusement out of his voice. "Amelia's done it this time."

She nodded. "I heard," she said. "Poor Amelia!" There was a curious expression on her face, in which interest, and contempt, and tolerance took part.

"Poor Amelia!" Francis laughed. "She seems to have done very well. There may be method in this madness."

"What makes you say that?"

He laughed again. "Five thousand dollars is a good haul," he said lightly. "I wish I had it, though I wouldn't hang it round my neck. I'm not sure but that Amelia's a smart woman." He listened again to the voices upstairs. They were lower now, almost inaudible, but Cousin Mart's tone had obviously changed. He seemed to be taking pleasure in Hutchinson's dilemma. Once or twice he chuckled. Francis sighed with relief. "You know," he went on to Mrs. Warden, "I believe that you and Amelia, in your different ways, have worked a miracle. He actually seems to be in a good humor again. Perhaps he won't cut us off with a shilling, after all."

"I don't believe he will," she reassured him almost maternally. "He always feels better after he's been very difficult." She laughed a little. "And he has put on a fine performance, hasn't he?"

"Splendid!" Francis agreed. "Wait a moment! They're at it again."

Hutchinson and Cousin Mart must have come to the head of the stairs. Their words were clear again to the ears of the listeners.

"I can't see why you can't manage her," Cousin Mart was saying.

Hutchinson was reduced to humility. "Well, I can't," he said. "I can't make her tell me what she's done with it or do anything but cry. If you would talk to her, she might——"

"Certainly I'll talk to her." Cousin Mart had become cocky.

"I think I'll be able to find out the secret in five minutes, Hutchinson. And without peering into cubbyholes, too. *I* believe in diplomacy."

Hutchinson laughed with relief. "That's very good of you," he said. "I've been worried sick."

"Leave it to me, then." Cousin Mart was very business-like. "Where is she now?"

"In our sitting room."

"Very well. Go downstairs. I'll wait here till she starts down for lunch and speak to her. You needn't worry any more about *that* subject."

"I'm everlastingly grateful to you." Hutchinson's flat voice tried to express his mingled thankfulness and contrition. Treading with renewed firmness, he came down the stairs and into the library. He stared suspiciously at his various relatives, now apparently very much occupied with books and their own concerns. No one looked up at him.

He sat down and passed an immaculate handkerchief across his forehead with evident relief. As he folded it neatly and put it back in his pocket, Cousin Mart's voice was heard from upstairs.

"Ah, Amelia! I'm glad to catch you alone."

"Alone?" Amelia sounded frightened.

"Only to tell you something," Cousin Mart soothed her. "It occurred to me—and I feel badly about it—that it has been a long time since I have given you any little presents. I must make up for my neglect." His voice was suffused with gallantry.

Amelia was pleased. "Why, Cousin Mart," she babbled, "how very kind! But you really have given me things."

"You surely won't mind if I give you just one more?" Cousin Mart overpowered her with graciousness.

"Oh, no! Not at all. I *really*——"

"Perhaps," Cousin Mart suggested, "you've seen something lately that you've taken a fancy to? Hutchinson seems to be hard up, and you might like some piece of jewelry?"

"Oh!" Amelia exclaimed. "Well, I don't know," she hedged vaguely.

"But you're fond of it, aren't you?" Cousin Mart persisted, a little annoyed. "Wouldn't you like me to give you a piece of jewelry?"

Amelia accepted his offer heartily. "That would be lovely," she said.

"I thought you might have your eye on something," Cousin Mart suggested again.

Amelia hesitated for a long moment. "I haven't seen anything lately," she replied finally, "but I'll look around at the stores. I always——" She took refuge in bright vagueness.

"No. I'll tell you what to do," Cousin Mart interrupted her. "There's one jewelry store where I usually deal. You call them up as soon as you can this afternoon. Ask them to send out anything you fancy, on approval, you understand. Then you bring it to me, and we'll look it over together, you and I. Of course, I like to help choose the presents I give."

"Of course," Amelia breathed, "of course."

They came down the stairs together, Cousin Mart's step brisk with confidence. His trap was set. A pace or two behind him, Amelia followed. At the foot of the stairs Cousin Mart turned to her again.

"I'd prefer to have you buy it at the store I mention, Amelia. That is, at Banks and Tiffany. You understand?"

Amelia's eyes widened. "Why, yes—Banks and Tiffany," she murmured. Suddenly over her face passed a look of instinctive cunning.

CHAPTER XI

A NOTE OF JEALOUSY

IN THE course of the afternoon, Cousin Mart was unusually active. He had no more fits of temper, but used his energy in making sudden appearances upstairs and down. In spite of his scorn of Hutchinson's methods, he set Giulio to watching Amelia, whose face became more suspicious with every minute that passed. Some instinct told her that the frequent appearances of the valet in her neighborhood were not fortuitous. If it had not been for her obvious nervousness she might have been taking a wily pleasure in leading him from one room to another.

Even if they had not overheard Hutchinson's conversation with Cousin Mart, the others could not have failed to guess, with Amelia's well known aberration in their minds, what was up. Possessed of all the facts, they watched the comedy with undisguised enjoyment. Stella alone refused to take part in the game and was shocked at their coldblooded pleasure in it. Even Blackstone, his lip curling with disdain, unbent to make sharp comments on his unfortunate cousin-in-law. Francis was the only one who understood Stella's attitude, and tried to explain to her that Amelia would come to no real harm, that Cousin

Mart was only trying to outwit her, and that he would like her all the better if he did. Seeing that she was still distressed, Francis offered to go riding with her or play a game of tennis, but she refused him, not without gratitude. All her disturbance of mind seemed to center on Amelia's tragi-comedy.

"I've never understood before," she said to Francis with sudden bitterness. "It's he who has made you all like this. I think I could easily hate him." Her very quietness shocked Francis out of his explanations. He did not try to keep her when she said she would go upstairs to her rooms, but his eyes assured her of his always quick sympathy.

Cousin Mart made one more attempt to get Amelia to betray herself. By elaborate chance he passed her in her peregrinations.

"You haven't forgotten my little present?" he asked her. "Did you phone Banks?"

"Why, no," she said almost gasping. "No. I haven't yet. I've been *so* busy!" And she continued hastily on her way.

Cousin Mart did not confess to failure. He was still confident. Hutchinson was tactful enough not to hint that more than five minutes had passed and that the necklace was still undiscovered and unreturned. The burden had been shifted from his shoulders, and in his relief he was jovial. And reasonably enough, Francis remarked to the others, for even if Cousin Mart's strategy failed, he would certainly make up for its failure by paying for the necklace.

The interest of the spectators waned as the day grew older. Giulio was taken off his clandestine duty. One by one the Greenoughs drifted upstairs to prepare for the birthday dinner, or outside on the wide lawns to amuse themselves for the couple of unscheduled hours that remained. Cousin Mart seemed at first inclined to take up his post in the library. Accompanied by Mrs. Warden, he made his progress down the hall, disappeared into the room for a few minutes, and a few minutes later emerged again, evidently having changed his mind. He went upstairs and for an hour shut himself up in his sitting room. At the end of that time he again sent the valet for Blackstone.

The latter was a long time in obeying the summons, and when he came he did not bother to hide his reluctance. There was a bleak, self-protective look in his face, as if he had taken refuge from his problems in a hostile withdrawal from the people who made them.

Without speaking, Cousin Mart motioned him to sit down. For a moment or two he stared at him shrewdly, as if he were trying to find an opening through which to penetrate Blackstone's antagonism. Finally he gave up the attempt.

"You've been thinking over what I said to you yesterday?" he began with unusual directness.

"I haven't needed to think about it," Blackstone threw off the accusation.

"It's a symptom of weakness not to admit what's obvious, Blackstone," Cousin Mart cut back at him. "Weakness or stupidity, and I can't bring myself to think that you're really stupid. At least you remember what we talked about."

"If you mean that there's no necessity for bringing it up again, I agree." Color had begun to rise to Blackstone's high cheek bones. His reddish, crinkled hair refused to lie flat under his nervously stroking hand.

"That wasn't exactly what I meant," Cousin Mart retorted. "In fact, I see a distinct necessity for bringing it up again. I said then that Miss Irwin was not the kind of girl I cared to have you marry." He could not keep out of his voice a thin note of triumph, which fed Blackstone's anger.

"Well, I'm not going to have any more of this," he said, and sprang to his feet.

"Blackstone!" Something in Cousin Mart's voice stopped him on his way to the door. He turned and confronted the old man again.

"I have to remind you," Cousin Mart went on more softly, "that I am not saying these things for my own pleasure and satisfaction, but on account of my interest in you."

For a moment Blackstone hesitated; then he walked back to his chair and sat down, tacitly acknowledging the other's sincerity.

"Something has come to my attention," Cousin Mart resumed, "that I think you should know about. When you *do* know about it, my part in your business is finished. You'll have to make the ultimate decision yourself. Will you ring for Giulio?"

Mechanically obeying him, Blackstone pushed the bell. They heard it ring in the corridor. Before the sound had died away Giulio had opened the door and stood waiting for his orders.

"Ask Mrs. Warden if she will kindly come here," Cousin Mart directed him. The valet bent his great shoulders in a little bow and disappeared as quietly as he had come.

The old man still kept to his chair, and to the inflexible position he had taken, but his sharp eyes, as he looked at Blackstone, were clouded with affection.

Blackstone returned the look with hard brightness. He made no answer to the appeal, but for once in his direct, unswerving life he seemed to have allowed himself to become confused by two conflicting emotions.

"What do you want her for?" he demanded sharply.

"I want you to have the evidence of an impartial observer," Cousin Mart said, and went on with a trace of bitterness, "I shall not ask you to believe my word alone."

"I'm willing to believe you," Blackstone replied with a queer break in his voice.

"Thank you, but——" Mrs. Warden had opened the door. He turned to her. "Will you come in and sit down, Edith? I want to tell Blackstone what you and I observed together. If I vary in the slightest degree from the truth, I want you to contradict me. You understand that?"

"Yes, I understand." She settled herself and waited, taking scrupulous care neither to avoid nor to catch Blackstone's angry, tormented eyes. He too waited, stiff with unvented resentment.

"You know, Blackstone," Cousin Mart began slowly, "that I did to-day what I do not usually do. I went down to the library after lunch—without telling anyone of my intention— that last by chance. You also know one of my peculiarities, which explains my second point. I didn't do so until I'd found out through Giulio that no one else was in the room. I like to get myself arranged in a certain privacy. Edith and I, then, went down together." He paused as if he were trying to make his story as clear and as brief as possible. "As you may remember, I had the furniture in that room rearranged this morning, and so I had reason to look at it more carefully than I might have otherwise. At any rate, my eyes are sharp, and an unusual object rarely fails to attract my attention. When I entered the library this afternoon I noticed, somewhat projecting from between two of the books on the upper shelf of the case to my right, an envelope. I'm naturally curious, so I pulled it out. I found it a plain white envelope, unaddressed. It contained a sheet of notepaper with a few lines written on it." He hesitated again, and then said to Mrs. Warden, "My dear, I want you to tell Blackstone either that what I have said is entirely true, or that I have varied from the truth in some detail."

She shook her head slightly. "It is all true, entirely true." She spoke with reluctance.

"What has this to do with me?" Blackstone's sharp voice cut in on them. His amber eyes glittered with irritation.

"A great deal, Blackstone." Cousin Mart took from the pocket of his dressing gown a plain white envelope. "Let me read you what was written in that note." He unfolded the sheet, his delicate hands shaking a little. He read off the words:

"*I must see you alone and talk things over. Don't misjudge me. You know how glad I would be to marry you if it weren't for the old man!*"

Cousin Mart folded the sheet again, running his finger nail along the crease. "It is signed 'F.'," he concluded. Silently he offered the note to Blackstone. "Do you care to look at it?" he asked.

Blackstone did not hear him. His hands were clenched together. Bright-eyed he stared into the glow of the lamp.

"You can't ignore this, Blackstone." Cousin Mart tried to stir him.

Still Blackstone neither replied nor moved. The color that had left his cheeks was beginning to flare back again.

"Do you want to look at it?" Cousin Mart repeated his question, and again held out to him the white sheet of paper.

Blackstone's stare focused on it. Suddenly he changed from torpor to violence. "No!" he cried, shrinking away from it and from Cousin Mart. "I won't touch it! This is a trick of yours to prove your point about Stella—to get your own way! But you can't take me in! No, thank God!" His very vehemence betrayed the completeness of his overthrow.

"I might have played a trick on you at another time," Cousin Mart answered him. "But in this case I haven't. I haven't needed to." His lips had taken on a bluish tinge, and his clear voice was low with weariness. "Edith vouches for me. I'm telling the truth."

Blackstone turned on her, an easy vent for his passionate fury. "I suppose you had a hand in this," he spat out. "I won't have you interfering in my life—you ought to know that by now!"

"Blackstone," Cousin Mart interposed dryly, "don't be absurd."

Blackstone was tormented with unappeased rage. His eyes flickered from the one to the other of them, blind with desperation. He tried to speak again but could not.

Mrs. Warden turned to him slowly. "I didn't want to interfere in your affairs." She tried to soothe him with the sincerity of her regret. "If I have, it is against my will. I think you, Martin, are making too much of this—incident. There may be an entirely innocent explanation of it. I advised you not to tell Blackstone what you have told him. I advise you both to forget it now."

Blackstone stared at her helplessly.

Cousin Mart followed the cue she gave him. "You may be right," he admitted. "We may all be making too much of this.

Forget it, if you like," he concluded brusquely, "but——" He made his nephew a gesture of dismissal.

When Blackstone had gone Cousin Mart sank back in his chair, his features pinched with exhaustion. "I'm more than ever convinced," he said to Mrs. Warden, "that one should not indulge in genuine emotion. I thought I'd given myself a sterner training than I have."

CHAPTER XII

THE SHADOW TAKES SHAPE

THE TIME appointed for Cousin Mart's birthday dinner was approaching. In honor of the occasion the house and its inhabitants took on a hush of solemnity. The servants, fear of Cousin Mart strong in them, moved quietly and hurriedly to make ready the celebration that he had ordered. Everything must be as he wished.

There was expectancy in the air. Upstairs the guests donned their dinner clothes with special solicitude, making their garments an outward sign of the deference they wished to show their host. One by one they came downstairs, having been informed that Cousin Mart was ready for them. All of them reacted to the prevalent excitement, Hutchinson with ponderous magnificence, Amelia with twitterings, George with nervous recklessness, Francis with a charming gayety that devoted itself now to Mrs. Warden, now to Stella, along the line of his always feminine inclinations.

They assembled as usual in the library. Again Mrs. Warden had made the cocktails. Again Cousin Mart sat in state to receive them. His mood had changed. He was once more urbane, saturnine, the living portrait of an ancestor. He threw into his manner an added touch of formality for the occasion. "I feel that I have reached a turning point in my life," he remarked. "It is something to feel that at seventy-five." He spoke of his age pridefully, as if he were a young man announcing that he was twenty-one.

With the first cocktail, they drank deeply to Cousin Mart's health. With the second, at his suggestion, to the coming year. Blackstone fell in with him.

"Yes," he said with forced hilarity, "next year! Better than the last. I agree. I've come to a turning point myself." Touching his glass to George's, he drank. He was flushed, for he had already had a good deal to drink. He looked as if he were riding the last spurt of a lost race. His cropped auburn hair gleamed in the light. He was stiff with rash energy.

"Perhaps we've all come to a turning point," Stella said with a gayety to match his, "in honor"—she smiled too brightly at Cousin Mart—"of your birthday."

"Thank you." He was impervious to the meaning that might lie behind her words. "Let me propose another and a last toast to—as they used to say—the ladies! What would we think about if it were not for them?" He glanced with affection at Mrs. Warden, with mockery at Amelia, with irony at Stella.

Blackstone laughed aloud. "Again I agree!" he said, and drained his glass.

Griggs hovered in the doorway, announcing dinner. Cousin Mart rose and offered Mrs. Warden his arm. In imitation Francis offered his to Stella. She took it, laughing up at Blackstone, who ignored her completely. Quickly she turned to flirt with Francis, and he followed her lead. He was thoroughly enjoying himself. Amelia, neglected by the unobservant George, trailed along a few paces behind Hutchinson.

The birthday dinner was a splendid affair. Under Cousin Mart's admonitions the chef had outdone himself in conceits and fancies. With each course, a different wine was served. Cousin Mart presided over the feast with, for him, an exuberant gayety. His frosty eyes sparkled as he surveyed the somber magnificence of the dining room, the table before him glittering with silver and delicate glass. He glanced from Mrs. Warden, dressed in dull blue velvet, to Stella, proud in scarlet. Even Amelia's baby pink and baby blue pleased him, but more than anything else some secret, anticipatory delight seemed to tickle his palate.

Suddenly silent, his long white fingers caressing the curves of his wineglass, he looked from the one to the other of his nephews, dressed alike to every detail in their immaculate evening clothes, and yet never to be mistaken in their separate individualities. Blackstone sat erect, his small head finely poised between his broad shoulders. His lips were curved in an almost mechanical smile, his small, bright amber eyes half closed, as if, like Cousin Mart, he were possessed by a hidden electrical excitement. His narrow pointed face was pale except for two hectic spots of color on his high cheek bones. He never looked at Stella. Once her laugh rose above the laughter of the rest, and his fingers tightened spasmodically, so that a little of his wine spilled over the edge of his glass to make a widening red stain on the white tablecloth. He stared at it, his lips still curved in the same fixed smile. In a minute he turned to Amelia and began in a rapid, abrupt monotone to tell her about a steeplechase he had ridden in, the fall before.

Francis, sitting between Stella and Mrs. Warden, was in fine fettle. He was a true gourmet, who ate not only with deep appreciation but somewhat to excess, in the same easy abandon with which he cultivated all types of pleasure. But he did not neglect his dinner partners. With facile, magnetic charm, he turned from the one to the other of them, entertaining them effortlessly with his light, clever small talk. Stella did more to second him than Mrs. Warden, upon whom a quiet reticence had fallen. Her reserve deepened as the conversation between Francis and Stella grew more vivacious. Once she made an effort to catch his attention.

"Aren't you seeking out trouble, Francis?" she said.

Francis was flushed. "Not trouble," he replied, laughing too much. "Only amusement." Under his lightness there was a strain of resentment at her interference.

"Is it always to be amusement?" she asked.

"I'm probably a worthless sort," he admitted, "but I think you're taking things too hard." His wide placating smile illuminated his face.

"So is Blackstone," she reminded him.

Francis was carelessly exalted. "Oh, let him look out for himself," he said, and turned back to Stella.

The interchange hardly made a ripple in the smoothness of the party. Even Hutchinson's stiffness had relaxed in the general warmth. With extraordinary adaptability and tact he was inquiring Cousin Mart's opinions on the stock market and listening to them almost too attentively. His humor mounted higher and higher as dinner progressed. He glanced speculatively at Cousin Mart now and again, as if he had a final trump card up his sleeve and were doubtful when to play it. At last, however, in a moment of silence he showed it.

First he turned to Griggs. "You've carried out my orders?" he asked mysteriously.

"Yes, sir."

"Orders?" Cousin Mart caught up the question. "What orders?"

Hutchinson smiled confidently. "I've a surprise for you," he answered.

"You often have surprises for me, Hutchinson. Only this afternoon——" Cousin Mart paused.

A grimace of discomfort passed over Hutchinson's face. "This is quite different," he said hurriedly. "For your birthday. I thought of it myself. The seventeenth being Bunker Hill Day reminded me."

"Ah!" Cousin Mart breathed his appreciation.

"You see," Hutchinson explained heavily, "I read in the newspaper that in China people always had fireworks to celebrate a birthday, and so I thought——"

"Fireworks!" Cousin Mart exclaimed incredulously. "You are going to entertain me with fireworks?"

"Yes." Hutchinson stammered a little. "Yes. I thought this evening we'd all set them off on the lawn."

"Not I," Cousin Mart announced decisively. "I hate the noisy things."

"But you'll watch, won't you?" Hutchinson was anxious.

Mrs. Warden helped him out. "Why, of course you will, Martin," she said. "Amelia was telling me the other day what very fine ones she had picked out for you."

"Very well." Cousin Mart was grumpy. "Very well, I'll watch.

But this is the first time anyone has set off fireworks for me. I must say, Hutchinson," he pinned his keen eyes on his nephew, "you sometimes have the most extraordinary ideas." Again he savored his secret amusement.

Hutchinson was gratified. "I think you'll like them," he said.

The dinner had come to an elaborate and magnificent end. Cousin Mart, presiding over his board, seemed to be in the best of humors. By Griggs he sent his compliments to the chef in words of exuberant praise. Smiling his thin-lipped smile, he again surveyed his nephews, the melancholy, spasmodic George, Hutchinson the impervious, rapier-like Blackstone, easy, charming Francis. He seemed to be passing a final judgment on them.

"I'm very sorry," he said at last, turning to George, "that your sister Anne is not here to-night. You keep in close touch with her, of course?"

"Yes, I do," George muttered. A spark of defiance flared up in him.

"It is always pleasant to see a brother and sister so devoted," Cousin Mart commented. "When you next see her, you will have news to give her—news she should find very interesting."

"News?" George straightened up in his chair. "What news?"

"I'm about to tell it to you." With a fine sense of the dramatic, he paused. Something in the tone of his voice arrested the attention of his guests. They stared at him, waiting as if they instinctively recognized a climax. But when he spoke again it was only to order Griggs to fill up the glasses with champagne. When the butler had done so, Cousin Mart dismissed the servants from the room.

"What I have to say," he murmured, "had best be said in the

privacy of the family. Of course I want you to know before I even talk to my lawyer to-morrow."

There was a flavor of subtle enjoyment in his words. "Yet," he continued slowly, "even in such privacy it is difficult——" A gesture of Blackstone's halted him. "Not yet, Blackstone!" he said, as his nephew started to raise his wineglass to his lips. "I shall have a final toast to propose to you!" Blackstone looked at him sharply without turning his head. He put the glass down again.

"I have come to a decision," Cousin Mart went on in a leisurely fashion, "not so suddenly as it may seem to you. It has been maturing in my mind for ten years." He looked around slyly to see the effect of his words, and then resumed more briskly: "As I said this morning, our lives have become too monotonous to be interesting. We shall all be the better for a change. Mine is to be drastic." His hand crept toward his glass. Slowly he raised it from the table. "My dear Edith," he said, bowing a little toward Mrs. Warden at the other end of the table, "I hope you will do me the honor of marrying me, day after to-morrow. To-night," his eyes swept around the table, "I shall ask you all to drink to our happiness."

He rose. The others pushed back their chairs and stumbled to their feet. Mechanically they raised their glasses and drank. The birthday party was over.

CHAPTER XIII

CARDS AND CONSEQUENCES

AFTER THE toast which he had called for had been drunk, Cousin Mart had risen to leave the table, saying to his nephews, "Perhaps the four of you would like a glass of port. I think I shall accompany the ladies to the library." Like a good stage manager he had left them alone, to appreciate to the full the effect of his announcement.

The four men sat like statues while Griggs filled their glasses, placed the decanter on the table, and vanished into his pantry.

Francis was the first to speak. Little beads of perspiration stood out on his flushed forehead. "God!" he said.

Hutchinson stared at him woodenly. The blow had come so suddenly—they had all been unprepared, and defenseless beneath it. In another moment, Hutchinson had summoned his faculties. "Something has got to be done about this!"

"What are you going to do, Hutchinson?" George mocked him wildly. "You may as well accept the fact that this is the end of all of us!"

"Not necessarily." Francis's eyes were intent on the marks his fingers drew on the tablecloth.

"Why not?" But Francis, absorbed in calculation, did not answer him.

"This is the situation, isn't it?" George went on savagely, as if he found relief in attacking his cousins. "Cousin Mart marries—*marries!* It's what we've thought ourselves lucky he didn't do! Well, he's going to do it. Then where does that leave us?—in the discard, that's all. I'll speak the truth, for once. I've been waiting for years for him to die! I've earned the money he said he was going to leave me! And now, I'm tricked! So are the rest of you! He'll see his lawyer to-morrow. We're ditched, I tell you!" His eyes were bloodshot, and the veins on his temples stood out.

"It won't do you any good to get hysterical, George." Even as Francis checked George's outburst, his own voice rose to shrillness. "You're exaggerating. It may not be as bad as you say. Of course, she—she will cut us out, but only partly, perhaps. If we behave decently, maybe——"

"Maybe," George cut in on him, "maybe we can still hang on. Great God in heaven! What a prospect! And maybe, after Cousin Mart dies, we'll have to curry favor with her for our bread and butter!"

Blackstone had not spoken. His face was as white as chalk. His eyes glowed and glittered with rage. "I won't stand for it," he said suddenly, and then fell fiercely silent again, gnawing his crimson lips.

"Look out what you do now," Francis warned him, "now more than ever. Remember——"

"Remember," George concluded bitterly, "that he's going to see his lawyer to-morrow."

They heard a slight sound. Griggs had come into the dining room and was busying himself at the sideboard. In a minute he came over to the table and ostentatiously filled the glasses again. Under his scrutiny they became controlled, stiffly normal again.

"That'll be all." Hutchinson dismissed him abruptly, but when he had gone there was nothing to say. They sat on, drinking mechanically, each one occupied with his own thoughts.

"There's no good staying here." Blackstone pushed back his chair with a clatter.

"No." Francis rose. One by one, they went to the door. From the library they could hear Cousin Mart's smooth, decisive voice. Automatically they paused and listened, although they could not hear his words, and then went on, each as he passed the doorway assuming his usual attitude, making the adjustment of features that would enable him to act as if nothing cataclysmic had happened.

Once in the library, nothing they said or did gave any obvious sign of their disturbance. Francis's amiability rang perhaps a little hollow. Hutchinson seemed stiffer. His face, always expressionless, was like a mask in which only his cold blue eyes showed signs of life. He was careful, passive, watchful. George was more nervous, more desperately melancholy, Blackstone overstimulated by his anger. But their training provided them with superficial ease.

Cousin Mart's bright eyes scanned them, as they now spoke mechanically, now were silent. He did not press his nephews for congratulatory comments, but rested content with the effect he had produced. It was he who conducted the conversation, which rapidly became almost a monologue, although his nephews managed to supply the commonplace remarks he called for. He spoke smoothly, with a suave relish, of his particular enjoyment of their visit. He was glad that it had been so pleasant, he said, since he might not see them for some time. He might possibly take a trip abroad, spend next winter on the Riviera. He was tired of the cold. Every word of his seemed to cut them off more completely.

Mrs. Warden, sitting in the midst of them, was still strangely isolated by Cousin Mart's pronouncement. It was not so much that his guests ignored her, as that an impassable barrier had been set up between her and them, across which their voices could not carry. Amelia, staring fascinated at Mrs. Warden's controlled, quiet face, made no attempt to reach her. Once or twice she herself tried to break down their restraint, appealing instinctively to Francis for help, but even he failed her. An active agent or a passive instrument in Cousin Mart's hands, it was she who had brought this ruin upon them. In the face of that fact, not even Francis could bring himself to slur over his true feelings. He avoided her almost beseeching eyes.

Like a marionette master, Cousin Mart played with them. His right hand gently stroking Lucy, who sat on his lap contentedly cocking battle-torn ears, he inquired of Francis if he were going to take his yearly summer trip to Dinard. Lost in thought, Francis replied, "Yes," and then, "No," and, stammering, "I haven't decided." Of Hutchinson, whether as usual he had taken a house at Cohasset. Of Blackstone, whether he was going to ride in the fall horse shows. His apparently idle questions brought sharply before them the fact that everything was changed for them. They answered feverishly, uncertainly.

As their numbness wore off, the excitement of desperation took its place. They began to talk quickly, in strained, unnatural voices. Their laughter rang too high, and underneath it ran a strain of hysteria. They became restless and looked for something to occupy their hands and their minds.

"What about setting off those fireworks?" Blackstone asked Hutchinson. "We may as well be about it."

Hutchinson glanced at the still bright daylight. "It's too early," he answered mechanically. "There's no sense in doing it till dark."

"Well," Blackstone replied impatiently, "let's do something!"

George roused himself suddenly. "We could have a game of cards," he suggested.

The idea fitted in with their overcharged moods, and they seized upon it with relief. "I'll get the cards," George said, as if he were glad to find something to occupy himself. He looked in the drawer of the table where they were usually kept, and, apparently unsuccessful, went quickly out of the room. They heard him taking the stairs two at a time. In a minute he was back, breathless in his haste. His eyes were bright with the born gambler's urge. George was himself playing cards as Blackstone was himself on horseback, or Francis, entertaining a pretty woman.

"Twenty-one?" he suggested. "If you like I'll be banker." His long, nervous fingers ruffled and snapped the pack.

They agreed and pulled up their chairs to the table which Griggs had brought in for them. George dealt out the chips. By common consent, it was only the men who played. Cousin Mart, for whom they had left a place, refused to join in. Games of chance, over which he had no control, did not appeal to him. Stella, Amelia, and Mrs. Warden watched.

Under George's nimble fingers the cards fluttered across the green table and fell. The players glanced at them and made their bets, sometimes asking for more cards, sometimes drawing too many and throwing up the hand. The stakes were high, and although at first they were moderate in their betting, the heat of the game caught them, and they began to indulge in recklessness. Now they won and now lost. Hutchinson was the first to demand more chips. He had developed an elaborate system which did not seem to be too successful, but his methodical mind refused to abandon it. When he might have won by keeping to his theories, he lost his nerve and threw up his hand, although he afterwards pointed with satisfaction to the proof of his idea.

"The proof of the pudding is in the eating, as you have often remarked to me, Hutchinson," Cousin Mart prodded him. "It amazes me, as it always has, to see your logic develop up to a certain point without a flaw, and fail so miserably in the conclusion."

However apt the description, Hutchinson was unmoved by it and went on in his own way.

Blackstone played with a savage ferocity. He hardly looked to see whether his chips slid away from him, or came back increased. He had plunged head first into the game and did not care whether he lost or not. Francis, too, at first cautious in his plunges, soon caught the fervor that possessed the rest and laid rash wagers.

The luck varied, but by some chance George remained banker. Several times the others announced the triumphant natural, but each time, with his uncanny good fortune at cards, George matched them. He was the only one who played the game with skill. He watched the draws of the others carefully and doubled or let the bets alone with a fine judgment. He won steadily, however the others suffered ups and downs.

After three quarters of an hour of play they had all reached a high pitch. Francis's awkward fingers trembled as he fumbled for his cards. Hutchinson, lost to everything but his manipulations, did not move except to pick up his hand and make his seemingly deliberate plays. Blackstone leaned far over the table, staring at the shining pasteboards flickering towards him. One look, and he pushed out his dully clicking chips. He did not seem to care what color he chose or what amount he was betting. Only George remained cool and skillful, but his dull brown eyes were lighted into brilliancy.

"Three more hands and stop?" he suggested. The others agreed, hardly hearing him.

He dealt again and doubled the bets they had made. When the cards were turned up, no one could match his twenty-one, an eight, a two, and an ace. The next deal he showed a natural, and again they paid. During the next he paused to double the bids before he went around for a second time. Francis called for an extra card. It was a five. He stood. Blackstone stayed with two. Hutchinson split his first two cards and drew on both. On one he overdrew and paid. On the other he rested with two. Slowly George looked around the table. For the first time he seemed hesitant. He glanced at the two cards before him face down, and fingered the pack he held in his hand. It was Francis's three cards that held his eyes. Suddenly he decided. His long fingers flipped a card from the pack. It fell face upwards— an ace! He turned up the others, a ten and a queen.

Francis laughed. "I thought I'd beaten you, George. But I ought to have known better. The colossal nerve of you, to draw to twenty!" He turned up two eights and added them to his five, and paid with his last chips the redoubled stake. Hutchinson, with a count of nineteen, and Blackstone, with twenty, paid up. They had only a few chips left. Practically all the chips they had started with were piled before George.

Francis suddenly woke up to the fact. "Good God!" he said. "We've lost fairly heavily."

"So I noticed," Cousin Mart said dryly. All through the game he had been watching George's agile hands. "Is George always so fortunate?"

"Not always." George's tone was strained, as if he were tired after the excitement of the game. He began to arrange and count the chips before him. "Will you check my count, Hutchinson?" The two busied themselves with their mathematics. George had won nearly a thousand dollars.

Francis whistled a little. "Settle with you tomorrow," he said.

"All right." The others agreed to do likewise. Hutchinson was disgruntled by the amount of his losings. Blackstone hardly knew that he had lost.

Idly Cousin Mart reached out his slim white hand and swept together the cards that lay on the table. Without looking at George, he arranged the pack and, apparently absent-mindedly, put it in his pocket. Then he glanced across the table at George, who had suddenly gone white.

"I think I shall go upstairs now," said Cousin Mart quietly. "Hutchinson, I suppose I shall be able to see your fireworks from my window? I don't want to come downstairs again. By the way," he turned his piercing eyes on him, "you remember that I want to speak to you alone in fifteen minutes or so. I telephoned Banks and Tiffany this afternoon." He glanced at his watch. "It's half-past nine," he went on. "I'll expect you at a quarter to ten." He rose and stood over them, one delicate hand on the card table. "I shall not be able to see you to-morrow," he said, "since I have a great deal to attend to with my lawyer. And the next day—I shall also be busy, as you can easily understand. Good-night." He turned to Mrs. Warden. "Will you come with me, my dear?"

She nodded and, followed by Lucy, went with him out of the

room. So Cousin Mart, accompanied by his two favorites, left his birthday party.

The cousins, left together, had very little to say to each other. The time for talking had gone by. Stella drew off into a corner, making a pretense of reading, but her eyes rested more frequently on Blackstone and Francis than on the unturned page before her. She seemed to be measuring them, and through them to be measuring herself.

George, the excitement of the card game having grown cold within him, was sitting with his face in his hands. The others paid no attention to him or to his sudden defiant exclamation, "Hell, it makes no difference!" He straightened up, poured himself a stiff drink, drank it down, and swiftly left the room.

Hutchinson was standing by the fireplace, staring into the coals. Their redness illuminated his face, but when he turned away from the fire, it showed gray and drawn again. Once or twice he glanced nervously at his watch. When Francis came up unexpectedly, to knock the ash of his cigar into the grate, Hutchinson jerked away from him, startled.

"Something affected your iron nerves, Hutchinson?" Francis asked him. Hutchinson made no reply.

Some time passed before the door into the hall opened and Mrs. Warden came in. Lucy hung purring around her heels. Outside the room George was speaking to someone in a muffled voice. A second later he came back to the library.

"Well!" he said nonchalantly. "Cousin Mart get tired of Lucy?" He seemed suddenly ready for conversation.

"Only for to-night," Mrs. Warden answered. "He thought the fireworks might frighten her—or him." She smiled a little at the standing joke. "So he's being put away now for the night." She rang for the butler. When Griggs appeared in answer to the summons, she merely nodded at the cat. The man understood at once, and, betraying a certain undignified embarrassment, caught the animal and carried it away.

"Is Cousin Mart ready to see me?" Hutchinson asked Mrs. Warden. His voice was distant.

"I think so," she said. "What time is it?"

"Quarter to ten." He nodded to himself. "I'll go up."

Amelia slipped out of the room behind him. Five minutes later Griggs appeared in the doorway with a tray laden with small glasses and a decanter. He passed before Blackstone.

"What's that?" Blackstone asked him.

"The special cognac, sir." Griggs looked reverently at his burden. "Mr. Greenough just ordered it served."

Blackstone laughed a little bitterly. "It's the first time I've been permitted to taste it," he said. "And I suppose it will be the last. A stirrup cup, I take it!"

His decorum unshaken by the speech, Griggs offered the brandy to Mrs. Warden and Stella, and then to the three men, who sat silent, each occupied with his own thoughts and plans. Blackstone's wild hawk eyes looked fiercely before him, into the depths of the fire. Francis sat quietly. A half smile, which was belied by the fretful, furrowed lines that crossed his forehead, hovered as usual about his lips. Now and again his short fingers, clasped about his knee, twitched suddenly. None of them was aroused until, a quarter of an hour after his departure, Hutchinson reappeared. He made himself heard coming down the hall, issuing abrupt, exacting directions to Griggs about the disposition of the fireworks, making certain that all his orders had been carried out.

"Listen to him!" George remarked impatiently. "Showing what a nuisance he can be!"

Francis stirred. "He is raising a fuss," he answered mechanically, his mind still busy with his own concerns. But when Hutchinson showed himself in the doorway he jumped to his feet with a burst of alacrity. "Ready to set off your fireworks, Hutchinson?"

Hutchinson's fingers brushed at his mustache. "In a minute," he said. He pulled out his watch. "Almost ten-fifteen," he said, "and dark as pitch. We ought to start."

"Fine." Blackstone sprang up as if he welcomed the signal for activity. "Where are they? Let's shoot the works." His words were loud and crisply metallic. He spoke hurriedly as if to divert attention from his pale face and his eyes, still burning with anger and a pain more desperate than anger.

"Where do we see them from, Hutchinson?" Amelia's voice, placating and over interested, startled them. She had slipped into the room unnoticed. "I mean, where do you want us to sit?"

"Sit?" Hutchinson was picking up match boxes and putting them in his pocket. "I don't want you to sit anywhere. We're setting them off ourselves, don't you understand?"

"Oh! I thought you'd got the servants to fire them." Amelia's eyes opened wide with comprehension, and she nodded her head brightly. "That *will* be nice."

"The boxes are out on the south lawn under the trees. We'll set them off there. Then, even if Cousin Mart doesn't care about coming down," Hutchinson concluded without resentment, "he can watch from his window."

"But will he?" Francis spoke to Mrs. Warden as Hutchinson turned his conversation to another quarter. "Fine idea to celebrate his birthday so dramatically, but," he laughed softly, "how he hates noises! He may even refuse to look at the things."

"Come on." Hutchinson was directing the others. "It's getting late." They got up, ready to follow him. "Mrs. Warden—Edith, aren't you coming?" he asked in surprise, for Mrs. Warden was still sitting in her chair.

"I don't believe so." She smiled at him reluctantly.

"Why not?"

"I'll watch from the house," she assured him.

"Well, if you want to———"

"Now, Edith," Amelia protested, "I want you to come. There's no earthly reason why you should go up to sit with Cousin Mart. If he wants to watch the fun from there, that's no reason why you should cut yourself off———"

"What are we waiting for?" Blackstone burst out. "Mrs. Warden knows whether she wants to come with us or not. I'm going." Without waiting for anyone else he went out into the hall. Hutchinson and Amelia followed him.

"Better come," Francis urged her as the rest disappeared. "Hutchinson's feelings will be hurt." He laughed as he spoke, but Mrs. Warden seemed to take his words quite soberly.

"You think they will?"

"I'm sure of it. Come along."

After a moment she stood up. "All right, then. I shouldn't want to do that." They left the room after the others.

CHAPTER XIV

PLAYING WITH FIRE

It was a dark, almost black night. The air was sweet and heavy, as if a storm were coming. Overhead the clouds moved smokily across the sky. The branches of the trees seemed to bend lower under the weight of the air, every now and then to stir languidly at a puff of sultry wind.

The ground was familiar to all of the party, but the darkness was so thick that they could see nothing, not even each other. "Over this way," Hutchinson directed them, and as best they could they followed his voice. "Over here!" he called again. "Between the wing and the house. Under Cousin Mart's windows."

"I can't see where I'm stepping," Amelia cried out. "Hutchinson," she called in sudden fear, "isn't this where they play croquet?"

But Hutchinson, some distance from her, was busy with his own affairs and did not answer, leaving her to stumble onward by herself.

The place to which he led them was a rectangle of lawn, perhaps fifty yards square, sheltered on two sides of the long low house. Beyond this open space, cutting it off from the rest of the grounds on a third side, were five or six trees and some shrub-bery, set out in an irregular fashion. The tops of the trees showed faintly against the black sky, and the bushes beneath them were distinguishable because of their bulk and deeper shadow. Nothing else could be made out. The flower beds, the sundial, the bench that stood near the croquet ground, the people themselves, disappeared in the impenetrable obscurity. Light from several windows fell across the grass, but served only to emphasize the darkness beyond.

Again Amelia was seized by panic. "Where are we?" she cried out. "Hutchinson, where are you?"

"Here!" he called to her impatiently. He must have lighted a match to guide them, for they saw a tiny distant flare.

"Hasn't anyone a flashlight?" George seized the arm of someone passing him.

"Not I." It was Francis. "And you might let go of me. Why, George, what makes you shake so?"

George did not answer. "He's a nervous fellow," Francis whispered to Mrs. Warden as they walked along, bringing up the rear of the party.

"It's so dark," she answered in a low voice, "it makes me nervous too."

Hutchinson was still lighting matches. As the others came near him they could see his face. He was standing over a large packing box, intent on sorting out its contents, bending his stiff knees as little as possible.

"Careful, Hutchinson," Francis mocked his sober mien. "A spark from that match of yours will put you among the angels."

"No fear," the other replied in a matter-of-fact tone. "I'll put it out before it does any damage. Now, in this box are punk, some of the smaller firecrackers, and Roman candles. I'd advise that each of us light a piece of punk. It's easier and safer. In the box over there. . . . "

From a spot fifty feet away there came a fearful reverberation. Even Hutchinson whirled in alarm. A succession of spurting flames, dropping sparks, and sharp explosions seemed to issue of their own accord from the trunk of a large tree. Only a moment later a burst of flame showed Blackstone standing alone near the tree, watching moodily the frantic leapings of the last firecrackers.

"That's a whole string," Francis pronounced admiringly, "and even that didn't shatter Cousin Mart's self-communion. Do you suppose he isn't going to pay any attention to your party, Hutchinson?"

"He can please himself, of course," Hutchinson replied stiltedly.

Amelia sprang to her husband's aid a little too obviously. "He certainly will want to watch," she cried. "I picked out such pretty rockets, and it was such a good idea of Hutchinson's. He'll want to see them and be so pleased."

In spite of her enthusiasm Cousin Mart's curtains remained drawn.

"Oh, yes," George stepped in with unusual tact. "He'll wait till we get really started." A sudden excitement seemed to have taken possession of him. He kneeled down and began pawing around in the box. "Hold a match, somebody. . . . All right, here we are. Good Lord, Hutchinson, you've got a lot of stuff. What'll you have, Amelia? Sparklers? Here's a bunch. Roman candles for Mrs. Warden and Stella——"

"Where do I light it?" Stella held the gaudy stick at arm's length, laughing.

"I'll show you," Francis answered. "We need a stick of punk first."

Mrs. Warden gingerly examined the tip of hers. "I remember how it's done. I can manage mine."

"Wait on yourselves after this." George got up from the ground, with a collection of pin wheels and rockets in his hands. "We'll start you off. Hutchinson," he concluded, his voice almost shrill with enthusiasm, "you had a great idea. This really is sport!"

The match that had showed them to each other for a moment went out, and the night closed in on them again. Hutchinson gave them a last warning. "Look out where you throw things," he said.

George gave a high laugh. "Look out!" he protested. "What good does it do to look out when you can't see your hand before your face?"

"Perhaps I'd better light a flare," Hutchinson suggested. "I have a couple here."

"Oh, don't," Francis answered him carelessly. "I like this stumbling around in the dark."

The rest seemed to share his opinion. For a moment they gathered around Francis, each lighting a long yellow punk stick from the match he held. Their faces, curiously illuminated and shadowed by the wavering flame, showed an excitement unusual to most of them, inspired perhaps by the pleasure and novelty of the occasion, perhaps by the opportunity it gave them to release their overwrought emotions. Their sensations were heightened by the darkness and the strangely still, heavy air of the night.

From far away there came a low rumble of thunder. "That means rain in about ten minutes. Look at the sky." George's voice, coming from a distance of six or seven feet, seemed absurdly disembodied.

"Nonsense. It'll hold off for an hour. We've plenty of time. Confound Blackstone," Francis exclaimed, as that aloof young man set off another raucous bunch of firecrackers. "He must have filled both his pockets. Well, come on, Stella. Let's touch off that thing of yours."

One by one they had begun to scatter over the lawn, each armed and ready to begin.

Amelia, preoccupied with her sparklers, came to a sudden realization. "Hutchinson!" she called in an anxious voice, "aren't you going to let Cousin Mart know we're ready?"

"Certainly." Hutchinson's tone was enough to tell her that her reminder was unnecessary. "Cousin Mart!" he called firmly, but Cousin Mart refused to pay any attention.

"Is his window open?" someone asked. "Perhaps he doesn't hear you."

In answer, Hutchinson walked across the lawn toward the house. Standing beneath the window of the study, he called again, more loudly, "Cousin Mart! We're going to start the fireworks."

The curtains jerked apart, expressing as clearly as Cousin Mart's voice could have his impatience and distaste of the celebration held in his honor. The old man was sitting by the window, the light opposite him half revealing, half hiding the outlines of his face.

"Isn't very encouraging, is he?" Francis muttered to Mrs. Warden. "He looks cranky to me." He laughed a little. "I don't think I'd prepare these surprises if I were Hutchinson. He's showing some generous interest though, Edith. He changed to your chair to see better." He laughed again. "It's tactful of him to——"

A sudden explosion startled him. "Damn!" he said, jumping aside. "Look out!" A burst of flame from Mrs. Warden's Roman candle had come too near him for comfort. "Hold it up in the air, not pointed at me!" He seized her wrist, and held it above her head.

"Infernal machines!" he exclaimed, as the candle blew itself out. They laughed together. From every corner of the lawn they could hear similar exclamations and explosions.

"I'd forgotten—after all," Mrs. Warden said nervously. Her voice was half fearful still, half relieved. They laughed again.

They could hear Amelia chattering as she ventured from sparklers to more dangerous and uncertain weapons, the steady machine-gun rattle of Blackstone's firing, George's high, "Look at that!" as he set off something worthy of special notice.

Rockets with fiery tails burst up from the ground, soared high in the air towards the lowering clouds, and exploded, falling to earth again in a shower of stars. From everywhere came hissing noises and sharp detonations, streams of fire that rose and died, and shoots of brilliant flame. They cut the darkness like flashing knives, but only for an instant, and then, where there had been bright glory, the dark fell back again. Mingled with the snapping of the firecrackers and the roar of the rockets was the sound of laughter and excited voices. A face and a figure would be illuminated for a moment, and then were gone.

Once, in an unexpected flare of light, Francis saw George standing, half hidden, near a clipped bush. He was talking rather furtively to a woman beside him. The woman held out something to him which he took and slipped into his pocket.

"Hello," Francis called to her in surprise, "when did you——?"

The light died suddenly. When he could see again there was no one near the bush.

"Who was that with George?" Mrs. Warden asked.

"I don't know. I thought for a minute—oh, it must have been one of the servants."

The volleys began once more, multiplied by the echoes thrown from the walls of the house. Hutchinson, methodically dealing out his supplies, had lighted a flare to see by and was kept busy with the incessant demands for them. Mrs. Warden noticed his difficulty and came to help him. The others ran to and fro, now calling to each other, now occupied each with his own toys. Like shadows they appeared and disappeared beyond the red glare of Hutchinson's torch. Under their ministrations the noise rose to a deafening crescendo and came to a climax in a loud report. There was silence for a moment.

"What was that?" Hutchinson's voice was peremptory. His tone startled Mrs. Warden, who stopped her work to look up at him. From the darkness beyond the circle of light they stood in, there came no immediate reply. Then, "What was what?" someone answered him sharply.

"That noise." Again Hutchinson's voice sounded queerly disturbed.

"Are noises against the law here?" George's reply seemed unduly petulant. "I thought we were here to make them. You provided these cannon crackers."

Hutchinson shrugged off George's answer and his own question. In a minute he turned away from the packing box, leaving his torch to die, and disappeared into the surrounding night. In another ten minutes the supply of fireworks was almost exhausted, and the enthusiasm of the company fell a little. The explosions came sporadically. Cousin Mart gave no sign of applause, although the performance for his benefit was obviously coming to a close.

"He might give this vaudeville act a hand," George grumbled. But Cousin Mart was noncommittal, sitting in his lighted window and accepting the honor like royalty on a throne.

"Hutchinson!" Amelia's still excited voice summoned her husband. "Come here, over by the box, I mean!" Hutchinson apparently did not obey her, for she called again. "Hutchinson!"

"What is it?" His voice came from far over in the corner of the lawn.

"You should sort out the rest of the things for us."

"You do it." Hutchinson was obviously no longer interested.

Francis came to her assistance. Between them they hunted around, and with the help of matches got out several packages of firecrackers, three or four pin wheels, and the few other remaining explosives. "I think that's all," Amelia said anxiously. "If only Hutchinson would look——"

"Perhaps he enjoys watching more," Francis comforted her. "Every time I've seen him for the last quarter of an hour he's been standing aside and—" but Amelia had scurried off "—leaving us to do the work," Francis finished to Stella.

Amelia was having difficulty placing Hutchinson, who made no effort to come to her or answer her. When she finally found him, he was standing alone. He received her coolly but with tolerance.

"There's just one rocket left," the others could hear her explaining to him. "It's the very best one I got, and I want you to set it off. Besides, I just felt a drop of rain, and——"

"I did too," someone confirmed her. "We'd better hurry."

Hutchinson, more amenable than usual, accepted the rocket. Blowing the ash off his punk, he leaned down. There was no excitement in his face, no pleasant anticipation of the sight to come. He might have been lighting his cigarette or his pipe as he touched the glowing tip to the stringy end of the fuse.

The projectile leaped from the trough into the air with a hissing, menacing roar. It soared upward toward the clouds, leaving in its wake a parabolic trail of fire to mark its flight. Minutes seemed to pass, and the rocket to have disappeared utterly into the night, when suddenly, high in the air, there was a burst of multi-colored radiance, which heightened and widened and then seemed to hold itself motionless above the earth. As suddenly as it had appeared it dropped, the fiery stars shifting and fluttering down like scraps of thin paper or brilliant flakes of snow.

It marked the triumphant end of the celebration. Now, in quickening drops, the rain began to fall, as if the rocket's flight had brought down the storm from the clouds. The wind came up and rattled the discarded wrapping papers across the lawn. There was a flash of lightning and a solemn roll of thunder.

Everyone rushed for the house to avoid a wetting. Laughing and breathless, the women surveyed their clothes and found them barely spotted.

"Let's go to the library and have a highball," George suggested in the midst of the confusion. In a body they went down the hall, Amelia in the lead like a stick forced by the tide.

She was the first at the door, where she hesitated in flushed embarrassment.

"Why—Anne!" she exclaimed, taking a half step backward.

By the table, facing them, stood a lithe, graceful girl, wearing a loose camel's-hair topcoat and no hat. She had a well shaped face, nicely cut around the chin, and small, boyish features. Her blonde wavy hair was cut short like a boy's and fitted her head like a cap except where the end of some rebellious curl escaped insolently upward. One hand was shoved deep in her pocket, while the other held onto the edge of the table, as if for balance. She smiled at Amelia a little defiantly.

"Hullo," she said abruptly. "Hullo, everybody."

Mrs. Warden passed Amelia and held out her hand to the girl. "Hello, Anne. When did you come?"

"Not so long ago," Anne stated in quick, clipped half phrases. "Passing the house . . . thought of Cousin Mart and his birthday, you know . . . thought I'd stop and see him."

"Well . . . " George offered this uneasily in way of greeting, as he came up and stood at his sister's shoulder. After kissing her in a brief, inadequate fashion, he looked uncomfortably at the floor. She glanced quickly at his worried face. It was clear that she knew and understood him very well. They were in odd contrast to each other for people of about the same height. Where he was slouching, she was straight and alert; when his eyes shifted and fell, hers were direct and almost offensively bold.

Anne spoke to the others and was introduced to Stella. Soon the surprise, but not the curiosity, in regard to her presence wore off. Francis summoned Griggs and ordered highballs. When the tall glasses were brought, the company found themselves cigarettes and places to sit. Instinctively each of them avoided telling Anne of Cousin Mart's announcement at dinner that night.

Blackstone sat down beside the newcomer. It was curious that his way of speech and his manner of bearing himself should resemble hers, when those of her own brother were so dissimilar. He held up a match for her, and skillfully she touched it with just the tip of her cigarette, which glowed in an instant.

"Cousin Mart ought to be down soon—if he comes at all," Blackstone told her. "He knows the fireworks are over, and we're waiting. Why didn't you join us out there?" he asked sharply. "You must have seen us when you drove up."

"I didn't come for fireworks."

"Then why?"

"To see Cousin Mart."

"And you think he'll be pleased to see you?"

"Some part of him will be—his vanity, maybe."

"Sure of that?" Blackstone glanced up at her skeptically. "Then why do you look so nervous at the prospect?"

Anne stared straight back at him, holding her cigarette to her lips without smoking it. "You're mistaken, Blackstone," she answered coolly. "I'm hardly ever nervous. But while we're on the subject of personal appearance," she looked away from him, around the group, "you might explain why you're so pale to-night. Is it lack of exercise, or because Cousin Francis makes too much hay while the sun shines?"

Blackstone could not have concealed his involuntary change of expression if he had not turned his face away instantly. However, he controlled his words more easily. "It's a healthy pallor, at any rate."

"Ummm." Anne got up, and before anyone understood her intention had slipped into her coat.

"What! You're not going!" Amelia objected from the other side of the room. "I thought you were staying to see Cousin Mart."

"Obviously he's not coming down. It's almost eleven-thirty."

"Well," the other meditated in some concern, "that's a pity. Why don't you just go upstairs and see him?"

"Not I. I know how he greets visitors without appointment." Anne turned up the collar of her coat. "Besides, my car's been sitting in the rain for twenty minutes now. I ought to push off."

"Wait, Anne." Mrs. Warden got up from the couch. "This is one time when I have no conscience about interrupting Martin. He ought to have come down long ago—at least to say he'd enjoyed the fireworks. We'll *all* go up. There's strength in numbers." She smiled. "Come along."

From certain members of the group there flashed a queer look which she could not see, a look which resented her tone of authority. George and Francis got up half-heartedly. After a moment of hesitation, Anne threw off her coat again. Finally they all fell in with Mrs. Warden's suggestion, even the remote Hutchinson.

As they climbed the heavily carpeted stairs toward the second floor, they made laughing conjectures about the nature of the reception which awaited them. Outside Cousin Mart's study, however, they grew more silent.

Mrs. Warden tapped lightly on the door. "Martin!" she called. Then she pushed open the door, and they followed her into the lighted room.

The air was damp and cold as a cellar.

"Why, the window's wide open in all this rain!" Amelia exclaimed. As she spoke, the draft from the open door caught the curtains and blew them out into the room. They were wet halfway up and dripping with water. Pools of glistening rain lay on the broad window sill.

Cousin Mart, seated where they had last seen him, regarded

the soaked curtains and the pools of water with wide-open, in-curious eyes.

"Martin!" Mrs. Warden called to him in fear. "Are you asleep?"

But one glance was enough to tell them all that Cousin Mart was not asleep, but dead.

CHAPTER XV

THIS IS MURDER

FOR A moment unendurably long no one moved or spoke. If Amelia had screamed when she first realized that the old man lay dead in his chair, she might have precipitated them all into a state of hysteria. But although she might have been expected to exhibit uncontrollable agitation, she was, of them all, the least in evidence. She merely stood, cowering, a few paces behind the others, as though their presence between her and the dead man protected her from the horror of his death.

The others, trained to conceal their deepest emotions, accepted the shock quietly, in an emotional torpor. Their tortured senses unrelieved by any exhibition of fear, they were stunned by the frightful happening that had overtaken them. The factor that had governed their lives was removed, the old man who had mocked them, indulged them, tyrannized over them, malevolently tricked them, was now powerless. Martin Greenough's terrific vitality was snuffed out. His body, sitting upright in the chair, held them off, sick with dread, even more than he, as a living man, might have done.

George cleared his throat. "He's had a stroke." The words

were whispered, but they rang like a shout through the silent room.

Only Mrs. Warden had courage enough to move. Her face ghastly, she dragged herself from their protecting company and approached the old man. She started to speak, but no sound came. She moistened her lips, and leaned down over him. "There's blood," she said. "It's on his face. I think—I think he's been—shot. Martin!" She called to him in a kind of defiant terror, as if she thought the sound of her voice would bring him to life again. Again she called his name: "Martin!" but this time her voice was heavy with despair. "Will someone——" She took the dead man's hand, and shuddered at the touch of the limp fingers.

Blackstone brushed her aside. "He can't be dead!" His harshness challenged her. He leaned over, and seized the old man's shoulder with his young, violent hands. "Cousin Mart!" Then he recoiled, unable to endure the rebellion of his senses. His arms fell slowly, as if he realized the presence of something that no anger of his could overcome. Standing rigid, he scrutinized the spectacle of death with feverish, burning eyes.

Martin Greenough sat in the chair as he might have sat when he was alive, except that his head fell too heavily back against the soft cushions. His body was not sprawled out, nor slumping. Over his knee lay an open gray-bound book, with its covers uppermost, as though he had put it there temporarily to keep his place. One thin, blue-veined hand lay on it; the other hung over the arm of the chair. His feet, in their polished, soft leather slippers, were stretched out comfortably before him. Nothing about him suggested that he was dead but his fallen head and chalk-white face. His mouth hung open, his lips pale and drooping. His face muscles had relaxed, leaving an unnatural smoothness around the jaw and on the forehead, beneath which his eyes stared out with glassy composure. Down his left cheek, that side of his face which was toward the open window, ran a few trickles of dark, thickening blood. They came, or had come—for the blood had now ceased to run—from a bullet wound in his left temple.

Without moving from his strained position Blackstone stared at the wound. Then, as if he dared not act too quickly, he turned his head, and the others, their attention riveted on his slightest motion, followed his glance. He looked at the open window. Instinctively he stepped back from it as comprehension dawned in him.

"Close it! Close it!" Seized with an uncontrollable fit of trembling, his jaw shaking as if with a chill, George stammered out the words breathlessly.

No one noticed him or his absurd demand. But Hutchinson, coming to himself at the sound of the other's voice, leaped past Mrs. Warden and Blackstone, stumbled by the chair in which the body lay, and, bracing his broad white palms on the window sill, thrust his head and shoulders out into the night. For a moment he stayed there, looking down at the dark lawn, turning his head from one side to the other.

Then he pulled himself back, catching uncertainly at the curtains as he squeezed by the chair. "I can't see anything," he said hoarsely. "It's black as pitch. Anyone could be down there."

He was gray faced, breathing hard from his slight exertion. It was as if this appalling horror, which stunned for a moment the others' more volatile fears, had had far greater proportionate effect upon him, in its liberation of his deeply buried emotions. He was completely shaken from his habitual thin-lipped control.

"What shall we do?" he stammered, shifting his eyes from one to the other of them. "I could . . . we could . . . go outside . . ."

"We ought to have a doctor," Francis said jerkily, looking at none of them.

"But he's . . ."

"I'll call a doctor." Stella's voice came from the hall. She had never been more than a few steps inside the room, and no one had seen her leave.

Anne shifted her weight from one foot to another and drew her hand across her eyes. "And the police," she said.

"The police." Someone repeated the words vaguely, as if they meant nothing.

The girl lifted her head with an effort and looked around at their dull faces. "This—this is murder," she said huskily.

She could not have been stating a fact they did not know. Yet they turned on her with sudden consternation.

Blackstone was the first to respond. "Yes, the police . . . of course," he said wonderingly. Then he pushed by them hurriedly and went out of the room.

"We'll have to get out of here, out of this room," Francis ordered. "They'll want . . . I think we ought to leave things as they are."

Five minutes later they were gathered downstairs, to wait. A dreadful silence hung over the library where the glasses they had drunk from and the unemptied ash trays stood to remind them how short a time destroys the most enduring circumstances. Hardly a word was spoken, yet not one of them would have dared to sit in the same silence alone. Hutchinson stood behind a tall-backed chair, drumming restlessly on its hard surface with his fleshy, soft fingertips. Down Amelia's tired cheeks ran a thin trickle of tears which welled slowly and inexhaustibly over her lower eyelids—the easy tears of fatigue and worn emotions. She was indifferent to their flow. Outside in the hall, Blackstone passed and repassed the library door, treading a monotonous path on the heavy carpet. Now and then he glanced sharply at the clock, whose brassy pendulum ticked away so evenly the minutes passed since he had put in a call for the police. Ironic fortune was bringing the help of the law to one who had consistently set the law aside.

PART II. THE CASE

(As Detective Sergeant Moran of the Bureau of Criminal Investigation formulated it)

CHAPTER XVI

THE TIME OF DEATH

SERGEANT MORAN of the Bureau of Criminal Investigation, with the medical examiner, a photographer, and two policemen, arrived as soon as they might reasonably have been expected. It was a bad night, wet and stormy, and Moran had scowled impatiently when the call from headquarters had come through to his flat in Dorchester. As he listened to further directions, however, his scowl vanished and his eyes grew round with excitement. "Greenough? *Martin* Greenough?" he shouted into the transmitter incredulously. "Oh . . . all right."

To his wife, who waited with a look of pleasant commiseration, he said, thrusting his thick arms into the sleeves of his best overcoat, "Greatest luck I ever had, getting this case. You know *the* Greenough—the hermit of the Fenway. Well, somebody's shot him." And he pulled his coat collar around his heavy jowls in a happy excitement which his wife had come to understand only with the passage of years.

As the police car in which he and his companions rode was admitted to the Greenough estate and rolled up the drive toward the porte-cochere, he stared through the isinglass at everything they passed. "You can't see much," he admitted to his subordinates, "but take a good look at everything you *can* see. This is your first visit, and it may be your last— but, even so, you've got a look-in at something no other policeman ever saw." They dismounted, and Moran smoothed down the collar of his coat neatly as he waited for his ring to be answered.

Now he stood in the broad, high-ceilinged hall, listening to the brief facts which Blackstone offered, looking curiously, even while he listened, at the arched doorways, the hangings on the walls, and the graceful, curving staircase leading to the floor above.

"We'd been downstairs in the library about a half hour," Blackstone was finishing in his resolute staccato. "During that time he was shot." He paused and then went on again, determinedly summing up the last details. "As far as I know, we disturbed nothing while we were in the room. Dr. Cavendish has been up since then, but he stayed just a minute and came down again."

"Ummm." Moran brought his eyes back to the young man. "I'll have you repeat that later. Where's the body?"

Blackstone winced at the question, but quickly controlled himself and told Moran the location of the room. "I won't go up with you," he said.

"Won't need you now," Moran told him. "That doctor you spoke of—is he still here?"

"Yes."

"Have him stay, then, until we come down."

Blackstone nodded and turned away. Moran ordered two of his men to make a search of the grounds outside, and then, followed by the medical examiner and the man with the camera, started upstairs. They found the study without difficulty, opened the door, and went in.

The lights were on exactly as they had been when the others first entered the room—four concealed wall lights, shedding a dull orange glow, and a reading lamp which burned beside the empty chair by the window.

At the other chair Moran looked, and for a moment hesitated beside his two companions, as if he were about to speak to the man who sat there, to explain that they had come into the wrong room. Then he caught himself up, gave a muttered exclamation of surprise.

"Lifelike, isn't he?" he said loudly into the silence, and walked over to stand in front of the chair.

As he looked down into the white face of the dead man, even as he noted the exact position of the wound, the placing of the narrow, delicate hands, and the posture of the body—even at that moment of cold, critical inspection, there was an expression on Moran's face which showed that he could not entirely cast aside a personal, hesitant awe of the man whose lifeless body he considered so professionally. He rubbed the edges of his coat with uncertain fingers.

"Where's he shot?" one of the others asked.

"On this temple." Moran pointed. "You wouldn't notice it from there." The two men came and stood beside him. "Shot from outside, y'see. Not much blood, Doctor."

"No," the medical examiner replied. "There wouldn't be, with the body in that erect position and the wound where it is."

"Well," Moran turned away, "let's get the pictures before we disturb anything."

The photographer arranged the lights carefully and set up the large black camera on its tripod near the door. From this angle, focusing his lens on the quiet figure in the chair, he took two pictures, then two more from each side of the room. While these operations were going on, Moran stood to one side, but his sharp eyes ranged over the room and turned abruptly from one object to another as if to pry a secret from every corner. He noted the wide-open window, the wet curtains, and the water on the sill, the book on the dead man's knee, and, last of all, a small table on which was lying a pack of blue-backed cards, four of which had been separated from the rest and lay face downward, to one side.

When the photographer had finished and started to stow away his plates, Moran went over to the table while the medical examiner began a closer examination of the body. He bent over the table to look at the cards, and then carefully, one by one, turned over the four that lay apart from the pack. An ace of diamonds, an ace of clubs—they were all aces. Moran considered them for a minute, then shrugged his shoulders and went on to further investigation of the room.

Apparently he found nothing of particular interest to him during the next five minutes. When the medical examiner stepped back from the body and picked up his bag Moran was waiting for him.

"Through?"

"Yes. Nothing much to report. Of course, he died instantly."

"How long ago?"

The doctor told him.

"H'mm." Moran pulled at his lower lip and stared into space. "That's interesting. Not quite what I——" His eyes came back to the doctor. "There's another man here who examined the body before we came. Let's see if he has any opinion."

Blackstone met them as they came downstairs, and at Moran's request, summoned Dr. Cavendish from the library. The latter, an elderly gray-haired man, anxious to be gone as quickly as possible from this disturbed household, talked in low tones with the medical examiner for a minute or two. He nodded gravely in answer to the other's queries. At the end of their conversation he was allowed to go.

As he opened the door to leave, one of Moran's men came in from outside.

"Find anything?" Moran asked him.

The man shook his head.

"Well, better look around a little longer. I'll see you before I go." Moran turned from him and with a heavy step went toward the library, where Cousin Mart's guests were waiting for him.

Although they were there by his orders, and had had time to nerve themselves for his appearance, they were startled as he entered the door. They stared at him with dread, as if, having assimilated the shock of Cousin Mart's death, they now feared what had happened less than what was to happen. Moran personified for them the inevitable, incomprehensible process through which they must pass—the unwinding machinery of the law. His short square figure threatened them with everything they feared; took away every hope they had dared to have.

From the other end of the room Blackstone hurried toward him with a nervous stride.

"Did your man find anyone outside, any traces?" He fixed the other with arrogant eyes which demanded an instant reply.

But Moran glanced away indifferently. "No." Standing with his hands in his pockets, his lips compressed, he looked around the room. He took his time about it, turning from one face to another with a slow, impassive stare. It was not a welcome scrutiny to most of them—one or two frowned and avoided his eyes.

Finally he spoke, turning to address Blackstone. "All of you here for a party or something—staying in the house?"

"We're all house guests, yes. It was Mr. Greenough's birthday. We've been here three days." Blackstone gave the details hurriedly, impatient to receive information rather than to give it.

But Moran was not to be drawn out too soon. His head a little on one side, he contemplated the young man from head to foot. "Who're you?" he asked curiously. "His son?"

Blackstone flushed and his sandy eyebrows drew together as they did when he was about to make an impertinent retort. But he bit his lip and answered steadily. "Mr. Greenough was not married. I'm his nephew. All of these people are relatives of his, except Mrs. Warden and Miss Irwin." And Blackstone introduced the company, one by one, to the detective.

Moran drew out a small black notebook and, licking the end of a pencil, made certain annotations. He had a way of glancing at the person whom Blackstone named, and immediately afterward jotting down a word or two on paper, which was not reassuring.

Finally he pocketed the book. "Guess that's all I can attend to now," he said. "Of course, I'll see to it the body's taken out of here to-night, but except for that," he executed a large generous sweep of the hand, "you won't be bothered before morning. Then," he folded his lips firmly about the word, "I'll be here to take a look around outside, and I'll want to talk to each of you. You'll all have to stay here in the house in the meantime. You may not like it, but it's police regulations." He fastened the lower buttons of his coat in a conclusive manner.

"But, Sergeant," Blackstone asked almost angrily as the other failed to go on, "can't you tell us something . . . give us some idea? We're very much upset. If you have any opinion, we'd like to know what it is."

"Pretty early for anyone to have an opinion." Moran considered him doubtfully. "But I'll tell you this, though." He rubbed his hands together and raised his eyes to the ceiling. "Your uncle was shot from outside, by someone on the lawn, as you know. Now, the criminal's got away for the time being, but," his eyes widened, "not for long. There'll be traces. And I'm leaving two of my men outside to-night to watch, in case anything turns up. To-morrow morning we'll know a lot more than we do now. By the way," he came back at them suddenly, "I take it that none of you heard the shot fired?"

Blackstone shook his head, but it was George who answered for them all. "We were here, in this room, then. It was right after the fireworks. We were talking—it was storming outside. We couldn't possibly have heard—the windows were closed——" George began to falter.

"H'mm," Moran murmured speculatively. "Now, let's see if I've got this straight. You were in this room from eleven to, say, eleven-thirty. Right?"

"Yes."

"And you didn't hear a shot?"

"No."

"Well, you wouldn't have heard a shot then, even if you'd been standing outside on the lawn."

"Why not? I don't understand."

"Because there wasn't any shot fired at that time." Moran tapped a thick finger on the palm of his other hand as he glanced around the group. "The medical examiner looked over the body a few minutes ago. He swears to it—and your own doctor says he's right—that Martin Greenough's been dead *two hours* at least. So you see the shot that killed him was fired *before* eleven o'clock."

And in spite of their incredulous, horrified silence, Moran would say no more that night. He would see them to-morrow and make further investigations which would clear up the whole affair.

CHAPTER XVII

WHO?

MORAN'S INVESTIGATIONS on the morrow were not of a secret nature. Early in the morning he arrived with men to re-
place those who had stayed on the grounds during the night,
and without coming to the house went directly to that part of
the lawn which had been the scene of last night's fireworks. His
derby pressed down hard on his head, he walked slowly over the
lawn, still soggy from the rain, occasionally stopping to kick at
something beneath his feet, and his men did likewise, but without the solid enthusiasm which dominated their chief. There
were many small pieces of paper, sticks, and tag ends of exploded combustibles lying about, and these they collected in neat
piles. The pacing off of distances seemed to enter into their work
also, and in every case the point from which they measured was
the window of Martin Greenough's study, which Moran regarded from time to time with calculatingly narrowed eyelids.
That other eyes, some awed, some frightened, and some only
indifferent, looked down on him and his movements from every
room on this side of the house, he was perhaps not aware.

For the members of the household and those who had been

temporarily forced into that status found the investigating methods of the police distracting, from a distance. After a bad night, they had awakened to a world removed from death and violence by the passage of only six or seven hours and the serving of their ordinary breakfasts. The servants, frightened of Martin Greenough alive, more than fearful of his death, moved like ghosts in the course of their morning duties. Only for Giulio, the valet, was the new day empty of routine. The big fellow cowered in the butler's pantry, leaning against the shelves as he fingered his red sash, the emblem of former office.

Over the main part of the big house, the dining room, the library, in the bedrooms, and the halls lay a curious atmosphere of vacancy. Their owner would not have thought to use them in these morning hours. Yet now, with their changed aspect, it seemed that in his lifetime he must have lived and breathed in each of them even while his corporeal body sat small and isolated in the one room he chose for solitude.

There was a cold blankness in the portraits and pictures on the walls, a lack of color in the tapestries and rugs he had bought, with careful taste, in foreign markets. The handsome, massive furniture, that carved ebony table from Holland, the set of Venetian chairs he had so admired, the wrought-iron chandeliers—all these objects of personal, sometimes romantic history, faded coldly in the light of this day to things of wood and metal, their spirit departed with him who had prized them. The muffled footsteps of the butler passing in the hall, the opening and closing of a door, were noisy and daring interruptions of the spell which lay over the house.

After breakfast most of the household avoided a return to their separate rooms. With an appearance of aimless indecision they wandered to the library, from the windows of which they could look out on the lawn where Moran and his men were at work. Some of them studiously turned the pages of magazines and newspapers. Their relations with each other were unnaturally stiff. Not one of them could conceal the strain under which he moved and spoke. But there were no tears, no uncontrollable manifestations of grief.

Martin Greenough's death left with them a sense of loss which was not, and could not be, affectingly personal. He had provided for them, stormed at them, shunted them imperiously from one course of action to another—but always he had held them, critically, at arm's length. Money had been the impersonal medium of exchange between them. Possibly it was the realization of that which kept him from allowing them, even from allowing Blackstone, to approach him more closely. They, on their part, had regarded him from his chosen distance, sometimes with admiration, sometimes hating him, but always with awe. He was a colorful phenomenon, now dangerous and now kind to them, a versatile actor on a moving stage. They could remember the tales he told them, always of himself, of what he had done before they knew him. They had watched the growing spectacle he shaped about his life and habits. His death was the end of the spectacle, the nature of it a stunning and, in a sense, fitting climax to all that had gone before. They were shocked and repelled, but they could not show sorrow over the death of the man who had been so far removed from them.

The morning was not made easier by the fact that they all shared a common thought and certain common speculations. There was not one of them but realized that the course of his life had been changed overnight, not one of them but caught the reflection of his own thought in the faces of the others. The fear that by word or gesture they might let slip these inner workings of their minds kept them scrupulously aloof, while in secret they fed upon the thought of possible tomorrows.

Only in regard to the police could they find any ground for conversation. From the window Hutchinson had watched them quietly for over an hour. Occasionally someone else joined him there.

"What are they looking for?" The question was asked by every one of them, in so many words, at some time during the morning. And each time Hutchinson shrugged his shoulders without answering and took a slow drag from his cigarette.

"It's a waste of time," Francis said, putting down his newspaper.

"What else can they do?"

But Francis was not listening. "Funny what that Moran said last night. I mean—that Cousin Mart was dead before eleven."

"Oh, he didn't understand," Blackstone said impatiently. "That's the only way to interpret that."

"But he did understand, Blackstone," Mrs. Warden interposed quietly. "You heard him asking George about the time we came into the library."

With one accord they all turned to look at her. She had been so silent all morning, so little in evidence at breakfast and afterward, that they had almost forgotten her existence. Now they remembered her—remembered also that in an interval of twelve hours she had become of little importance to them, that her circumstances were altered, by Cousin Mart's death, to a far greater degree than theirs. None of them would have gone so far as to wish for her a different fate. So they let her words fall into a silence that was only broken by a halfhearted suggestion from Francis.

"We'd better explain the situation to him again."

"You'll soon have a chance to," Hutchinson said from the window. "I think he's coming in now."

In a moment they heard Moran's gruff tones in the downstairs hall and Griggs's voice replying to him. In the library the flagging conversation had stopped altogether. Mrs. Warden rearranged the folds of her skirt, while Anne shifted her position in the chair and began quickly turning over the pages of the magazine she held in her lap. Hutchinson looked even more studiously out the window. When Moran, still in his overcoat, appeared in the doorway, they presented too obvious a picture of unconcern.

Again he favored them with his slow, searching stare. "'Morning," he said at last, without a smile.

"Good-morning."

"Come in, Mr. Moran. Better take off your coat. It's warm in here." Francis half rose, stretching out a hand to assist him.

But Moran drew the edges of his coat more closely about him and shook his head. "I'll keep it on," he said as he walked across the room to an unoccupied chair.

"You people must have done quite a lot of celebrating last night," he remarked when he had settled himself, "at least, judging by the litter there's out on that lawn." Having delivered himself of this, he sat quietly for a second or two, as if preparing himself for a plunge into deeper waters. But Blackstone, clearing his throat hurriedly, was before him.

"Look here, Mr. Moran, there's something I—we all want to straighten out with you before you go any farther. Something about the exact circumstances last night. From what you said the last time we saw you, it's obvious you don't understand what they were." The young man fixed his intent eyes on Moran, while his forehead wrinkled into a dozen sharp creases.

The other frowned impatiently, as if his course of action had been interrupted. "All right, what is it?"

"When we finished the fireworks last night," Blackstone tapped a nervous hand on his knee, "we had to run for the house to keep from getting wet. I know I looked up at Cousin Mart's window as I went across the lawn. Some of the rest of us did too. We distinctly saw him sitting there. He was alive then, I'm sure of it."

Moran contemplated his derby meditatively and fingered its stiff edges with a broad thumb. "Well, now, Mr. Greenough," he said at length, "here's how I look at it. Would a living man have kept on sitting at that open window in a storm like we had last night? Wouldn't he have closed it? And wouldn't he have pulled his curtains to again?"

Blackstone bit his lip in silence.

"You've got a point there," George burst forth unexpectedly from the other end of the room. "But tell me this—if you think Cousin Mart was shot while we were all out there. Why wouldn't we have noticed a sudden change in his position?"

Moran turned to face this new attack. "Because," he replied doggedly, "there probably wasn't any sudden change in his position. Listen! You don't make much of this, but I do. The body was sitting easy in that chair, it wasn't slumped over. Like this." To illustrate, he leaned back in his own chair, and stretched out his feet before him. Then he resumed his own stiff-backed position. "That means," he went on, "that from the lawn you wouldn't have noticed anything unusual. The change would have been so slight. Besides," he challenged, "how many of you can swear you kept your eyes on him every minute from the time he pulled his curtains back to the time you went in the house?" He looked around the group, and no one answered him.

"But, Mr. Moran, the shot!" Francis objected incredulously. "We would have heard it!"

"Hutchinson!" Amelia whispered in sudden excitement, "do you suppose that was what you heard when you——" But Hutchinson's scowl silenced her.

"No, sir," Moran was saying in answer to Francis's question, "you wouldn't, not necessarily. Not with fireworks. Not with the rest of those things popping and exploding around you."

Blackstone again called Moran's attention to himself. "What I can't realize," he began more quietly now, "is the possibility of any prowler being around last night. He'd have a hard time getting into the grounds, for one thing. And then, we would have seen him. It was dark, I know. But one of us would have spotted a stranger. He would have had to shoot from approximately the locality where we were."

"That's so," Moran agreed. "There can't be two opinions about that. I've been looking around out there," he jerked his head toward the window, "pretty carefully. And my mind's made up that whoever shot the old gentleman stood within a certain radius to be able to do it. And that radius is pretty well spotted with burned-out firecrackers and pieces of the other fireworks you set off last night. That means that a good many of you were standing around there at one time or another. And you'd be bound to catch sight of anyone who didn't belong to your party."

"But we didn't! We didn't see anybody!" Amelia cried in despair.

Moran heard her absently. "No. No, you didn't," he said, and went on methodically. "The servants all have watertight alibis.

They were having a party, by your uncle's orders, to celebrate his birthday. Even that valet was with them. No, you didn't see any-body . . . else."

He let the appalled silence hang about his words for a second or two. Then he drew a long breath. "Now," he announced, "it's my turn to ask for some information." He dug into the pocket of his overcoat and pulled out a heavy object, rolled in a handker-chief, which he unwrapped and held on the palm of his hand. "Any of you ever seen this before?" he asked. It was a dueling pistol with a long, slender barrel.

All of them stared at it, fascinated, and as they looked Mo-ran watched their faces. For a moment no one moved. Then Blackstone's eyes flickered away from the pistol, but they did not meet Moran's, and he said nothing. Nor did Francis or George, whose sudden change of expression betrayed them.

"Any of you ever see it before?" Moran repeated grimly. Still no one answered him.

But Mrs. Warden got up from her chair with a strange look on her face. Quickly she crossed the room toward the door where a heavy table was standing. With a jerk she pulled out the small center drawer and looked inside. Her hand went slowly to her lips, and she stood motionless, with her back to the rest of the company. Then she turned around and looked vaguely to-ward the detective.

"It's Martin's pistol," she said softly. "You took it out of the drawer."

But Moran shook his head. "No," he said with slow signifi-cance. "This pistol's been lying out all night in the rain. I found it hidden in the shrubbery, out there on the lawn. It shoots the same kind of bullet we found in Martin Greenough's body."

CHAPTER XVIII

HEIRS APPARENT

THAT AFTERNOON Moran began his systematic questioning. Gradually the many witnesses, the servants, the guests, blocked out the story for him. With a fine exercise of common sense, he confined himself at first to its outlines. He learned of the invitations sent by Cousin Mart to all his nephews and nieces, except Anne, to attend his birthday party, of his guardianship of and complete control over them. He had no trouble in placing the relatives in his mind. Stella—it was Amelia who, more communicative than the rest, explained the fact to him—was of course Blackstone's fiancée. But Mrs. Warden's status puzzled him.

"When did you get here?" he asked her. "Along with the others?"

"Oh, no," she replied, the suggestion of a smile illuminating her tired face. "I was here, you see."

"You mean you came *before* they did?"

"Not exactly." She hesitated a moment. "I live here," she explained finally. "I've lived here for ten years now."

"Oh!" Moran's rubicund countenance lightened and then became puzzled again. "I didn't know you were one of the family too. What relation——"

Again she avoided him. "I'm not one of the family," she said, "except in a very broad sense. Mr. Greenough was not married, and he needed someone—" she chose her words with care—"to look out for things for him."

"You mean—" at last Moran was able to define her—"that you're his housekeeper, sort of."

"You might call it that," she agreed.

Moran was left with a germ of bewilderment in his mind, but he did not press her any further.

Only when he talked to Blackstone, next on his list, was the situation elucidated for him. After Blackstone had answered the questions of fact which Moran put to him, the sergeant turned back instinctively to the subject of Mrs. Warden.

"What d'you know about your uncle's housekeeper?" he asked.

"His housekeeper?" Blackstone looked at Moran with sharp surprise. "I didn't even know he had one! Griggs did all the housekeeping, as far as I know, unless there's some woman downstairs——I don't know anything about the arrangements."

"Well, you do know her," Moran insisted, resentful of the other's manner. "You spoke to her when you passed her in the hall a minute ago. Mrs.—" he looked through his list—"Mrs. Warden."

Blackstone's sudden laughter made him look up. "What's so funny?" he said in irritation.

"Who told you she was a housekeeper?" Blackstone asked curiously.

"She did—no—that is, she said you might call it that," Moran answered him.

"I prefer to call her his mistress."

"What!" Moran jumped up, astounded. "Do you mean to say . . . Well!" He sat himself down again. "Now you *have* told me something." He chewed at his lower lip, nodding his head triumphantly. "His mistress, you say. Well, that puts a different face on it, yes, a different face altogether."

"What makes you think that, Sergeant?" Blackstone asked maliciously.

"It's immoral, isn't it? Well, then, if you'd been in this business as long as I have, you'd know that crime and immorality are hand in glove, so to speak. Of course I'm not making any statement, you understand."

Blackstone grimaced to hide his smile. "Oh, my God!" he muttered to himself.

"It works this way," Moran went on, lost in his subject. "You take the average woman—well, she's married. Her husband, he's forced by law to keep to the contract he's made. That is," Moran waved a decisive hand, "he has to support her, he can't mistreat her—and he can't just leave her and take up with some other woman."

"Oh, no-o-o!"

Moran glanced at the young man suspiciously, but the latter's face looked quite innocent of guile. "Well, he can't," he repeated with emphasis, and changed quickly to the next point. "What I'm getting at is that the courts protect the married woman. If the man she's married to doesn't stick to his bargain, she can go to the law about it, and it . . . they . . . " Moran was annoyed by the grammatical confusion, ". . . anyhow, she can get redress. But someone like this Mrs. Warden . . . what redress has she got? If her—er—if her—" Moran sought for and found at last a suitable word—"if the man doesn't do what he says he will—if he doesn't support her—oh, well," Moran shut down on that argument hastily, "that doesn't apply here, I suppose. Neither does the mistreatment, I expect." But he looked hopefully toward the other man.

Blackstone's amusement had faded into contempt. "Cousin Mart was not given to muscular chastisement," he said dryly.

Moran was undeterred. "You see what I'm getting at. A woman in Mrs. Warden's position—well, the law wouldn't be on her side. She wouldn't have any legal come-back. And if a woman doesn't have a legal come-back she's liable—oh, it happens all the time—to take things into her own hands," he concluded portentously. "You see what I mean?"

"Perfectly!" Blackstone announced in a loud, serious tone.

Moran hurried on expectantly. "Did you ever," he asked, "hear him say anything about sending her away, or that he was tired of her, or something like that?"

Blackstone laughed aloud. "No, I never did."

"He wasn't paying attention to any other woman, was he?"

"No!" Blackstone spat out the word, his patience exhausted.

Moran regarded him severely. "*You* might not know everything that went on." But he shifted to other ground. "Do you mean to say that your uncle had her here all these years with the rest of you?"

"It was his house," Blackstone said after a short pause.

"And you had to put up with her?"

Blackstone turned on him in a sudden, impotent fit of rage. "She's still here, isn't she?" he said savagely.

Moran accepted the answer. "All right," he said, and let Blackstone go. But his eyes were bright and his step brisk as he went to find Amelia.

"I thought maybe, Mrs. Greenough," he said with some trace

of embarrassment, "that you might be able to tell me about—about Mrs. Warden."

Amelia agreed amiably. "Oh, yes," she said. "I'd be glad to." She waited expectantly.

"You knew—" Moran coughed—"you knew her position in the household."

For a moment Amelia did not understand him. Then a faint flush rose to her cheeks. "Why, yes," she admitted, a little breathlessly. "Cousin Mart was *so* unconventional. It was very hard on her, I always thought, and at first I didn't like it at all, but then I found she was so sympathetic, and I felt sorry. Such a shame," she went on aimlessly, "just when he was going to make it right."

"Make it right! You mean he was going to tell her to go away?"

Amelia stared at him round eyed. "Oh, no!" she exclaimed. "She wasn't going away. They were going to be married—it would have been tomorrow."

"Married!" Moran ejaculated. And then words failed him. He stared at Amelia with annoyance and suspicion, looking like a man who has been thoroughly tricked.

At exasperating length, Amelia told him the story of the dinner party and Cousin Mart's announcement. At the end of her narrative, he sighed. "Well, I'll be damned!" he said in honest disappointment.

"Why, what's the matter?" Amelia asked sympathetically.

"Nothing—nothing," Moran muttered. "Except that nobody ever gets anywhere."

Amelia regarded this answer in some confusion.

After a moment of thought Moran seemed to forget his disappointment. His eyes lighted up again as he turned to her.

"He said he was going to be seeing his lawyer to-day, you told me?"

"Cousin Mart? Oh, yes." Amelia faltered a moment. "He said 'I'll be busy to-morrow with my lawyer.' Those may not be his exact words, but——"

"He said that just after he said he was going to get married?"

"Just *before*, I think." Amelia was making every effort to be exact. "Yes, I'm sure it was just *before*."

Moran waved away the correction impatiently. "That makes no difference," he said. "I meant that he hitched the two together." He changed the subject abruptly. "How'd he intend to leave his money?" he asked.

"I—I really don't know. No one could ever be quite sure." Unconsciously Amelia betrayed the family's interest in the question. "We always thought, that is, Hutchinson said it ought to be divided equally, if he didn't make some special provision about the eldest. But Cousin Mart never told anyone. He *suggested* that that was the way——"

"But, of course," Moran cut in on her, "his getting married would change things."

"Why—" Amelia was bewildered—"why, I never thought . . . Of course, Hutchinson was upset—I could see that last night—but I never thought . . . " Her voice faded into murmured protests.

Moran, off on another scent, ignored them. "McBeath!" he called out.

McBeath, the imperturbable, appeared in the doorway. "Yeah?" he said.

"Find out where to get hold of Mr. Greenough's lawyer for me and tell him I want him here right away."

"There's some lawyer here now," McBeath announced. "He

tried to get in, and they wouldn't let him, at first, till they found out who he was, and then——"

"Bring him in." Moran cut the explanations short.

"All right."

Amelia did not know what she was supposed to do. "Do you want me to stay?" she inquired mildly.

Moran had forgotten all about her. "No," he answered absent-mindedly. "That's all."

She left in some haste. A few minutes later, McBeath appeared again. "Here he is," he said shortly.

A shrewd-faced man of middle age stood in the doorway behind him. "My name is Judson," he said to Moran, "and I represent the firm that has taken care of the late Mr. Greenough's affairs. This——" he passed his hand over his face—"this is a shocking thing."

"It's going to be more shocking than it is now," Moran remarked, biting the end of a fat cigar. "How'd you happen to come out here?"

"I had an appointment with Mr. Greenough for to-day," Judson answered. "When I learned of his death, I came out anyhow, thinking that the police . . . "

"Would want to find out what was what," Moran finished for him. "That's right. We do—*I* do."

"You've decided that the will is going to have some bearing on this?" The lawyer frowned.

Moran avoided his question. "When was this will written?" he asked.

"A long time ago, in 1918. That's almost thirteen years." He looked sharply at Moran. "Of course, you may be expecting some strange quirk in the bequests. There's no such thing. No one is mentioned outside the family."

"But how about Mrs. Warden?"

Judson obviously knew the person he spoke of. "She doesn't come into it," he said. "I believe that was before they had met. But I happen to know that Mr. Greenough settled a fairly large sum on her a few years ago."

"You knew that he would have been married to her to-morrow?" Moran asked him curiously.

"Ah!" The lawyer was only slightly surprised. "So that's why he wanted to change his will!"

Moran looked at him eagerly. "He said to you thàt he was going to change it?"

"Yes, he did."

Moran rubbed his hands together with satisfaction. "That clinches the motive," he remarked. "Now—who was going to profit most by the old will?"

"Most?" The lawyer looked at him inquiringly. "That's difficult to say. Let me tell you briefly what the will says. To each of his nephews and nieces, that is, to George and Anne Pickering, to Blackstone, Francis, and Hutchinson Greenough, it gives a million dollars outright. The remainder of his fortune, quite a sizable amount, incidentally, Mr. Greenough left in a way that, I think, particularly pleased him." Judson smiled. "He had a unique sense of humor," he commented drily. "He directed that, ten years from the time of his death, this fortune should be divided equally between two of his heirs—the one who had made the most of his original inheritance, and the one who had *spent* the most. You see," again he smiled, "a great part of his wealth was left in the balance. It is," he chose the word with precision, "to be competed for in the future."

Moran was annoyed. "The future," he remarked sarcastically, "that doesn't provide me with a motive, now. You're sure he didn't leave Anne out?" he asked with some insistence.

The lawyer answered him positively. "She shares with the rest."

"And he didn't mention Amelia Greenough, Hutchinson's wife?"

"No. I suppose that he considered she would benefit along with her husband."

"Then," Moran came to a conclusion distasteful to him, "they were all in the same boat. But—wait a minute." He pounded his fist against the palm of his other hand. "He didn't say to you what he was going to do in his new will, did he?"

"Nothing specific," Judson admitted.

"D'you think he would have left everything to his wife—nothing to the others?"

"That I can't say," Judson answered patiently. "He might have left the bulk of his fortune to her. Again, he might not have—I don't know. Of course, if any one of them had displeased him recently . . . "

"That's it." Moran was satisfied. "That's what I've got to look for. Money's back of it, of course. But the one most likely to be cut out of the new will on account of something he'd been up to—that's the person I'm after!"

CHAPTER XIX

THREE PATHS

Moran tramped up and down the small room on the first floor of the house which he had chosen for his headquarters. His round, red Irish face was set in a mold of stubborn perseverance. Now he puffed furiously on his cigar, now let it die. Lighted or unlighted, he rolled it furiously between his lips. It was his constant aid to thought.

His coat was unbuttoned, and from its inside pocket a dog-eared notebook half protruded. As he walked it flapped against his barrel-like chest. Gradually he was reminded of it. He fingered it once or twice, and finally, with a sigh, took it out, sat down by the table, and began to turn its pencil-smudged pages. From beginning to end he ran through it, and then turned back to the beginning again. There he paused. As he considered what he had written he mouthed the words he read, frowning in the depth of his concentration upon them.

It was a rough time schedule, which he had painstakingly made for himself, that he considered so carefully. In his patient, obstinate zeal, he had gone back far before the time of the murder. Beginning with days, he had narrowed down his list to hours and minutes as he approached the crisis. Over and over again he read his phrases, drawn out in his flourishing copybook hand.

13th June.	Francis came.
14th June.	Hutchinson, wife, George Pickering came.
15th June.	Blackstone came. Girl, Stella Irwin, with him.
16th June.	Everybody here.

(He considered this a moment, and then added, "except Anne Pickering.")

17th June.	Evening of murder.	
	7:00.	Dinner, all in dining room.
	8:15.	All in library. Till 9:30 playing cards.
	9:45-10:00.	Saw Hutchinson upstairs.
	10:15-11:00.	Setting off fireworks. He watched from upstairs. 10:45 (approximately) people hear a loud report.
	11:00-11:30.	All in library. Anne Pickering there.
	11:30.	Murder discovered.

Painfully he mulled over his list, only to resign it helplessly. With an effort at clarifying his thoughts, he wrote a question after it, "Who'd have been cut out of new will?" But this took him no farther along, and after going over the schedule once more, he began on a new tack. A gleam of triumph came into his somewhat dull blue eyes. He underlined one sentence, "9:45-10:00. Saw Hutchinson upstairs." He sent for Hutchinson.

When the object of this sentence came in, Moran looked him over with more care than he had awarded him before. The sergeant was impressed by Hutchinson's neat, conventionally distinguished appearance. Already Hutchinson wore on his left sleeve a band of black; already his expression was composed into the lines proper to a mourning heir. His attitude denied the impossible truth—that the fate that had overtaken Cousin Mart was an unnatural and horrible one—but something in his face betrayed it. His flat, clean-shaven cheeks had become grayish-white and flabby. A muscle in his temple twitched with unfailing regularity. Still his decorum was statuesque, perfect.

Moran wasted very little time in getting to the point. "Want to ask you some questions," he said. "Sit down."

Hutchinson composed himself, uttering a clipped, "Very well."

"It's this," Moran said. "You were the last one to talk to your—uh—uncle, weren't you?"

"I believe so. Yes, to talk to. All of us saw him, of course——"

"I know about that," Moran interrupted him. "That makes no difference. What I want to know is this—he wanted to see you for some special reason?"

"Yes." Hutchinson admitted Moran's allegations coolly.

"Well," Moran pursued him, "how about that reason?"

"You mean," Hutchinson corrected him precisely, "what was his reason?" In answer to Moran's impatient nod he went on, "He wanted to discuss with me the payment of a bill." Hutchinson coughed. "A bill for a piece of jewelry my wife had just bought."

Moran was nonchalant. "Oh, yeah?" he said. "What'd he have to say about it?"

"Not very much. Simply that, since my wife seemed very much attached to the thing and didn't want to return it, he would settle the bill."

Moran was in no position to appreciate the comedy of Cousin Mart's phrasing as rendered by Hutchinson. "Why didn't you pay it yourself?" he asked bluntly.

"It was a large bill," Hutchinson replied stiffly. "I didn't feel that I could give my wife such an expensive present."

"H'm," Moran considered the answer. "Didn't he care how big it was?"

"He was a very rich man," Hutchinson explained coldly. "He had no reason to be upset about the amount."

"Well," Moran became more general, "how'd he seem to you? Bothered by anything, or mad, or——?" He waved his large hand suggestively.

"Not at all," Hutchinson replied indifferently. "He was in an excellent humor."

Moran let him go, watching his tailored back disappear down the hall. "First time I ever heard of *anybody* being in a good humor about a big bill," he muttered to himself, and hailed Francis, who was passing his door.

Moran, like everyone else, was at his ease with Francis. Something in the other's large geniality expanded his own simple nature. He liked, too, the fact that Francis seemed genuinely disturbed over Cousin Mart's death. None of the rest of the family showed what Moran called "a decent feeling." Mrs. Warden's grief could not be counted, slurred as it was with impropriety.

He was prepared to speak openly with Francis. "What's this

about your cousin Hutchinson's having a big bill that your uncle was going to pay for him?"

For a moment Francis was mystified. "A bill?" he inquired.

"Something about a piece of jewelry," Moran prompted him.

"Oh!" In the midst of bereavement Francis allowed himself a smile. In answer to Moran's questions, which, as the story went on, needed to be put less and less frequently, Francis unraveled the tale of Amelia's failing, of Hutchinson's attempt to cope with it, of Cousin Mart's share in the activities. Embarked on the story, Francis warmed to the humor of it. With the gift of a born and witty narrator he outlined the situation for Moran's benefit, dealing frankly and openly with the family's private affairs. Moran was somewhat shocked by his unsecretive attitude, but listened eagerly.

"I *thought* there was some funny business going on," the sergeant said with satisfaction, when Francis had come to the height of his conclusion. "I as much as *knew* it!"

"What do you mean?" Francis looked at him, at first with curiosity, and then with a dawning amazement. "You surely don't mean—— Why, it's only amusing! I'd never have told you if I'd thought——" He finished in a last flourish of astonishment: "You can't be connecting that with—murder!"

"Why not?" Moran wheeled on him. "Suppose your cousin's story isn't true? Perhaps his uncle never said he'd pay for the necklace. Then, if Hutchinson was hard pressed, why——"

"Wait a minute, Sergeant," Francis replied with easy tolerance. "You're off on the wrong track. There's no doubt at all that Cousin Mart was perfectly willing to give Hutchinson the money to pay for the necklace. I heard him say so—we all did."

"Well, anyhow——" Moran dismissed the subject. "I'll think it over."

Before Francis's eyes he refused to give up his idea, but when he was alone again he yielded to discouragement. With thoroughgoing exactitude, he made notes of what he called the "necklace business," but there was no enthusiasm for it left in him. Wearily he returned to the perusal of his outline.

"Who'd have been cut out of new will?" He turned his key sentence over and over, running through a list of names and making absentminded stars and crosses beside them. "Who especially?" he added to his pencilled question. Again his face brightened with a new idea. He buttoned up his coat in a determined fashion and set out from his room.

He found Anne Pickering in the library alone. If he had come to deal with a distressed and uneasy young girl, his expectations were disappointed. It was a question whether Anne had ever been what is usually described as a "young girl." Now, at least, looking twenty-three, she was thirty, and her thirty years had given her experience enough to back up the assurance she was born with.

The windows were open, and a cool breeze came in through them. Sitting by the fireplace, in which for the first time in years no logs were burning, she had thrown her careless sport coat about her shoulders to protect her from the draft that ruffled her cropped hair. She wore no mourning band on her sleeve. Visibly Moran disapproved of her.

"What time was it you got here last night?" he asked.

"I didn't look at my watch," she answered as coolly. "I believe it was a little before eleven. The others were on the lawn when I drove up. They may know."

"You came right in here?"

"Griggs let me in," she replied. "Perhaps he can tell you the *exact* time." She flicked the word at him.

"How'd you happen to stop?"

"For no particular reason. I thought I might wish Cousin Mart a happy birthday, and that sort of thing, and I'd been out driving, and there was a storm coming up—and so forth," she came to an indifferent conclusion.

"I thought you didn't like your—uncle." Moran wheeled on her quickly.

"You mean," she took him up, "why did I bother to wish him a happy birthday? Well, I thought it might be the part of worldly wisdom, to tell you the truth. As another matter of fact, since you seem to be interested, I disliked him as much as I ever expect to dislike anybody in this world." Somehow her frankness did not disarm Moran.

"You'd had a fight with him, hadn't you?"

She nodded. "Certainly. What about? About money, as usual. I'm careful about money. I'd been putting small sums by for a rainy day. And worse than that, I'd been speculating successfully on the stock market. He forgave Hutchinson for losing. He wasn't so tolerant of my winning. He liked us to be"—she smiled scornfully—"entirely dependent on him."

Moran was answered. For a minute or two he did not continue his cross-questioning. His broad, low forehead, above which his stiff hair bristled pugnaciously, was knotted in thought. He stared, not at Anne, but out the window, as if he wanted to sum her up without being distracted by her physical presence. Two figures, standing on the lawn, caught his wandering eye, the finely drawn, graceful figure of a man, his hands deep in his pockets, his shoulders squared, his head thrown back, and the equally slim but more rounded and yielding figure of a woman. They were not far away. The man turned abruptly. It was Blackstone. His voice carried clearly to the two in the library.

"I've nothing more to say." There was no indecision, nothing but a severing finality in his tone.

"You mean," Stella turned to him, "that you believe everything your uncle said of me?"

"So," Blackstone insinuated brutally, "you have reason to guess the kind of things he may have said!"

"I'm not guessing anything," Stella replied bitterly. "Your attitude is enough to tell me."

Blackstone's voice was lower as he replied to her. Moran could not hear, and turned back to Anne, a little ashamed of his distraction. She was watching him, her gaze cool and inscrutable.

"Well?" she prompted him, serenely antagonistic.

"I want to be sure I've got this right." Moran came back to his business. "You'd been out driving, and came past here, and decided to stop. You wanted to wish your uncle a happy birthday and get out of the storm too. So you came in about when the others were finishing up the fireworks. Griggs let you in, and you sat here a few minutes till they came. That right?"

She nodded.

"You're sure I haven't slipped up on anything."

"Quite sure."

"All right." Moran paused. "Where do you live when you aren't here?" he asked with sudden curiosity.

"I have a place on the Hill," she answered.

Moran paused again. Then he tore a sheet out of his notebook, and wrote a few lines on it laboriously. He read it over, "Call garages around Beacon Hill," it said. "See where Miss Anne Pickering," he spelled the name over carefully, "keeps green Ford roadster. What time did she take it out last night?" He turned to the doorway. "McBeath!" he called. His corpulent shadow appeared. "Follow out these directions," he said, and handed the man the note. "Give me the answer as soon as you can make it."

With his usual "All right" McBeath took himself ponderously away.

Still Moran sat on in silence. Anne did not prompt him again. Apparently she was willing to meditate as long as he. Outside the window Blackstone and Stella stood where they had been for the last fifteen minutes, speaking abruptly, disjointedly, after long intervals. Stella's voice was soft, almost pleading. Her words were difficult to catch. "We can start again now," Moran heard her say. "Won't you say you're willing, Blackstone—now?"

"Why—now?" he answered sharply.

"It's hard—" a gust of wind carried her voice away, and then her words were clear again—"what I have to say. I can see—" she was making every effort to reach him—"I understand better now about the money. I used to resent it. I don't now. I know you couldn't have stood being poor. But now—now that he's— dead"—the word came breathlessly—"that doesn't stand between us."

"You mean to intimate," Blackstone asked rapidly, "that I was afraid of losing his money?"

"I can see that you might be, reasonably," she answered him.

"I wasn't. I'm not." Fiercely Blackstone thrust away her generous understanding.

"Then it is the things he said to you about me?" Her tone was less tolerant.

"Things he *said!*" Blackstone's voice had risen to the pitch of fury. "He didn't need to say anything. I can believe the evidence of my own eyes!" After a moment he concluded more quietly. "I don't want to see you again."

Pride sprang to the girl's defense. She laughed a strained little laugh. "Very well," she said, still smiling. "As far as I can help it, you won't. The police won't allow me to leave here, as you know. But I'll not bother you again. Perhaps Francis will keep me from utter loneliness." Quickly she left him.

"Blackstone seems to be in hot water." Anne's indifferent voice in the library startled Moran. "He's no longer matrimonially inclined, apparently."

Moran cleared his throat softly. "Mr. Greenough seems to have made a fuss about the girl he picked out," he said with an awakening interest.

"It seems so, doesn't it?" She refused to make any further comment.

It was the grinning, malicious Giulio, less obsequious now, and entirely willing to confess to eavesdropping, who informed Moran about Cousin Mart's attitude towards Stella and Blackstone, and who, with relish and graphic detail, described Cousin Mart's finding the note in the bookcase. Moran whistled softly as he listened to the anecdote, and later on he outlined it in his ready notebook, supplying his own connotations.

Things were moving faster, but Moran reined himself in with a firm hand. Again and again he went over the events of the preceding evening, again and again his lips moved to form the key words of his structure, "Who'd have been cut out of new will?" Once again he mounted the stairs heavily and, unlocking the door, entered Cousin Mart's study.

Nothing in the room had been touched since the removal of the body except that the windows had been put down to prevent disturbance by the hand of nature. The chairs stood in their accustomed places. The curtains were drawn open, not as Cousin Mart would have had them in the middle of the day, but as he had left them the night before, no longer able to raise his fine white hand to pull them to.

The sun, shut out so long, streamed through the panes, struck in a long finger that touched the arm of the old man's chair, and glanced across the table that had always stood by his side. It illuminated the dark-blue cards that lay on its surface, four of which, face down, were separated from the rest.

Moran, suddenly curious, leaned over and, with careful fingers that touched only the edges of the cards, picked up the four that had been sorted out. Still careful, he turned them over. His eyes fastened upon them. As he already knew, they were the four aces.

Moran stared into space. "They played cards last night," he said aloud, as if to assure himself of the accuracy of his facts. "George, he won. And the old man picked up the cards and took them away with him." He fell silent again, thinking. Again his eyes scanned the backs of the cards, as if he were trying to make the truth appear on their noncommittal shining surfaces.

"McBeath!" he called out, and as the door opened, "Have these sent to be examined, and get them back to me p. d. q.! Find out if they've been marked!"

CHAPTER XX

BLIND ALLEYS

MORAN HAD set the wheels of his investigation turning. So far he was satisfied. There was nothing for him to do at this moment but wait—wait and think. About Anne—McBeath had not yet brought him the answer to his query about her case. As to George, if he had cheated at cards, and Cousin Mart suspected him of it—well—Moran wrote that much on a blank page of his notebook but held his hand from adding after it any premature conclusions, whatever his inner conviction might be.

Alone in the room he had established as his office, he sat down and committed himself to thought. His pudgy fingers gripped his pencil hard, but instead of adding to his notes he let the point wander idly over the blank page before him. Once or twice he heard voices outside—the ban that lay on the great Gothic house permitted its inmates to use the grounds, since they were so securely walled in from the outside world—and raised his large round head as if he expected to see outside his window the two alien figures he had seen before and to hear their bitter voices continuing in difference. But each time he saw nothing but the sun-flooded, empty lawn. On the white sheet before him he drew meaningless designs and shaded lines. Once his pencil, guided by some subconscious, sentimental fancy, created a wavering outline heart across which ran a heavy breaking line. He stared at it for a moment; then turned his page and wrote a name, "Blackstone."

Under it he noted down laboriously, "In love with Stella." And again, "Jealous of Francis." Then, "Hot-tempered; found out that Stella had double-crossed him—note." For himself he added in parentheses to this last remark: ("See Mrs. Warden and find out if valet's story about note is true.")

His wandering pencil drew a line of question marks. Finally he sighed, and disconsolately finished his argument concerning Blackstone with, "He was fond of the old man."

He flipped the page over and started again. This time he chose the name "Stella." His mind worked with her quickly and easily. "Suppose," he scribbled, "she knew the old man was going to tell Blackstone about the note and wanted to keep him quiet. But," he added with a frown, "Cousin Mart saw Blackstone at least five hours before he was killed, and she knew that. What good would it have done her if she'd killed Cousin Mart *after* he showed Blackstone the note?"

He chose a new tack, underlining his next sentence heavily, *"How did she know that Cousin Mart found the note at all?* Cousin Mart wouldn't have told her. Blackstone was too mad to tell her. Mrs. Warden might have." Ponderously he considered his last point. For a moment he stood by his table and drummed on it. Then he made a decision. Quickly he turned to McBeath.

"Where's Mrs. Warden?" he asked.

"Upstairs in her sitting room, I guess."

"You go up," Moran directed him, "and ask her if I can see her for a second."

When Mrs. Warden's permission had been given him, Moran went slowly upstairs, his mind busy with the questions he had to ask. On the threshold of the room he had been bidden to he paused, and his eyes opened wide with surprise. If he had expected to find the apartment filled with some exotic fragrance and furnished with divans, its cheerful, comfortable chintzes must have startled him.

"Won't you come in?" Mrs. Warden's voice brought him out of his abstraction. She greeted him with a faintly troubled smile. "Sit down," she went on, "and be comfortable." Her fine hands were busy with a piece of needlepoint. "Sewing makes me nervous," she remarked, "and therefore at this moment makes me less so."

Moran did not follow her train of reasoning. He cleared his throat. "I just wanted to ask you a few things," he said. "H'm. Sort of to check up. That Italian fellow, he may be a liar for all I know. Anyhow, he said you were with Mr. Greenough yesterday afternoon when he—" Moran hesitated—"went into the library and found a note hidden in the bookcase."

Mrs. Warden studied his face for a moment, as if she wondered how much he already knew of the family's affairs. "Yes?" she prompted him.

"A note," Moran went on, "signed 'F.' and written to Blackstone's girl."

If she had intended to conceal the story from him, she gave up the attempt. "Yes," she admitted, "I was there."

Step by step Moran went over Giulio's story with her and found that it was true.

"There's just one other thing," he said when he had finished his review. "You didn't happen afterwards to tell the girl about that note, did you?"

Mrs. Warden was startled. Her eyes, dulled by the trouble they had seen, sparkled a little; her broad, generous lips faintly suggested a smile. "Why, no," she said, unable to keep the signs of humor out of her voice. "No, I didn't. You see, if I had, it might have created even more of a situation." She was trying, as tactfully as possible, to explain a point of delicacy to him. "No," she repeated, "I couldn't and wouldn't have done that."

Moran excused himself and went downstairs to his office again. To his notes he added, "Valet's story was true," and "Stella did not know Cousin Mart had shown Blackstone the note from Francis to her." Two names, Blackstone's and Stella's, he crossed off his list. Biting the end of his pencil he ran through the others, "Hutchinson, Amelia, Francis——" There came a knock on the door to interrupt him.

"Come in," he shouted impatiently, and as McBeath appeared, "Well?"

McBeath was ruffled. "You told me to find out, didn't you?" he asked crossly. "Well, I been talking on the telephone ever since."

"A—ll right," Moran stopped him. "What have you got?"

McBeath held out Moran's penciled instructions. "'Call garages around Beacon Hill,'" he read out. "Well, I did. 'See where Miss Anne Pickering keeps green Ford roadster.'" He paused to look at Moran.

"Well?" Moran prompted him.

"She keeps it at a place in Bowdoin Square." McBeath nodded in ponderous triumph. "The fellows there know her all right. She's been keeping it there for two years. Same car, same girl," he concluded.

Moran was exasperated. "Do you mean to say," he turned on McBeath, "that's all you found out? You never paid any attention to the only thing I wanted to know! Go and find out what time she took it out last night!"

McBeath stared at him stolidly. "Wait a minute," he said. "I know all about that." He picked up the scrap of paper and deciphered the figures he had added after Moran's last question. "Last night she took it out at—the floorman said he *knew* because it was just when he came on duty—she took it out at exactly ten twenty-five. That's right."

He turned slowly and propelled his massive figure toward the door.

"You're sure of that?" Moran called after him sharply.

McBeath continued on his way. "Dead certain," he said, without bothering to turn his head.

"Well, tell the butler to come here," Moran shouted after him.

"I'll get him." McBeath sighed patiently, and stumped away.

It was an ashen Griggs who appeared, for the fifth or sixth time, before the sergeant.

"Yes, sir?" he queried, his voice trembling a little.

"I'm not going to hurt you," Moran remarked sourly. "I just want to ask you one question. What time did you let Miss Pickering in last night?"

The butler drew a long breath of relief. "At ten minutes of eleven, sir, exactly. I noticed the clock in the hall."

"All right." Moran grinned as he watched the man making a quick escape down the hall. Then he turned to his notebook, no longer undecided about a name.

"Anne," he wrote, and added rapidly, "She'd quarreled with her uncle. She said she came to his house the night he was killed for no special reason—that she was out driving anyhow and decided to stop. *She lied—because she took her car out just in time to come straight here.* Therefore she had a definite reason for coming."

In a new paragraph he carried his case farther. "Anne would have been cut out of any new will Cousin Mart made. She could have stopped on the lawn just long enough to shoot him."

With sudden amazement, Moran leaned over his paper. There was something else. He worded it rapidly. "Was Anne the woman they saw talking to George right in the middle of the fireworks?"

Moran's honest red face had cleared. He slung his pencil down on the table and rose, stretching his cramped muscles. "Little things—" his manner seemed to say—"you have to be smart to catch 'em."

"It's too good to be true," he muttered to himself. Anne's case fitted together neatly—opportunity, motive. He turned back to the fateful words, "Who'd have been cut out of new will?" He nodded. No flaw there. As soon as she knew about the new will—Moran's expression fluctuated rapidly, and he stopped in his eager stride. Cousin Mart had told his guests about the new will at dinner. Anne had not been there.

Moran swore heavily. In his disappointment he clenched his stubby fingers. In their grip his pencil broke in two. He stared at the pieces, threw the blunt half away, and with the other conscientiously added to the case he had drawn up, "But Anne didn't know he was going to get married; she didn't know anything about his making a new will."

With incredulity he examined the words that he himself had written. They must be wrong—they had to be, since everything else fitted into a perfect case. He shook his head slowly. They weren't. No desire of his could change the perverse facts. Anne had not been asked to the dinner. She had not come to it. She did not know that Cousin Mart intended to change his will.

Moran's face clouded in a protest against his ill luck. His own honesty, his own burning eagerness to be right in Kane's eyes, had robbed him of one of his suspects after another. He had just one opening left to him.

He summoned McBeath back to him again. "You got any report yet on those cards?" he asked his right-hand man.

"You only gave 'em to me an hour or so ago," McBeath expostulated. "They've got to go to town, and get to that expert, and get back here again. But they ought to be here soon."

"Well, then," Moran went on, "I've got something else to get from you. How about that necklace? Has anyone been looking for it?"

"They been looking all morning," McBeath reported. "And they ain't found it yet."

For fifteen minutes more Moran condemned himself to an impatient solitude, reviewing his labors. Stella, Blackstone, Anne—he had done with them. He had caught up many loose threads, answered many questions. But nothing he had done seemed to lead him further along. He had simply been going up so many blind alleys. Just one hope remained. On the result of his one unanswered question his ultimate success depended. Again he asked McBeath for a report on the cards, to find again that it had not yet come.

He walked up and down his office, his face now hopeful, now discouraged. Soon his optimism began to predominate. His round cheeks reddened. His lips moved as if he were making ready his triumphant report. He struck the table with his fist, muttering to himself, "I'll beat Kane to it!" He spoke, not in a spirit of jealousy or envy, but in honest anticipation and pride.

Someone outside the door was speaking to McBeath. Moran sprang toward it, his hand outstretched for the knob, but before he got there McBeath had already opened it from the hall.

"Well?" he asked, his voice cracked with excitement.

"I don't know," McBeath answered him. "See for yourself."

Moran tore open the envelope McBeath gave him. The four cards fluttered out of it and fell to the floor. Moran disregarded them, fumbled at the folded note it also contained. He read it once, twice. Then he looked up at McBeath.

"They aren't marked," he said dully. "There isn't a mark on 'em."

★　　★　　★

For an hour Moran sat at his desk, his head in his hands. Then he roused himself, and straightened his coat as if he were pulling his courage together.

"Start all over again," he said to McBeath with determination. "I'll see 'em all once again, and maybe twice, and maybe three times. By God, I may not be smart enough to guess things, but I can find 'em out and remember 'em. Shoot 'em in, one by one, family, servants, everybody!"

McBeath nodded with heavy sympathy. "That's right," he said. "You get it straight. Kane'll do the rest."

All that evening and all the next day Moran conducted his unremitting examination. At the end of it he had the story letter perfect. The rest, as McBeath had said, he left for Kane.

PART III. THE SOLUTION

(As Inspector Kane discovered it, by using evidence given him by me, and by following out the clues rejected by Sergeant Moran.)

CHAPTER XXI

THREE CLUES TO FOLLOW

IT WAS dawn before I finished telling Kane the whole story, a cool dawn that foretold a hot, clear June day. During the night we had built a fire in my grate, but by morning the embers had burned down to gray ashes. They reminded me of Martin Greenough's fireplaces, untended now, and of the fiercer flames the old man must unconsciously have fed—flames that in the end destroyed him.

I was exhausted when I had come to an end. In all my long training in the law I had never had so complicated an argument to follow out, nor an argument in which so much depended on slight shades of interpretation and expression. I knew that in so far as it was possible ever to reconstruct the past, Moran and I had done it, but now that my part in the labor was over, I was distrustful and tired and discouraged, ready to abandon any plea for my accuracy if Kane questioned it. I glanced at his face, expecting to see in him a perplexity and a hopelessness equal to my own.

It was almost a shock to me to discover that his eyes were bright and that he was smiling.

"You think you can make something out of this, then?" I asked him.

"If I am as good in my business as you are in yours, I can," he said. "No," he threw aside my unspoken doubts and fears, "I don't question anything you have told me. It all hangs together too well; it all leads too definitely to a solution. What the solution is, I admit I can't say—yet. But there is a plan, a plan made by an active, logical mind, behind this. We have to discover the plan, and—" he hesitated, choosing his words carefully—"analyze the mind before we'll know who killed old Martin Greenough."

He was smiling no longer. His face had fallen into stern lines that emphasized his harsh, ugly features. Once or twice he passed his fingers through his dark hair. His eyes seemed to have sunk deeper into their sockets under his heavy brows. He appeared to be making every effort to get the facts of the case firmly before him. Not until he had everything straight would he allow his delicate intuitions full play.

His hand crept toward his pipe, but it was not on the table beside him. He got up slowly, stretching his lanky limbs, and walked toward the mantelpiece to fetch it. His movements brought him out of his momentary abstraction.

"I want to reduce this to even simpler terms," he said briskly. "Otherwise we won't see the woods for the trees." He struck a match and held it above the bowl of his pipe.

"Now," he began, "we have eight people to deal with. I leave out, with your permission, Giulio the valet. He has served us enough as a spy, and if he had the wit to plan Martin Greenough's murder he wouldn't be a valet. Certainly, also, we can leave out the rest of the servants, except as you have used them for evidence. Then we have as our characters Anne and George

Pickering, Blackstone, Hutchinson, Amelia, and Francis Greenough, Mrs. Warden, and Stella Irwin. I am convinced of one thing, though it would be difficult to prove, and that is that each one of them, whether consciously or unconsciously, has contributed to this problem. To find out which one is the center of it, we must scrutinize every action of theirs, past and present."

I nodded. It was strange to me to hear the people with whose intimate lives I had become so familiar reduced to lay figures. Yet I knew that Kane, once having so reduced them, would build them up again and disclose in the process the mainsprings of their characters more truly than ever I could.

"These eight people," he went on, talking more to himself than to me, "were a week ago the puppets who moved according to Martin Greenough's whim. One of them rebelled. You see, Martin had overstepped even the wide territory of his tyranny. Moran was saying that, although his statement was too limiting, when he asked himself who would be cut out of Martin's new will. He was undoubtedly right in supposing that Cousin Mart's announcement of his approaching marriage and the contingencies, obvious to every one of them, arising from it, supplied the immediate cause of his death. Broadly speaking, there's your motive, Underwood."

Kane drew himself out of his chair, and, still smoking, began to walk slowly up and down the room. His head was a little bent, and his shoulders stooped as if his ungainly height were too much for him to manage. Once he leaned over, and reached out a thin hand for a pin that lay on the floor. He considered it thoughtfully as he moved to and fro.

In another minute he continued his monologue. "You've done me a great service," he said. "Without what you've told me I could do nothing. You've given me all the evidence up to the murder, all the bricks and mortar for the building we've got to set up." He paused reflectively. "Moran's done a good job, too. He's cleared the ground for me. He's narrowed the field. But he hasn't, as I see it now, followed out his points quite far enough, though, on the other hand, in certain instances he has gone too far and too subtly. It's the middle path we've got to follow.

"You know," he said slowly, "if Martin Greenough had ever learned the old school-book moral of the golden mean, he would probably be alive now. It's a very dangerous thing to be too rich a man, as he was, but he was too clever a man as well. So clever that he underestimated the wits of other people. So set on what he wanted that it didn't occur to him that other people might want things too, and work to get them in spite of him. In a sense you can say that he killed himself. But—" he caught himself up briskly—"it's a sense we don't have to take into account. We have too much else to do."

He began to gather up from the table the notes that he had made on my story during the night. He stuffed them into his pockets without looking at them, along with his tobacco and a handful of matches. When he had cleared up everything to his satisfaction he turned to me again.

"This is our day's program," he said. "Bath and breakfast. Then we'll go to Martin's palace. We have three things, and, as I see it, *only* three things, to follow out there. If we fail in them, we fail entirely. Those three things are—let me label them— the cards, the necklace, and the note. The cards with which the Greenoughs played a game of twenty-one. The necklace that Amelia hid away. The note that Francis wrote to Stella."

"But Kane," I protested, "Moran's done everything there is to be done with them. He's worked them over and over, and found that each one came to nothing."

"Nevertheless," Kane smiled down at me, "I set my faith on them. This case will be proved by those three things. Or else—" he became suddenly grave—"it will never be proved."

He shifted quickly. "Now," he said, "I'll have a bath, and tell your man to cook me plenty of scrambled eggs."

By nine o'clock we were on the Fenway. I pulled up before Martin Greenough's gates. The lodgekeeper, and the policeman who had been posted there, evidently recognized my car, for they opened to me without question. As we passed through I heard a sibilant whisper, "There he is! He's come!" It was a salute to Kane.

As we drove up through the long avenue of trees, the noises of the city seemed to die away behind us. Even the sound of the engine was muffled beneath the drooping boughs of the elms that overhung the road. For a minute or two the immense, low Gothic house was hidden from us by the shrubbery. Another curve, and we saw it stretched out before us, bathed in sunlight, and yet secretive, as if it consciously hid from our eyes the thoughts and actions of the people who still lived in it.

Moran met us at the door. He shook hands clumsily, and greeted the two of us with a gruff "Hello!" in which were mingled embarrassment and pleasure at seeing Kane again. In the same manner he made his brief report, covering the ground that I had already been over. Kane listened to him, making no interruptions.

"You've done a good job," he commented when Moran had finished.

Moran flushed heavily. "I don't know," he said. "We aren't any farther than we were before."

"Oh, yes, we are," Kane reassured him. "And I think we'll soon go a great deal farther."

His first hour in the house Kane spent in wandering around with Moran and me. He made no effort to see any particular person, but in some unexplained way, before the hour was over, he had unobtrusively made the acquaintance of everyone he might have sought out. He made very few comments on them, except to tell me that he recognized each one from the descriptions I had given him.

It was Moran who conducted him through the house and over the grounds. When they came to the place where the fireworks had been set off, the sergeant pointed out the measurements that he had made, the spot where he had found the pistol, and the line along which the murderer must have stood to fire his shot. As I followed Moran's pointing finger to the window of Martin's study, I half expected to see sitting by it the sardonic figure of the old man, but the casement framed only the empty chair.

As Moran talked Kane sketched for himself a rough plan of that part of the lawn, which he thrust in his pocket along with the rest of his crumpled notes.

From there, Moran wanted to take him to Martin's study, but Kane shook his head. "Not yet," he said. "I want to see your tangible collection of evidence first."

We went back to the house, and the sergeant turned over to him the few objects that he had been able to collect, the note, the pistol, the pack of cards. Kane examined them one by one, the note in a cursory reading, the pistol with more care.

"A very fine dueling weapon," he commented. "Beautifully

made and accurate at long range. Would make very little noise too. Were there any fingerprints on it?"

"Not a one."

"That leaves us free to use our imaginations," Kane remarked drily. "Now the cards."

These he looked over with keen attention, first the four that Moran had found separated, and then the rest of the pack. When he had finished, he began to shuffle them idly between his long fingers. Every once in a while he sorted out the four aces and looked at them again.

Moran watched him with a worried frown. "That fellow didn't make a mistake, did he?" he asked anxiously. "They ain't marked?"

"Oh, no," Kane reassured him. "With my naked eye I can see that they aren't marked. Even old Martin's sharp eyes would have discovered that there's not a mark on them, except—" he laughed a little—"what the manufacturer printed there."

Suddenly he roused himself. "I want to talk to your friend the butler," he said.

Moran, a little perplexed, sent for Griggs. While he was waiting, Kane began a quick, nervous striding, up and down, up and down.

When the man got there, Kane asked him only one question. "Has anyone dressed for dinner since Mr. Greenough's death?"

"In dinner clothes, you mean, sir? No, sir. They haven't, I couldn't say why." Griggs evidently regretted the relaxation of decent ceremony.

When he had gone, Kane was ready for action. "Where are they all now?" he asked McBeath.

"Some outside," McBeath answered him briefly. "Some in the library."

"Nobody upstairs?"

"Nope. I see them all when they come down, and they ain't gone up again."

Kane led the way up the stairs.

"Where are George's quarters?" he asked Moran when we had reached the upper hall. Moran pointed them out to him.

Kane walked to the door and knocked. No one answered, and he opened it quietly. Without hesitating he passed through the outer sitting room into the bedroom. There he made for the closet. Five or six suits were neatly hung along the pole. Of them he chose one, a tuxedo. With nimble hands he went through the pockets. In twenty seconds he had found what he wanted. He stepped to a lighter part of the room and stared at the object he held in the palm of his hand.

"Ever see a pattern like this?" he asked quietly.

I went to his side. He was looking at another pack of cards. I felt a little shock run through me, I did not know why.

"Eh—yes," I stammered, hardly realizing what I was saying. "They're—they're exactly like the pack you had downstairs."

"Exactly like them," he repeated after me, thrusting the second pack into his pocket. "Or they are—as far as we know now."

CHAPTER XXII

DISCORD

KANE CAME downstairs to the lower floor slowly, sliding his hand thoughtfully along the heavy banister as he descended. At the second landing, he caught sight of Griggs passing in the hall below.

"Griggs," he asked suddenly, "will you put in a call to Banks and Tiffany for me. I want to speak to the store manager."

"Yes, sir."

Kane finished the stairs more quickly. We had just time enough to sit down in the library before the butler came in to say that the call had been put through. Kane followed him out of the room to the telephone. He was gone no longer than a minute or two. I glanced up as he came back.

After a moment he said, in answer to my look, "That's the store where Mrs. Greenough picked up the necklace."

"Yes, I know that." I waited for him to sit down and tell me the rest of the story.

But he continued to stand behind the chair, looking absently around the room. Finally he came to a decision. "There're several other things I'd like to do now. First—well, suppose we see Mrs. Warden."

"Wait a while, Kane," Moran protested. "How about George? How about those cards?"

"Later." Kane was already leaving the room. "Coming?"

We found Mrs. Warden in the upstairs living room, reading. She marked her place carefully and laid the book on the table, preparing herself, no doubt, to give this new police representative a complete resume of the facts of the last three days.

Kane, however, did not go back to the beginning. "Mrs. Warden," he asked her, "do you remember what liqueur Mr. Greenough ordered served on the evening of his death? That is, after dinner, and after the game of cards?"

Mrs. Warden looked at him in surprise; then recovered herself quickly. "Yes, I remember," she replied. "It was a brandy. I couldn't tell you the vintage, but I know that Martin was extremely choice of it. He had only a few bottles left."

"Brandy is very hard to buy now," Kane commented.

"Oh, but," she protested, "this couldn't be bought. Martin always said that it was supreme even compared with other pre-war vintages. It was one of his most cherished possessions."

"Yet he ordered his small stock served on the evening of his birthday."

Mrs. Warden nodded.

"That surprised you?"

"A little," she admitted. "Perhaps——"

"He was in such a generous frame of mind towards his guests," Kane finished for her, "so generally good-natured, that he couldn't help expressing it in that way."

She looked at him doubtfully.

"Do you think that was the reason?" Kane persisted. "Do you think he was in a good temper that evening?"

Mrs. Warden hesitated. "He seemed to enjoy his dinner party a great deal."

Kane recognized the evasion and smiled a little. "Appearances are sometimes very deceiving," he said. "But while he seemed so amiable, I understand from what I've heard that he had reason to be annoyed with several people. With the Hutchinson Greenoughs, for instance."

"There had been," she admitted reluctantly, "a number of irritations, small and large, through the day." Perhaps she feared that she was to be questioned as to their nature, forced to particularize against a definite person. Certainly she had avoided repeating the name Kane suggested to her.

"Then," Kane insisted, "beneath appearances, which do not interest me, you think that he may have been annoyed?"

She seemed relieved that he had gone back to generalities. "Yes, I do." She spoke more freely. "You see, Martin wasn't very patient, and things had happened, and——"

"He had worked himself into a vile mood?"

"Yes," she admitted frankly. "I should say so."

"I suspected as much. Then let me sum up the situation briefly. He seemed agreeable and in good spirits. Actually he had reason not to be. And any person who had displeased him might have expected to suffer for it."

Silently she acquiesced.

Apparently Kane was satisfied with such general information as she had given him, for in a short time he got up.

In the hall, at the top of the stairs, he paused to light a cigarette. "Are you finding anything that interests you?" I asked him. "Making any progress?"

"Some," he admitted, studying the gently burning match between his fingers. "Things shake down little by little. New ideas. Different possibilities. For instance," he blew out the match and nodded his head in the direction of the living room, "Mrs. Warden is under the impression that Mr. Greenough was in a bad temper on the evening of his death. Hutchinson Greenough, on the other hand, who went up to see him before the fireworks, seems to think that he was in an amiable frame of mind. Now that," he said, thrusting one hand into his pocket, "is something to think about." Kane poised one foot over the edge of the top step, as if to start down.

Down the hall a door opened and a woman came out. It was Amelia, on her way downstairs.

Kane drew back. "Wait a minute," he said to me softly.

Amelia came toward us in her fluttering fashion and would have passed us with a hasty, genial nod if Kane had not stopped her.

"Will you help us settle something, Mrs. Greenough?" he asked her.

Amelia drew up, astonished.

"It's not very important," Kane said, to calm her. "But Mr. Underwood and I have been wondering about Mr. Greenough's disposition—that is, the night he was killed. Now," he said, lowering his eyes to avoid Amelia's really devastating stare, "there are conflicting reports. One person says he was bad-tempered and disagreeable, the other claims he was good-natured and cheerful."

"Oh, he was," Amelia burst out, seizing her cue. "Cousin Mart was pleasant, oh, very pleasant, to me. It was his birthday. I had no idea . . ."

"Your husband says he was very agreeable."

"Oh, yes, Hutchinson thought so—I'm practically sure he did. Cousin Mart was very nice to us both."

"Now, let's see, Mrs. Greenough. Your husband went up to see his uncle about quarter to ten in the evening. And I believe . . . " Kane looked at her vaguely ". . . didn't you follow him upstairs soon after?"

"Yes. I went to my room. For my handkerchief. I needed one."

"I see. Your room is next to the study, isn't it?"

"Yes, it is."

"So that," Kane said smoothly, without warning, "if your husband had been quarreling with Mr. Greenough, you would have heard them."

Amelia's eyes widened with consternation.

"You would have heard them, wouldn't you?" Kane repeated.

"Heard them?" she asked faintly, and then went on, gradually recovering her voice. "Oh, yes, I would have heard them. I didn't mean to say I wouldn't *hear* them. But quarreling! Hutchinson didn't say they quarreled! Wha—what did you ask me?"

"I asked you—*could* you have heard them if they had been quarreling? Apparently you could. But did you?"

"Oh!" Amelia caught her breath. "No," she said.

"There was nothing that they might have disagreed on, Mrs. Greenough?"

"Goodness, no!" Amelia shook her head solemnly. "Why, I can't imagine their quarreling. They were the best of friends."

"Then that's settled," Kane announced heartily. And he drew aside with a slight apologetic gesture for having kept her standing on the stairs. Amelia sailed down them with suddenly renewed momentum. As he watched her hurried retreat Kane muttered something which I did not catch.

"What?"

"I said she should be more careful not to slip." He smiled as Amelia completed her skittering progress across the lower hall.

"Yes," I agreed absently, "those loose rugs down there are treacherous. Now," I asked him, "what's next on the program? What more do you want to do?"

"We'll take a short look at the study," he decided. "The photographs you gave me aren't entirely satisfactory, Moran. Where is it, up or down?"

"On this floor." We turned away from the stairs, and I took him to the door of the study. He unlocked it, and we went in. I told him that the room had been kept locked at all times, that no one except Moran and myself had entered it since the body was taken away.

Kane looked around quietly for a minute or two without making any remark. Then he went over to the side of the room and fingered a short length of green wound tubing which was set into a panel in the wall. "Speaking tube," he said.

"Yes. Connects with the butler's pantry," Moran informed him.

He walked to the window and stood there for some time with his back to us. Finally he came over to where I was standing and took out the envelope of photographs which Moran had had taken before the murdered man's body was removed from the room. Kane looked them over carefully, glancing up now and then to compare a picture with the actual details of the room.

Over one photograph, a close-up of the body, he paused for several minutes. "He must have been reading," he remarked. "There's a book in his lap."

I looked over his shoulder. "Yes. He might have been reading while he pretended to watch the fireworks."

"Ummm. But there's no light by his chair." Kane glanced up from the photograph. "See, Underwood, the reading lamp is beside the other chair."

"You're right," I said. "That's where he generally sat, by the reading lamp. The other chair, I believe, was usually, if not always, where Mrs. Warden sat when she was up here with him."

"I see." He took one more glance at the picture before he put it with the rest in the envelope. "Cousin Mart chose a poor light to read by. Well," he said as he turned away, "that's all. Let's go down to the library."

"I take it we've gained nothing by that examination," I remarked while he was locking the door of the study.

Kane made no answer, but I knew by the way he hurried us down the stairs that some part of his morning had been successful and that we were soon to hear about it.

CHAPTER XXIII

TWO IN DREAD

With the library doors closed behind us, shutting us in and away from possible intruders, Kane did not settle down at once but walked from one corner of the room to the other, inspecting a picture, fingering a book or magazine, hardly conscious, it seemed, that we were waiting for him to speak. However, his restless, indecisive manner more than ever convinced me that he wanted to discuss something with Moran and me. I was sure of it when he pulled out his pipe and filled it. So I waited quietly without trying to hurry him.

His first words disappointed me. "People," he said, thrusting the pipe stem into the corner of his mouth, "are clever at hiding their real feelings and the true state of their emotions in a crisis. Sometimes it's more instinctive than rationalized. Even so, that trait makes me a lot of trouble. I've got to be a downright ferret."

"Well," I volunteered absently from the depths of my armchair, "you can't expect a host, even such an unconventional one as he was, to brandish his irritations at his own dinner table."

"Are you talking about Martin Greenough?" Kane asked unexpectedly.

"Certainly I am."

"Well, I'm not." Then he went on more patiently. "I'm referring to his guests and relatives, Underwood—two of them, in fact. They were much more disturbed than their host—and in a far different fashion. Cousin Mart was irritated, and very angry, but these two I speak of were overwhelmed with horror at the thought of what was before them. Even more clearly than the others, they saw the comparatively pleasant lives they'd been leading torn up by the roots."

Kane had come around to stand in front of my chair. I nodded at him understandingly. But he shook his head.

"No," he said, "I'm not referring to Cousin Mart's threat of marriage and the effect it would have had on his heirs. This is different. The dangers which hung over these two people were separate things and entirely personal." He removed his pipe and blew out a thin stream of smoke. "On the evening that Cousin Mart died, George and Hutchinson were both faced with extremely disagreeable situations."

Surprised, but unwilling to acknowledge it, I waited for him to go on. He had gone over to the fireplace. "I like a fire to watch while I talk," he said as he leaned over and touched a match to the kindling in the grate. The flame spread quickly, and Kane came back and sat down on the couch. He crossed his legs and leaned against the cushions. Then he began to speak.

"That necklace affair—I told you we must follow it out. Well, I have." He drew a long breath. "Hutchinson hasn't talked about it lately, hasn't seemed to worry about it, even though it was such a valuable necklace that he couldn't afford to pay for it. In fact, I don't believe anyone has heard him worrying about it since Cousin Mart's death. Isn't that right?"

"As far as I know, it is. But, Kane," Moran objected, "you've got to be fair to him. It would be pretty mean of him to think about a necklace in the face of murder."

"Or, Moran," Kane put in, "pretty unintelligent of him not to know that he needn't worry any more over bills for a mere five thousand. He'll be almost able, in his present state of inflated credit, to let Amelia wander where she will. Yes, those are two excellent reasons, I grant you, for Hutchinson's relaxation."

Kane stretched his arms behind his head and smiled. "As you must have said to yourself, Moran, when you heard about the necklace—wouldn't it be awful to have a wife like that? I agree. It must have been terrible for Hutchinson, for a long, long time. They haven't much money, you know—or hadn't—though you'd never guess it from the way he acts. Then think of those noncommittal little bills which floated in the first of every month, bland little bills mentioning a three-dollar hand-kerchief purchased by Mrs. Greenough, a twenty-dollar hat ornament, or a fifteen-dollar scarf. Think of the man's rage! He couldn't avoid those bills as he avoided his own, or his wife would be exposed as a thief. And that would reflect on his own dignity. Half of the things he'd probably never see— Amelia would hide them away like a squirrel. But the bills remained. Hutchinson would have to sell a share or two of stock or beg from Cousin Mart to pay them. That tided him over for a while, but it didn't prevent the bills from coming the next month. Nothing would, except keeping Amelia indoors, and no man could do that."

I began to laugh. "I'm sorry not to be properly sympathetic," I said, "but the whole affair is funny—you'll have to acknowl-edge that. The picture of——" I stopped in surprise, for Kane was not laughing with me.

"Go on," he said slowly. "It is funny, and I'd enjoy it with you, only that—" he paused and then continued soberly—"I know the end of the story."

"The necklace," he said after a moment, "was a theft hardly to be compared with the rest of the things Amelia had picked up in her light-handed fashion. So far she'd confined herself to trifles which caught her eye. This—to put it mildly—was a departure. At least, Hutchinson seemed to think so. Five thousand dollars—why he could hardly have raised it if he'd sold everything he owned! You know how he went at Amelia, pleading with her, even threatening her. And Amelia acted about the necklace just as she'd acted about the scarf pins and the handkerchiefs. She hadn't taken it, she hadn't hidden it, she didn't know where it was! And that was the end of it, as far as she was concerned. Hutchinson tried hunting for it himself, burrowing around in bureau drawers, in desks, and all other unlikely places. Cousin Mart caught him at it. At first he was irritated— he'd never cared very much for Hutchinson, and to see him at this undignified pursuit exasperated the old man. But the performance lasted longer, and Cousin Mart became interested and amused. *He'd* get it out of Amelia, or know the reason why! He tried. But Amelia stuck to her guns. So, having failed, Cousin Mart finally gave Hutchinson to understand that he would do the generous thing and furnish him the five thousand to pay for the necklace.

"Think of Hutchinson's relief! He dropped his hunted look and his persecution of Amelia at the same moment. He had an appointment with Cousin Mart for that evening, at the end of which he would certainly be presented with the check. Hutchinson is a greedy man—you can picture him feeding on the thought of that five thousand, enjoying it more than he could be expected to enjoy anything else. Those were probably the happiest moments of his life—the three or four hours after he understood that Cousin Mart was ready to pay for the necklace. Then the bolt fell—and to Hutchinson it was lightning from a clear blue sky, for it had never entered his calculations that such a thing could happen. It is safe to say that never had he been so horrified, never in his life had he dreaded anything as much as his coming interview with Cousin Mart. For that wily old man, and his trick of doing what was least expected, had been his undoing. Just as they had been the undoing of George."

I waited for Kane to go on, for he had paused to suck meditatively on his pipe. Before he spoke again, however, he reached into his pocket and pulled out the pack of cards I had seen him take from George's room. He thumbed through them for a moment.

"This pack," he said finally, "is just like the pack which was in Cousin Mart's study. They are identical, in fact—except for four cards. And those four cards are marked." He spread the pack out like a fan. "Here's one of them," he said, picking out a card and handing it to me. "Look it over carefully."

It was the ace of clubs. I held it face down and examined the back. There were two small holes on it, like needle pricks, one in the top right-hand corner, the other in the lower left. "But you'd never notice them if you didn't suspect they were there," I said.

"No. However, once you knew it, you could rake in a pile of chips. The other three," he went on, "are pricked in the same unobtrusive fashion. They're all aces."

I gave him back the card. "You're saying, then, that George is a card cheat."

Kane shrugged his shoulders. "Not always, perhaps, but once, certainly."

"But you don't mean he cheated the night he played here."

He did not answer.

"Why, Kane," I insisted, "that isn't the pack he played with."

"Not the *pack*, no. But he did play with these four aces. Look!" He pushed the cards together compactly, and held them so that I could see the edges. "Those four aces do not belong to this pack. Don't you see that their edges are dull, as if they'd been played with more often. The rest of the edges are bright."

"You're right," I admitted.

"These four cards were originally in the pack found on Cousin Mart's table. The two sets of aces were transposed—that's the explanation."

"And a very simple explanation too," I complained. "But I don't follow it."

"Wait a minute, and I'll help you out. Look here!" Kane leaned forward with his hands gripping his knees and looked into the fire as he spoke. "George raked in a sizable pile of chips · that night, as you've told me. Probably he could have got away with his cheating, if it hadn't been for that last hand. But there was too much at stake then. George's *coup* was too spectacular, on top of the extraordinary luck he'd been having all evening. You remember how long he looked at the cards Francis held. Well, he knew where all the aces were. He had them in the pack. Therefore, only Francis with three cards could, with a possible twenty-one, beat the two court cards he—George—already had. But he also knew that he could give himself an ace on the draw, and he did. He won a lot of money on that hand, but he overreached himself. It was unfortunate for George that Cousin Mart had been following the game pretty closely. He might have put it over on the others, but the old man was too sharp to fool.

"Cousin Mart said very little, as I understand it, but after the game was over he picked up George's pack of cards, put them in his pocket and went upstairs with them. George had no need to be told what that meant. Cousin Mart suspected him of cheating and intended to verify this suspicion at his leisure.

"You can imagine George's state of mind at this moment. What Cousin Mart would do when he had verified his suspicion was no subject for conjecture. The old man would waste few words and very little emotion over the simple matter of casting his nephew off for all time.

"George had good reason to act very quickly in some fashion. In the midst of his torment he hit upon an idea. You told me, Underwood, that he left the company almost when Cousin Mart did, that he was heard talking to someone, you didn't know whom, soon afterwards. Well, I think he was speaking over the telephone. I'll tell you why."

Kane looked into the bowl of his pipe and pushed down the ash. "I'm thinking," he said, "of Anne's curiously unexplained presence in the house that night. She said it was just a whim, her coming there, but we know better. She wasn't driving aimlessly around the city as she said. Moran checked up on the time she took her car out of the garage, and it was very shortly before she was seen here. She must have driven as fast as she could—and that means there was more purpose than whim in her coming.

"Needless to say, she didn't come to wish the old man a happy birthday. That's absurd. They were sworn enemies, and everyone knew it and was surprised to see her in the house. Well, Anne could have explained that very simply. She hadn't intended to come into the house, but the storm caught her out on the grounds, and she had to take refuge somewhere. Why she was on the grounds in the first place is, of course, a different matter—for she was there during the fireworks. Francis caught sight of her talking to George, but she slipped away when he called to her.

"In short," Kane said thoughtfully, "Anne's conduct sounds very odd, until you begin to put two and two together. Then you realize that her actions might have been governed by another person, by her brother, for instance. She's very fond of George, in spite of a great many things. She would do almost anything for him—even when it came to the point of helping him cover up his cheating. For that, Underwood, was the one and only reason she had for coming to this house."

Kane looked up to see if I understood. "George had telephoned, you see, giving her certain directions. She came as quickly as she could and met him out on the lawn during the fireworks. She brought what he had asked for—a pack of cards identical with the ones Cousin Mart had taken up to his study. But the aces of this pack were not marked, and that was the essential point of George's scheme. For he intended to substitute these four cards in place of the marked ones." He got up and went over to the fireplace. Bending over to knock the ashes from his pipe, he remarked, "As you see, that's a full explanation of Anne's behavior that night, and of George's, as far as we've gone."

"But just a minute," I objected, "even that doesn't answer all my questions. You say George intended to substitute one set of aces for the other set that Cousin Mart had in his study. But how did he know that Cousin Mart hadn't already looked the cards over?"

"He had to risk that. Presumably he thought that the old man wouldn't have an immediate opportunity to do so. Also he knew that Hutchinson was going up to see him at 9:45. The interview would occupy him for some time, and after that, the fireworks. At any rate, it was his one chance, and he had to take it."

"But how could he accomplish such a thing? How could he go up to the study and change the cards without Cousin Mart's seeing him?"

Kane straightened up and looked down at me with deliberate coolness. "Have patience," he remarked exasperatingly. "I'll tell you this and no more. George *did* substitute the cards." He took out a penknife and began scraping the inside of his pipe, but as he scraped he went on more kindly. "What you don't see, Underwood, is that if I explained any one case completely, I should involve you in a mass of details which require their own separate explanations. The evidence in George's situation interlocks tightly with other situations, and to show you how all evidence and all clues to Martin Greenough's murderer point in one direction, and to one person only, I must tell my story in the only way I can.

"I started by saying," he continued, "that on the night of the murder there were two people in far worse states of mind than you would have guessed by seeing them. One of them was George, and I've explained why. The other was Hutchinson, and he had good reason to be horrified by the events of the day. I haven't told you in so many words what that reason was, but you must have guessed it."

"Guessed!" I threw my cigarette impatiently into the fire. "I haven't guessed anything."

"Well, then, I'll tell you." Kane slipped his knife into his pocket before he went on. "Cousin Mart," he said at last, "had taken it upon himself to telephone Banks and Tiffany."

I looked at him blankly for a moment, and then my dignity asserted itself. "Look here, Kane," I said doggedly, "you've told me just this much about Hutchinson. He was in a terrible state because Amelia had stolen a necklace which he could neither find and return nor afford to pay for. Cousin Mart finally promised to give him a check for five thousand to cover it. He was overjoyed, naturally. Now, why he should have become horrified because Cousin Mart telephoned the jewelers, I don't——"

"Wait a minute," Kane interrupted. "What you don't seem to have guessed is that there never *was* any such thing as that necklace!"

CHAPTER XXIV

WHAT THEY FEARED

"There *was* no necklace!" I repeated incredulously. "But—what on earth do you mean?"

Kane was refilling his pipe, calmly and methodically. "Just that," he said, as he pressed down the tobacco with his thumb. "Amelia did not steal a necklace."

"How do you know that?"

"First let me tell you how I came to *suspect* it." Holding a match to the tobacco, he explained between puffs. "Primarily I asked myself, 'What proof is there that she did steal it?' Well, Hutchinson's word and the fact that Amelia is in the habit of picking up things. Then I realized to my surprise that there was no actual proof at all. No one had troubled to check up on the fact—that is, no one that could help me now. It was simply taken for granted, and in my business I've learned that such an attitude of mind is dangerous. So, having once questioned the fact, I decided to verify it. Nothing was easier. I called the jewelry store where the theft, supposedly, had been committed."

Kane tossed the burnt match into the fire and threw one leg over his knee. "First of all I got the store manager at Banks and

Tiffany. He hadn't an idea of what I was talking about. But I told him who I was, and he transferred me to another man, a confidential kind of duck, who gave me all the information I wanted in two minutes' time. Yes, he knew Mrs. Hutchinson Greenough by sight and by reputation—they all did. She'd been in the store on the afternoon I mentioned—brought some shirt studs to be replated and asked the repair department to telephone her husband about the charge as soon as they knew what it would be. They did telephone him. And that was all there was to it. He laughed when I asked him about the stolen necklace. Nothing like that had been missing so far. I asked him how he happened to have the details of Mrs. Greenough's visit so well in hand, and he explained, even more confidentially, that the late Mr. Martin Greenough, the day before his death, had telephoned to ask the very questions I was asking."

Kane tapped the pipe stem reflectively against his teeth. "Now you see that the affair of the necklace, with its superficially amusing aspect, is pretty ugly at the base. Hutchinson was coolly and systematically using his wife's well known aberration to cheat Cousin Mart out of five thousand dollars. And, you know, his plan was danger proof in ninety-nine chances out of a hundred.

"The scheme was good principally because it was so simple. He sends Amelia to Banks and Tiffany with his shirt studs which need replating. They are to call him to tell him what the charge on the work will be. Amelia faithfully carries out his directions. The next day at lunch the butler tells Hutchinson that Banks and Tiffany are calling him. He goes to the telephone and comes back to the company with as horrified an expression as he can assume. But he won't say what the trouble is—not then. That's smart of him. Perhaps one or two people suspect that this is another of Amelia's misadventures, and the fact that Hutchinson won't admit it makes that suspicion more plausible. But now Hutchinson plays a few more cards—he searches the house, supposedly on the quiet, but he makes sure that Cousin Mart catches him at it every time. He sinks more deeply into gloom, is overheard threatening and pleading with Amelia. When Cousin Mart finally becomes exasperated and forces him to explain himself and his actions, it sounds as if Hutchinson were delivering up his most painful life secrets. Oh, it was a well played farce, and, as we know, it convinced the audience.

"Amelia was thrust into the piece just as she was. God knows, she needed no rehearsal. Hutchinson managed her like a skillful director, and she played her part without knowing it. Had she stolen the necklace? Certainly not—she denied it flatly. She hadn't taken it, she hadn't hidden it away, and, finally, she didn't know where it was. She was terribly frightened, reduced herself to tears—all in all it was an exact replica of her reactions to all former accusations. She always lied about picking up handkerchiefs and scarfs, and everyone knew she lied. Therefore she was lying about the necklace. You see," Kane remarked appreciatively, "Hutchinson was playing on the old, old Boy and the Wolf motif. Amelia had lied and cried too often. He knew no one would believe her now. And no one did.

"With the result that Hutchinson's little game was highly successful. Cousin Mart agreed to pay for the necklace that was causing so much worry. There was no reason he shouldn't—he'd helped Hutchinson out before in similar though less expensive situations. So he told Hutchinson to see him that night at 9:45, and he intended to make out the check for the five thousand.

"All was going well, and Hutchinson was, to speak mildly, pleased with the reward of his cunning. He completely forgot that hundredth chance." Kane frowned at the fire in silence for a moment or two. Then he went on slowly: "How Cousin Mart happened to telephone Banks and Tiffany, I'm not certain. I'm sure that he didn't doubt the stolen necklace. And Hutchinson hadn't foreseen that there could be any other reason. Probably Cousin Mart took it into his head that the jewelry store would want to be assured of payment. At any rate, he did telephone, and we know just what he found out."

Kane looked over at me and hit his fist on his knee. "There was nothing in the world—nothing—that could so infuriate Martin Greenough as the knowledge that he'd been made the dupe of another man's game. And duped by someone he really despised. He must have been beside himself with rage. Probably the thoughts of revenge were the sweetest thoughts he had. But he would not vent his anger until evening, until his interview with Hutchinson. So he controlled himself, and only Mrs. Warden knew that he was very angry. But he did allow himself one subtle blow. He dropped the remark, in Hutchinson's hearing, that he had telephoned the jewelry store.

"That was the utmost in horrifying information that Hutchinson ever expected to hear—the lightning from the clear blue sky. Oh, he knew what that remark meant. In one fatal second he saw what was in store for him that evening and for the rest of his life. He was done for.

"Meanwhile Cousin Mart was suave and cool, holding a firm rein on his anger. Nine forty-five was time enough. And, as he waited, you can imagine that his resentment grew no less. Hutchinson would be cut off once and for all. But first he would give him a touch of the cold steel, for Cousin Mart loved the excitement of battle."

Kane flung out his hand in a gesture of dismissal. "All that is clear enough," he announced. "You can interpret men's reactions to a given situation fairly accurately, once you understand their characters. So we can see that a terrific quarrel between Hutchinson and Cousin Mart was impending. But when we go farther," he said sharply, "we hit upon a curious bit of evidence.

"For Hutchinson, when he came downstairs after seeing Cousin Mart, was cool and collected. He said nothing to indicate that the old man was in a vicious temper or that he had quarreled with him.

"Of course, you can say that Hutchinson wouldn't want to talk about the quarrel with the rest of the company. Granted.

"But Amelia goes even farther. You remember she went upstairs immediately after her husband—to her room, apparently, which is next door to the study. Yet she corroborates Hutchinson's intimation that there was no quarrel.

"So," Kane gave a short, hard laugh, "Hutchinson came out of the lion's den—unscathed. Without ruffling a hair on his head, it would seem. Well, so much for him, for the present."

He got up to push a half burned stick onto the dying coals in the fireplace, and remained standing, with one arm resting on the mantel. "I'm about talked out," he admitted wearily.

After a moment's silence he went on. "But there's the other man we were speaking of, who was as much perturbed as Hutchinson. George was caught in his cheating just as Hutchinson was—and George, like Hutchinson, came off unscathed.

"I told you that he managed to substitute one set of aces for another. But the substitution was not made while Cousin Mart was alive. No, George had to wait too long. His first opportunity to enter the study came when the old man was dead. But he carried out his fixed idea, despite the dead man's presence, despite the seven other people who were in the room at the same time. He picked up from the table the four marked aces, and left in their place the four from the other pack.

"In that way, George removed the clue to his cheating. And in removing those particular cards from the scene of the murder," Kane said slowly, "he also removed one important clue to the murderer."

CHAPTER XXV

THE END OF THE GAME

As HE had asked me to, I stopped by for Kane the next morning in my car. He was waiting for me on the corner, and I had hardly maneuvered out of the main stream of the traffic before he opened the door and jumped in beside me. His gaunt cheeks were white and looked even thinner than usual, but he moved quickly and accurately, and his deep-set eyes were very bright, as if his vitality were at its highest pitch.

"Did you get any sleep?" I asked him. "It was a hot night."

"Was it?" he laughed a little. "I didn't notice. I was too busy." He was silent for a moment before he answered my question. "Yes. I got some sleep," he went on. "About four hours of it, after ten of hard thinking. And"—a jubilant note crept into his voice—"it was the sleep of the just, Underwood. The sleep of an easy mind. Now I know what I know, and," he finished softly, "I think I know what I'm going to find out."

"You mean——?" Again I felt the electric shock of excitement pass through my veins.

"Just this," he caught me up. "Certain things are going to

happen to-day, I think. And I also think that I am going to get a definite confirmation of a guess of mine."

He shot a quick glance at my eager face and laughed again. "Oh, I'm not going to be a prophet," he said. "And I'll spare you the irritation of hearing me say this evening, 'I told you so.' Besides," he had become serious, "I may be wrong. There may be some flaw in my logic. If there is——" He frowned and sighed. In another moment he had fallen into one of the sudden fits of depression that sometimes afflicted him.

We were silent the rest of the way. My own thoughts were chaotic. The faces of the Greenoughs, the scenes between them of which I had been a witness, others which I could reconstruct so well by hearsay, flashed through my mind. George and Hutchinson, both of them tarred with the same brush, both proved unscrupulous. But that was no longer the question. The question had become this—what greater consequences might have come of their intrigues? How were their fates interlocked with those of the others?

In ten seconds I could see the shifting field of action and emotion with which Kane had spent ten hours the night before. The conclusions to which he had come—they were hidden from me. What did he expect to see happen, what guess of his was to be confirmed to-day?

Before I realized where we were, we had come to our destination. One of the chauffeurs already held open the door of the car and stood ready to put it away for me. On the step Griggs bowed his conventional welcome to us. Kane was ahead of me, walking briskly down the hall towards the library. Moran joined us on the way.

"You want to work here this morning?" he asked. "Then I'll tell that fellow we don't want to be disturbed."

"Oh, no," Kane smiled at him. "Don't do that, Moran. I want to be disturbed."

He stretched himself out in a deep chair. "Have a cigarette?" He offered us his rumpled pack, and then chose one for himself, carefully smoothing out its creases with his long pointed fingers. He lighted it and began to smoke placidly. His eyes were half closed, as if he were willing and ready to take a nap. But when he heard voices in the hall, he sprang to his feet with a tigerish quickness and went quietly to the door.

"Amelia," he announced, relaxing as quickly. He returned to his chosen chair again and settled himself comfortably.

Moran stood for his inaction as long as possible. Then he said fretfully, "What are we sitting here for? I'd like to get busy."

"I am busy," Kane replied with a serenely irritating inflection. "I'm busy—smoking."

Moran slumped disgustedly on the sofa and began to chew on his thumb nail. He hardly looked up when Kane roused himself sufficiently to walk over to the window. He stood there, with his back to us for a long time. Finally curiosity overcame my inertia, and I went to see what he was looking at, but he was not looking at anything, unless a flock of robins interested him. One of the gardeners was putting up a croquet set. Mrs. Warden was languidly crossing the lawn to sit down on a rustic bench near by. She had a book under her arm, and in a moment had begun to read.

As we watched, George and Anne came by the windows from the rose garden. George's face was haggard, his eyes bloodshot. He had a twig in one hand, which he was breaking into small pieces. I could see that his fingers were trembling violently.

"Regret!" I heard him say harshly, and then, "What a word!"

"I've no use for it myself." Anne's cool voice cut across his feverishness. They passed out of sight, but at the front door they must have encountered another couple, coming out, for I heard Anne again, and Francis answering her.

In a minute, I saw him, and with him Stella. They were laughing and talking, as if they had made a compact together to ignore the shadow of horror that hung over the house. Francis was directing her toward the croquet ground. On the way Francis waved a ready greeting to Mrs. Warden, who smiled and nodded to them. Then he busied himself with mallets and balls, chatting all the while with low-voiced gay intimacy to Stella, who answered him in kind.

"Francis is a great one for games, isn't he," Kane commented suddenly, "games of one sort or another." He fell silent again, watching the two players, who made their shots with idle laughing indifference and gave themselves time in between for a more absorbing interchange, inaudible from where we stood, but of an obvious tenor.

Abruptly Kane began to speak, less to me than to himself. "Cousin Mart interfered once before with Francis's love affairs, didn't he?" he asked, but went on without waiting for a confirmation. "He'd have been wiser if he hadn't interfered the second time, particularly when two of them were involved—both Blackstone and Francis, and both in love with the same girl."

For a few minutes longer he watched them. "She's quite lovely," Kane remarked. "And as Cousin Mart said, not a ninny. I can understand their feelings—Blackstone's and Francis's. No wonder Cousin Mart had such poor success in managing them."

"I don't believe he'd think he was unsuccessful," I answered. "At least he's shifted Stella from Blackstone to Francis. He was fonder of Blackstone and wanted more for him. He didn't care much what happened to Francis. He might have preferred it this way."

"I doubt it," Kane replied. "If he had known better what he was doing—if he hadn't been so busy with his own plans that he hadn't time to look beneath the surface of things. He was so occupied with his own intrigues that he didn't suspect other people of strategy. I doubt if he would have preferred it this way, really. Look!"

I turned sharply, hearing the thud of a horse's hoofs. Down the driveway I saw Blackstone, riding toward us at a steady trot. As he passed Mrs. Warden his horse shied, but he steadied him skillfully, glancing over his shoulder to see what had startled the animal. As he did so, he must have seen Francis and Stella, absorbed in their game. With a violent and unmerciful hand he reined in his horse, so that its four hoofs slid in the gravel, and it reared, pawing the air. Blackstone's face was drained of color except that his thin lips showed scarlet. Whether Stella saw him or not, she gave a sudden gay laugh. Blackstone spurred his horse and galloped away.

Moran had jumped up at the sound and stood beside us. "All right for him to do that?" he asked Kane. "He can't go off the place."

"Yes, I think so," Kane answered absentmindedly. "He's got to work off his emotions somehow."

Moran stared at the croquet players. "They don't seem to care much what's happened," he grumbled, and then added sentimentally, "Still I like to see 'em, sort of. At least somebody's having a good time."

"Well, I don't like it, personally." Kane's retort seemed to me unduly sharp. "I don't care for it, knowing Francis."

The difference of opinion did not add to Moran's sorely tried good-nature. "I don't see any use in my hanging around here," he protested finally. "I got some things to do. D'you want me any longer?"

"No, you go along, Moran," Kane answered vaguely. He turned away from the window, intent upon some problem that he was turning over in his mind. After Moran had left us, he looked at me meditatively. "I said that Cousin Mart was foolish to interfere with people in love, didn't I?" he said. "And he was. That's why I dislike my present duty. For I've got to interfere with them too. Now," he took a long breath of determination, "let's go outside."

I followed him across the lawn towards the croquet ground. Stella and Francis had finished their game. She was sitting, and he was half-lying down, at her feet. He sprang up, as we came towards them, with a swift change of expression. She watched our approach with passive attention.

"I'm sorry to bother you," Kane said, "but I want to speak to Miss Irwin. And—" he turned to Francis with an unspoken dismissal—"may I see you in about a half hour?"

Francis nodded, his eyes suddenly intent. He picked up his coat from where he had dropped it, and quickly walked away. Kane looked around to make sure we were alone. Mrs. Warden had left her bench. Kane motioned to it. "We may as well talk sitting down, don't you think?"

Stella acquiesced silently and led the way to the place he had indicated. Her charming frivolity had fallen away from her. Her face was strained and shadowed with illegible emotions.

"I have to intrude on your private concerns," Kane said to her, sitting down in the opposite corner of the bench from the one she had chosen. He took a package of cigarettes from his pocket, and stared at it thoughtfully for a moment. "By the way," he went on more lightly, "will you smoke?"

He offered her a cigarette, which she accepted, and held a match for her. In the pause I suddenly realized what he must be about to say to her, and instead of sitting down where I had intended to, I walked away a few paces and stood behind them. If I had not realized that Kane must have brought me there for some purpose, I should have left them entirely.

"It's useless for me to make any attempt at delicacy," Kane went on. "Suppose I come straight to the point."

Her faint stiff smile acknowledged his reasonableness courageously.

Beneath his lids Kane gave her a keen glance. "What did you know of Mr. Greenough's attitude towards you when you came here?"

"I knew that he disliked my father," she answered steadily. "I knew that he had used his influence over Francis—I know now I should never have come!"

"But Blackstone over persuaded you?"

"Partly, and partly I thought—" a note of self-ridicule crept into her voice—"that perhaps, if he saw me, he might be less—opinionated."

"You realized that he didn't become so?"

She evaded him. "I realized that something had been said to change Blackstone—in his attitude toward me." Her face was flushed, and she bit her lips.

"You realized nothing more?"

Her eyes searched Kane's face, as if she were trying to make out how much he knew of her affairs. "What more was there to know?" she countered, with an attempt at lightness.

"Perhaps that Blackstone was becoming furiously jealous of Francis on account of various incidents," Kane suggested softly.

She turned to him with swift, well bred insolence. "I think, Mr. Kane, you intrude too far on my private concerns—concerns that have nothing to do with what you are investigating."

Kane's face had hardened. "I'm afraid that I must be the judge of that." His eyes bored into her like a hawk's. "I can't force you to tell me what more there was to know, but I can tell you . . . " He paused. In the silence, I heard a twig snap. A little to my left, behind Kane's back, I saw Blackstone. He had just caught sight of Stella and Kane. He walked towards them, as if to interfere, but a few steps away he hesitated.

"There was this to know," Kane went on with cruel directness, "that while you stayed in this house as Blackstone's fiancée, you were also carrying on an intrigue behind his back with Francis. Mr. Greenough found a note from him which told the story, and showed it to Blackstone. Naturally he realized that you were using him as a cover for an affair between you and Francis."

Stella raised her head, about to speak. At that moment she saw Blackstone, standing behind Kane's back. She hesitated. Her eyelids flickered a little, and she turned away from his steady gaze to stare at the ground. She drew deeply on her cigarette.

"That's—not—so," she said, her voice faltering. "No, I—know nothing about—such a note. I—" she chose her words with strained care—"I was flirting with Francis—to teach Blackstone a lesson." She shrugged her shoulders. "I care nothing for Francis," she finished, and glanced quickly up at the place where Blackstone had been standing. But he had gone away.

Stella turned back to us. She was apparently cool, but the

cigarette she had been smoking had dropped from her fingers. "Is there anything else you want to ask me?" Overheedfully, she bent over and put the cigarette out.

"No."

"Then I'll leave you." With trained ease, she got up and walked away. Kane looked after her with a curious expression on his face. Then he turned to me. "Blackstone's gone, has he?"

I was startled. "You saw him?"

"No." He shook his head. "I heard someone come up, and I saw her face. Well," he got up, and straightened his shoulders, "what do you think?"

"About the note?"

"No." Kane brushed it aside. "I suppose she wouldn't have known about that. After all, Cousin Mart found it before it could reach its intended destination. I'm asking you how this whole situation strikes you."

"I don't know," I answered lamely.

Kane laughed in a strained fashion. "I think I do," he said dryly. "Now I must see Francis, and it had probably better be alone. I'll pick you up later."

He left me, walking slowly towards the house. I stayed where I was, glad enough to be there. We were pushing our way through the tangle, thanks to Kane's unerring, probing mind. But I turned away with instinctive dislike from the conclusions he left to be drawn. I knew enough of humanity to condone most of the faults of men, but this flirting with unscrupulousness, this denial of valid, straightforward emotion—suddenly I pulled myself up. I was thinking foolishly, for no one knew better than I that, in one of these people, emotion had mounted to such heights as I had never experienced, for it had found its satisfaction in murder.

In the distance I heard voices. As the sounds came nearer I realized that it was Kane and Francis who were walking towards me.

"Well, yes," I heard Francis say uneasily, and then, as if he were trying to reestablish himself in his own eyes, "Why not? Yes, I was having an affair with her. Of course. And really, she's as much the sinner as I. She won't admit it, naturally. As for me, from now on, there's not going to be anything to admit. I'm what you might call repentant." I could visualize his quick, charming smile.

"And so," Kane prompted him coolly, "you're going to save yourself?"

"Women," Francis had turned fretful, "women always go too far. She even wanted me to defy Cousin Mart. Well, I wasn't going to do that. I'll clear out."

"Very well," Kane assented. "But, by the way, I'd give some sort of explanation to Blackstone before you go, as near the truth as you can make it, without being—unchivalrous."

"Oh, all right," Francis replied. "I'll do that." He was silent for a few seconds. When he went on, his voice was determined. "I'm going to tell her this time I'm definitely through, but not exactly in those words. I don't see why"— his tone was protesting—"I have to hold the sack in this unpleasantness."

"I wonder," Kane spoke right behind my shoulder, "I wonder if I can't help him to find out." I turned in time to see Francis walking with his cheerful springing step toward the house. Kane sat down beside me.

"It's very dangerous," Kane went on, "to play at love. Some people think they can swim the Atlantic, but they don't go a hundred yards before they're caught by the undertow."

I hardly listened to him. Kane had disclosed the lie and the truth pitifully easily.

"I don't want to believe it," I said slowly. "It might have been the one decent element in this business—so it seemed to me."

"Don't do what Cousin Mart did," Kane cautioned me. "Don't hold so strongly to your preconceived ideas of people that you are blind to what they are. Francis is a ready liar, but at this moment he's telling the truth."

"Even when he says she doesn't want to release him—or intimates it?"

"Undoubtedly. Love and marriage are different things, very different to Francis. It was easy for him to write a few days ago, 'You know how glad I would be to marry you if it weren't for the old man.'" Kane sighed. "It's too bad that Francis was so unwise as to put that on paper. It makes the present circumstances pretty difficult for him. You see, now the old man is out of the way, and the situation changes. Now, in spite of what he said and wrote, Francis doesn't want to marry her. 'A woman scorned'"— Kane's voice was very grave—"you know the beginning of that quotation, Underwood."

We walked on in silence, until I felt Kane's hand on my arm. I looked up. He was staring across the lawn at two people. I recognized the two I had least expected to see together—Blackstone and Stella.

"Things move quickly in this place," Kane said. "Francis must already have made one of his plausible explanations. Well, Blackstone must have accepted it."

We watched them as they wandered off together, apparently reconciled.

CHAPTER XXVI

THE END OF A DECEPTION

WE HAD come back to the library, where Moran joined us. On the way to the house Kane had not quickened his long, lounging step by a single second, and yet as I walked beside him and looked at his noncommittal face, I knew that in his own mind he had reached the climax he had spoken of early that morning. My conviction was based less on the scenes I had witnessed, though they gave me the facts, than on some intensity in Kane which communicated itself to me.

Again Kane stood apart from the two of us, but this time he stared, not out the window, but at a blank wall, as if he were afraid of the distraction of objects. Moran started to ask him something, but was answered only by an impatient, "In a minute! In a minute!"

He leaned over to me. "What's happened?" he asked anxiously.

I told him briefly. He drew a whistling breath when I had finished. As I reviewed the events of the morning for him, a queer conviction came over me that there were more and stranger events coming upon us soon.

Kane had come to the end of his meditations. I looked at his face as he joined us. His eyes shone with a melancholy exultation, such as a psychopathologist might feel when he had probed the depths of some hideous obsession.

"You see it now?" he asked softly.

"See what?" Moran asked in astonishment.

"The answer to this puzzle," Kane replied, "the end of the case, the identity we have been seeking out."

I could summon up no coherent answer to him. For an instant I was dumb, hearing through the tumult of my mind the pounding of blood in my ears. When I could speak my own voice had an alien, far-away sound to me.

"No," I said. "No, I don't see."

"You can't have found out," Moran followed me up. "You can't!"

"But I have," Kane answered him. "I have. I knew last night before I went to bed, partly by guess-work. This morning I found out that my guess was right. You two have all the evidence before you, every single bit of it, except one thing which has only served me as a confirmation of other evidence. I told you yesterday, Underwood, that this case would be solved by following our three leads—the note, the necklace, and the cards. On that basis I've solved it, beyond the possibility of a doubt." He paused. "One of the eight people with whom we're dealing has committed murder. Can't you pick out which one it was—haven't you suspected it all along?"

He looked from me to Moran, and from Moran to me, but we were silent.

Kane drew a long breath. "Very well," he said. "That means I'll have to go back for you, over ground that you know even better than I. Because without what the two of you have done, I could never have brought this to a conclusion."

He sat down on the edge of the table near us, and took his pipe out of his pocket. The mechanical gestures of filling and lighting it seemed to make it easier for him to speak.

"I'm not going to review the whole story again," he said. "We all know it by heart. But I want to point out to you the importance, as a silent giver of evidence, of the character who is no longer before our eyes. Think for a minute of Cousin Mart. You, Underwood, gave me a complete portrait of him. Without it, I'd not dare to say what I am about to. You both collected for me a minute account of his actions, which were especially important on the night of his death."

Kane turned his head away from us, so that we saw his face in profile. His brows frowned a little over his keen eyes as he strove to bring back to us the things we had not measured for ourselves.

"I had complete information then," he went on. "I was thoroughly intimate with his temperament and with his habits. And, I found out—" he faced us to emphasize his point—"that on the night of his death he seemed to have acted in a way contrary to both. I'll show you what I mean."

He laid his pipe down, and with his long forefinger he drew on the shining surface of the table a figure one, as if he were numbering his points.

"On the evening of his birthday he ordered served to his guests a cognac of which he was very choice. That was, supposedly, his gesture to crown the celebration, an indication that his mood was pleasant and generous towards his nephews and nieces. Yet the person who knew him best, who would be in the best position to judge his inner temper, Mrs. Warden, tells us that he was in a disagreeable frame of mind. And we know that she was right in saying that, for several things had conspired to make him angry and resentful. Yet, in spite of his more than irritation, he ordered the cognac served."

Kane's glance questioned us, asking if we anticipated his conclusion. Then he went on. "Another thing." His finger added below the figure one a two. "When he watched the fireworks he sat in Mrs. Warden's chair, opposite his own. Now he invariably sat in his own chair, the one that faced hers."

Again he paused, and again went on. "In the third place," he said, "there was a book open in his lap, as if he had been reading it while he pretended to watch the fireworks. Yet the reading lamp stood beside the *other* chair, the one he would ordinarily have occupied. This may seem a small point, but it is important. Cousin Mart was not the sort of person who puts up with a bad light."

He picked up his pipe again and held a match to the bowl. "There," he said, "you have the case from one direction. Now, I'll take it from another. You remember, both of you, that during the fireworks someone heard a sound that so attracted his attention that he in turn called attention to it, saying 'What was that?'"

For the first time I stirred. "Yes," I said. "I remember. It set the moment for us when Cousin Mart must have been shot."

"Exactly," Kane confirmed me, "that's what it did. It set the time *when Cousin Mart must have been shot*. Remember that, and remember this. *That was what it was intended to do.*"

I jumped up. "Then——"

Kane answered me. "Cousin Mart was dead at that moment, and had been dead for at least three quarters of an hour. He was not shot during the fireworks."

Moran's face blazed with excitement. "God!" he said. "What a fool I am! What a——"

"He never ordered the cognac," Kane went on, brushing Moran aside. "Voices sound alike over a speaking tube. He was sitting in his own chair—not in Mrs. Warden's chair—reading under the reading lamp when he was shot. These are the conclusions we are forced to draw from the evidence we have. There are no two ways about it."

Moran worried over Kane's words. "I can see," he muttered, "yeah, I can see. But that's theory, Kane, and there's a fact that doesn't fit it. You say he was dead, and the man who killed him ordered the cognac. All right. You say he would have stuck to his habits, and sat in his own chair, and read by a decent light. All right. But—" his voice became heavier—"how'd his body get into the other chair?"

"That's very simple," Kane answered rapidly, hardly able to speak fast enough to keep up with his thoughts. "It was moved there after he was dead. Why? Because the murderer had shot him from within the study. The body was moved into the opposite chair so that its whole position would be *reversed*, so that the wound in Cousin Mart's temple was toward the *window*, and not toward the room. That made it appear that he was shot from outside, from the lawn where, very shortly, the fireworks were to be set off."

It was plain, as plain as day. Yet why had Moran and I not thought of that? There must have been something to throw us off. Suddenly I realized what it was and that it destroyed Kane's ideas.

"Wait, Kane!"

But he waved me aside. "I'll explain that in a minute," he said, as if he understood my unspoken objection. "Let me finish first with this one aspect of the case. What else was there to make you think he was shot from outside? The placing of the pistol, of course. The explanation of that is simple. It was carried downstairs from the study, and when the whole company went out to set off the fireworks, it was thrown into the shrubbery. The police would, of course, find it there and take it as marking the place where the murderer stood. You did find it there, Moran, and you did consider that the pistol was dropped there immediately after it was fired. So far the plan was completely successful in substantiating the assumption that the murder was committed by someone standing on the lawn."

He was about to go on, but I could not wait any longer to frame the objection that, for me, completely canceled Kane's scheme of things. "You say he was dead, Kane, before the fireworks were set off?"

He nodded.

"But that can't be. It isn't possible. You don't remember as well as I do what happened that night. They were all outside, about to start their celebration. Only Cousin Mart was inside, and he was alone in his room with the curtains drawn. If he was dead then, how could he have pulled his curtains apart? For he did. Seven people saw him do it!"

"Seven people saw the curtains pulled apart." For a moment I thought Kane was assenting to my objection, but then I saw the distinction he made. "You know, both of you," he went on, "how those curtains are manipulated. They are on rings which slip across a brass pole, and by an ingenious but common enough arrangement a pull on one cord opens them, and a pull on another brings them together again. Cousin Mart did not draw apart his curtains—they were drawn apart *for* him. You will find, attached to the cord that opens them, a tiny fragment of string, so small as to be unnoticeable. After the murder was committed, a long string was tied to the cord, and let down outside the window. By that means the curtains were afterwards manipulated from the ground. Later—I could point out to you the exact moment when it was done—the string was removed. But the hand that cut it off, in that moment of nervous fear, was inaccurate, and so left us with a tiny piece of circumstantial evidence, unimportant except that it proves beyond a shadow of a doubt what we might have known, and what I did know, before I saw it."

Kane's words came faster, beating the tempo of his implacable reasoning. "Remember!" he almost commanded us. "The call to Cousin Mart. They were about to set off the fireworks. He wasn't watching. The curtains were closed. There was no answer. Someone ran beneath the window. From there his voice could carry to any but deaf ears. He called again. Then the curtains did part, for the person who had called to him had also pulled the string attached to the curtain cord."

I fumbled in my thoughts for a name I could not yet shape. I knew, but——

"Remember," Kane commanded us again, "the mind that Cousin Mart himself accurately described. So amazingly logical up to a certain point, and then so fraught with weakness. Remember——"

Hutchinson!

CHAPTER XXVII

CAT'S PAW

"So we come near to the end," Kane said. "You know now why Amelia did not hear Cousin Mart quarreling with Hutchinson. The dead have no quarrel with the living." He paused and sighed a little, as if his burst of superhuman nervous vitality had left him exhausted.

"Let me explain to you"—he picked up his narrative again—"exactly what happened. Hutchinson had about fifteen minutes to work in, as we know. He left the library at nine forty-five to confront the angry and outraged old man whom he had tried to cheat. At ten o'clock he was downstairs with the others. In those fifteen minutes, horrified and appalled as he was by Cousin Mart's dead body, afraid, shrinking for all his cold unscrupulousness from the word that was ringing in his ears—the word 'murderer'—he still was able to collect himself, and to face the inexorable facts. He had to save himself, and up to the point where his plan conflicted with facts of which he knew nothing, he did save himself.

"He remembered the fireworks and the noise of their explosions. He remembered how necessary it was that Cousin Mart should seem to be alive after he himself had left the study. Two things, the time of the murder, and the direction of the shot he could control, as far as might ever appear.

"This is what he did: He lifted the body from the chair in which Cousin Mart had been sitting to Mrs. Warden's chair, thus reversing the position of the wound. He arranged it naturally so that from the lawn the body would have a lifelike appearance. Then he put the book that Cousin Mart had been reading when he was shot back into his lap.

"But something more was necessary to clinch the supposition he was building up. Cousin Mart must *do* something, so that it would be taken for granted that he was alive. Hutchinson could not make him speak; he could not, no matter how much ingenuity he had, with the time and means at his disposal, show a dead man in actual motion. But he could *imply* a movement on Cousin Mart's part. So he tied the string to the curtain cord, and let the other end of it down where it could be reached from the ground."

Kane drew a deep breath. "So far, so good," he said. "But now Hutchinson made a little mistake. He called the butler on the speaking tube and ordered the cognac. That was another ruse to make it appear that Cousin Mart was alive. He was, however, overdoing things. He should never have ordered the special cognac, which made it so conspicuous a gesture on Cousin Mart's part. But, after all, he was too rattled to consider carefully the first vintage that came to his mind.

"Last of all, he put the pistol into his pocket and went down to the library, composing himself, as far as was humanly possible, into outward calm. Apparently concerned only with the success of his birthday celebration in Cousin Mart's honor, he started the others to setting off the fireworks. When he had an opportunity, he got rid of the pistol in the shrubbery. Finally he chose his moment and asked in such a fashion that it would be remembered, 'What was that?' Then he had finished. He had put a complete screen between himself and the murder. He had, that is, after he had cut the dangling piece of string from the curtain cord, which he did when he looked out of the window—when he, with the others, had come into the study to find Cousin Mart dead. Presumably he was then trying to see an escaping criminal."

Kane had proved his case beyond the shadow of a doubt, but still doubt lingered in my mind. He had fulfilled all the requirements of the old tag, "who, what, when, where, for what reason." I hesitated a little. I was not, in spite of the logic of Kane's explanation, entirely convinced.

"It's funny," I said slowly, "that it should turn out this way. I distrust Hutchinson, and I should never want to have any dealings with him. I know he's sly and treacherous, but——"

It was Moran who interrupted me. "Never mind this talking it over business," he said, with satisfaction. "It's a watertight case, isn't it?" He looked to Kane for support.

"Yes, it is," Kane nodded. "We have only the final step to take."

"You've got the warrant in your pocket. Why don't you fill it out?"

Kane looked at the sergeant with mingled amusement and wonder and dismay. "I've already filled it out," he said.

I pursued my point obstinately. "I still don't think Hutchinson is the type to commit murder."

Kane turned back to me. "There's no such thing as the type that commits murder, Underwood. You should know that by this time. The facts are as they are, but"—he looked swiftly away—"if you had been more particular in the statement you just made, I'd have been forced to agree with you."

He got up and stood over us, his face calmer now that he had finished with his explanation. Moran half rose, impatient to bring the case to its conclusion, but Kane waved him back into his chair. I started to say something and then stopped.

"What were you going to say?" Kane prompted me.

"I was going to ask you—" I frowned a little—"I didn't quite understand what you just said. Something about being more particular——?"

"I said," Kane repeated patiently, "that if you had been more particular in your statement I'd have been forced to agree with you. In fact"—he thrust his hands deep into his pockets—"in fact, if you had said that Hutchinson is not the type to have committed *this* murder I certainly would have agreed with you."

"What in——" Moran's face had become a gaping mirror of stupefaction.

"But, Kane!" I cried. "You've been proving it to us, telling us——"

"I've been telling you the truth," Kane finished for me quietly. "And the end of the truth is this—Hutchinson did not murder Martin Greenough." He spoke with heavy emphasis.

"No," he went on, answering our unspoken protests, "think of the person he is. You said yourself, Underwood, that it was strange to think of Hutchinson as a murderer—at least, I think you meant that. Considering what he is, I agree with you. You also said that he is sly and treacherous. And, above all, we both know that he is a colossal coward. To commit this murder required boldness and daring. Hutchinson has only the false courage that comes of scheming, prompted by a cunning instinct for getting *out* of trouble. He could never have acted with such directness as the murderer did. I tell you again—it was not Hutchinson."

"Then, *why*"—Moran was outraged—"have you been telling us this funny story? About what Hutchinson did, and the mistake he made, and——"

"Everything I said to you was true, Moran," Kane broke in upon him. "Hutchinson went upstairs to see Cousin Mart and found himself faced with a worse disaster than he had anticipated. The old man was dead. He sat in his chair with a bullet wound in his temple. Who had shot him Hutchinson didn't know. But I daresay he used up no precious time in pondering on that. The main fact was horribly apparent—here *he* was in the room with the murdered man. The pistol was lying near by. Well, a straight-thinking man, with nothing to hide, would immediately have given the alarm. Such a man would have been numbered among the chief suspects, naturally, because he had the weapon and the opportunity to commit the crime. But you can't convict on circumstantial evidence alone. However—add a strong motive to that evidence, and you have a case. Now Hutchinson realized that in an instant. He had the opportunity and the weapon—and, above all, he had what the law would certainly interpret as a motive for murder. That necklace affair—if Hutchinson were accused of the crime—would come out: the fact that he had tried to cheat Cousin Mart and that Cousin Mart had found him out.

"No," Kane shook his head, "Hutchinson could not run downstairs to the rest of the company and say that Cousin Mart had been murdered when he, more than anyone else, had a strong motive for committing the crime. Suppose—" Kane's fist, pressed hard on the surface of the table, enforced his words—"suppose he had given the alarm immediately. He would have been arrested as immediately. And," he shrugged his shoulders, "he probably would have been convicted. A watertight case, as you say, Moran.

"No, he couldn't say that Cousin Mart was dead. Instead, he did what his sly mind told him to do. He changed the body from one chair to the other, tied a string to the curtain cord, placed the book, put the pistol in his pocket, and dropped it on the lawn. Once outside, by asking, 'What was that?' he induced the company to remember a strange noise and to think, later on, that Cousin Mart had been shot then. So he shielded himself, and, but for a stroke of chance, very nearly convicted himself as well. For certainly there is no jury in the world that, if the evidence we have were presented to it, would refuse to convict Hutchinson—an innocent man."

"But, Kane," I objected, "if Hutchinson did what you say he did and still isn't the murderer, all his self-protection didn't do him any real good. Suppose he had let things be, run downstairs, and said that Cousin Mart was dead and that someone else had killed him. Certainly we'd have found out that he had a motive and an opportunity for committing the murder. But his giving the alarm would have spoken for him. As it is, by doing what he did, he has condemned himself. Why should he not have seen that, in the end, the added danger wasn't worth the strategy?"

"There," Kane replied, "you hit upon the great flaw in Hutchinson's mind, his dependence upon logic and his inability to follow logic beyond a certain point. You know how he played twenty-one. He shielded himself in the same obstinate and mistaken way. And remember the plot he founded on the necklace. A perfect plot, up to a certain point. But he didn't foresee that Cousin Mart would telephone Banks and Tiffany. Well, this

more horrible plot of his runs the same course. Excellent logic and reasoning in its inception. He made himself one of eight
suspects instead of one standing alone. *But* he failed to realize
that his own scheming would be his certain destruction, once
his scheme was detected; he failed to realize that he was snaring
himself in a vicious coil."

Moran had sat frowning for a long time. "Look here," he
broke in suddenly. "You've *said* that Hutchinson wasn't the
murderer. But you've done nothing but say so. You haven't
proved it."

"That's true, Moran," Kane agreed quietly. "I'll give you
proof of what I've said and do it now." He paused for a moment
and then went on. "Hutchinson is not a complete answer to the
problems we've had before us," he said. "He doesn't explain everything. You realized, yourself, at the beginning of the case
that there were three things to follow in this investigation—the
note, the necklace, and the cards. All three concern the murderer. Hutchinson is concerned with only one of them—the
necklace.

"And I can give you a concrete bit of evidence which shows
that it was impossible for Hutchinson to have killed Martin
Greenough. I can prove to you with a certainty far beyond that
of any 'watertight case,' beyond the faintest question, who did
kill him, and when I do it will seem so simple to you that . . .
but never mind, now.

"To get back to the point," he said, "Hutchinson's part in the
solution is just this—he was a cover-up for the murderer. He
was, in fact, a cat's paw—nothing more. For the real murderer
was in possession of these particular facts—" Kane ticked them
off on his fingers as he spoke—"that Hutchinson was to see
Cousin Mart *alone* at quarter of ten, that he would find himself

in the room with a murdered man and the weapon with which the murder was done, and that he had something to hide, in other words, the necklace fraud. Obviously Hutchinson would have two courses of action open to him. First, he could announce the murder. Well, he would have been arrested, everything would have gone against him, and the real criminal would have been shielded. Secondly, Hutchinson could plot to protect himself from suspicion. In either case he would cover the identity of the criminal. In either case he would serve the murderer as a cat's paw.

"It's strange," Kane said with a short laugh, "that Hutchinson should be proved to be no more than a cat's paw *by* a cat's paw."

We looked at him with a mixture of bewilderment and anger. Why should he choose this moment to confuse us?

"You're not making sense, Kane," I said shortly. "You'd better put it in other terms."

"I can't," he insisted. "It's what I mean." And he repeated his strange sentence. But he went on. "A *physical* cat's paw, Underwood. The paw of a cat. The *print* of a cat's paw. Hutchinson's innocence is proved by that. Do you understand?"

"No."

"It's as if the god of evil had chuckled," Kane said, "and printed that sign manual on the case. But I'm afraid there's nothing as supernatural about it. I'll tell you how it happened. This," he added, "is where our second element, the element of the cards, comes in."

Out of the jumble in his pockets, he drew a pack of cards. "This is the pack I found in George's dinner clothes. It has the marked aces, as you know—the aces that were in the room when Cousin Mart was shot and which George removed later on. You remember my saying that George, in taking these aces away, had not only removed a clue to his own cheating, but a clue that confirmed the identity of the murderer. Well, I'll explain what I meant by saying that."

He separated the four aces. "These cards," he said, "are marked with pin pricks, for George's purposes. But on one of them, the ace of diamonds," he held it up, "there's another, a very different kind of mark, which has nothing to do with George or with George's purposes. He doesn't know it's there. I doubt if he even looked at the cards after he secured them from Cousin Mart's table. If he had looked at them, he might have observed this——"

Again Kane searched his pockets, this time to bring out a magnifying glass. He handed it to me, and with it the ace of diamonds, back up. I examined the shining dark blue surface under the glass. I saw what he meant. Wonderingly I handed the card and the glass to Moran. He did as I had done. Then he looked at Kane.

"What——" he began.

"The print of a cat's paw——" Kane answered softly—"in blood."

"It was chance," he continued in a low voice, "that Cousin Mart's cat was sitting on his lap when he was shot, chance that it got blood on one of its paws and then stepped on the card that lay on the table beside him. But all these chances work together to corroborate what we know from other evidence—that Hutchinson did not kill Cousin Mart.

"For we know that the cat went upstairs to the study when Cousin Mart went. And we happen to know, too, when the cat came down again and was put away for the night. Therefore, after the time when it was shut up in the room where it sleeps, it could *not* have made the bloody mark on the cards in Cousin Mart's study. Now you see what I mean—that the cat's paw clears Hutchinson."

But our faces showed plainly that we did not see.

Kane explained it simply. "Hutchinson went upstairs *after* the cat was put away. So the mark on the card must have been there *before* he ever entered the study."

"The cat left the study with the murderer. That should tell you."

We were silent.

"Let me put it to you as I saw it myself," Kane went on. "In the first place I considered the motive. We knew already that it must have grown out of rebellion against Cousin Mart's tyranny. He tyrannized over them all. Yet of one person he suddenly demanded—although his demand was cloaked in beneficence—a more complete subjection than he required of any of the rest. If that person had revolted—from the beginning, the possibility caught and held my attention. So much for motive.

"The second thing I had to consider was, of course, opportunity. The time element was decided for me by many things, all of which I have told you, and fixed beyond the shadow of a doubt by the cat's paw on the cards. My suspect on the grounds of motive was still more strongly to be suspected on the grounds of time. But whoever killed Cousin Mart had also to know how Hutchinson would behave. And the same person was the only one who could have known that Amelia had never taken the necklace.

"So a consideration of the motive, together with two of our clues—the cards and the necklace—brought me to identical conclusions. Do you begin to see?"

"No!" Moran cried in shaky self-distrust. "No. I don't see."

"Then," Kane caught him up, "you've forgotten our third element—the note."

He was about to go on when some sound attracted his attention. It came from upstairs—heavy footsteps thudding on the floor, as if a struggle were going on. Kane raised his head quickly.

We heard a scream. Kane sprang to his feet and made for the open door.

"Hurry!" he cried.

We ran down the hall. He led the way upstairs, taking the treads four at a time. At the head of the stairs we heard something else which, for a second, brought us to a halt. It was the sound of a shot.

CHAPTER XXVIII

WHO KILLED HIM

A DOOR to our left stood ajar. Kane made a lunge toward it. It was the door to Francis's room.

Someone blocked his entry. I heard Kane say harshly, "No running away now!" and saw him push Francis aside. Moran, thrusting in behind Kane, seized Francis by the shoulder and spun him around. I had barely got in before the sergeant had slammed the door to and blocked it with his massive frame. I took one look at Francis's pallid, abject face, and then I saw, lying on the floor, the body of a woman. Kane knelt beside it swiftly and gazed at the face. It was Mrs. Warden. She was dead, shot through the heart.

Through the thick silence I heard Francis's once pleasant voice, whining now and terrified. "I only defended myself," he cried out. "I caught her hand, tried to get away. She wanted to kill me! She shot herself!"

His words reechoed in the room. Kane got up slowly from his kneeling position and for several seconds stood looking down at the body. Finally he raised his head and turned to face Francis. There was a cold glitter in his eye.

"No," he said quietly, "you didn't kill her, I know that. But it was on your account that she killed herself. You pretended to be in love with her, you told her you would marry her if circumstances were different. Then you taunted her, made love to another woman, refused to marry her. Drove her——"

"I didn't know—I didn't know it mattered to her," Francis stammered.

Kane went on inexorably. "You wrote to her 'You know how glad I would be to marry you if it weren't for the old man.' She was clever enough to let Cousin Mart think that that note was addressed to Stella. But she wasn't clever enough to know that the writer of it didn't mean what he said."

"I never meant to marry her. She should have known——"

"You said you would—if Cousin Mart were dead."

"But he was alive—I never thought—he was alive then."

"He's dead, *now*." Kane turned on him brutally. "She believed you and everything you said. So she killed him."

THE END

DISCUSSION QUESTIONS

- Were you able to predict any part of the solution to the case?

- After learning the solution, were there any clues you realized you had missed?

- Would the story be different if it were set in the present day? If so, how?

- Did the social context of the time play a role in the narrative? If so, how?

- What role did the geographical setting play in the narrative? Would the story have been different if it were set someplace else?

- If you were one of the main characters, would you have acted differently at any point in the story?

- Did you identify with any of the characters? If so, which?

- Did this story remind you of any other books you've read?